BRAVO

ALSO BY GREG RUCKA

THE JAD BELL SERIES

Alpha

THE QUEEN & COUNTRY SERIES

The Last Run
Private Wars
A Gentleman's Game

THE ATTICUS KODIAK SERIES

Walking Dead
Patriot Acts
Critical Space
Shooting at Midnight
Smoker
Finder
Keeper

A Fistful of Rain
Batman: No Man's Land
Perfect Dark: Second Front
Perfect Dark: Initial Vector

BRAVO

GREG RUCKA

A JAD BELL NOVEL

MULHOLLAND BOOKS

LITTLE, BROWN AND COMPANY
New York Boston London

Mulholland Books/Little, Brown and Company
Hachette Book Group
237 Park Avenue, New York, NY 10017
mulhollandbooks.com

First Edition: July 2014

Mulholland Books is an imprint of Little, Brown and Company, a division of Hachette Book Group, Inc. The Mulholland Books name and logo are trademarks of Hachette Book Group, Inc.

The publisher is not responsible for websites (or their content) that are not owned by the publisher.

The Hachette Speakers Bureau provides a wide range of authors for speaking events. To find out more, go to hachettespeakersbureau.com or call (866) 376-6591.

ISBN 978-0-316-18230-0
LCCN 2014934037

10 9 8 7 6 5 4 3 2 1

RRD-C

Printed in the United States of America

This is for Angela.

BRAVO

Chapter One

"You look tired," she says, moving out of the doorway to let him inside. "Do you want to talk about it?"

The soldier enters, moves his cover to his hands, holding the hat in a way that makes him feel half her age, though he's most of the way through fifty and she's not seen the edges of thirty yet. He doesn't speak, doesn't move as she shuts and locks the door behind him, comes back to put a gentle touch on his elbow. She looks at him curiously, concerned, then shakes her head in such a way that her hair shifts and gently sways, exposes bare neck from collar to jawline. He sees her skin, feels an almost magnetic tug, an immediate urge to wrap his arms around her and inhale her scent. He's too old to believe that doing so will make it all better, but it's what he feels. He thinks about the fact that he should've waited before coming here, before talking to her. He thinks that he doesn't have a choice.

"Jamieson's dead," the soldier says.

She nods slightly, a touch of sympathy in her expression, in the movement, and he thinks it's for his sake, and not for the dead man she has never met, hardly even knew.

"I'll make you a drink," she says. "I've got some of that rye you like."

He nods, moves into the large front room. Floor-to-ceiling windows that would show the gleam of the capital at night, but the curtains are drawn, the way they always are when he arrives. He's never seen them open, never seen the view out of her condo here in the West End. This town, he knows, keeps a secret like a four-year-old at a birthday party. When he visits, he visits at night, drives straight into the underground lot, takes the spot that's always open. Normally, he changes out of uniform before coming here.

Tonight is not normal.

The soldier takes a seat, sets his hat beside him, loosens his tie and his collar. When she comes back with the drink, he takes it from her hand, sets it aside. She raises an eyebrow.

"You don't want a drink you should've said so."

The soldier pulls her to him, meets her mouth with his own. She kisses him back with full hunger, uncaged; it's what she's been waiting for.

When they reach her bedroom, he keeps much of his uniform on, at least for a while.

Afterward, embracing every cliché, she lights a cigarette and shares it with him, resting on her elbow, the ashtray balanced on his sternum. He stares at the ceiling. It's the lost hours, between three and five in the morning, and the only sounds are the hum of the air-conditioning and, just beyond, the muted tick of the clock on the bedside table. He can feel her gaze, studying him. Her patience is unnerving, and he cannot stop his mind from spinning into questions. He knows what she's waiting for.

"He can name his price."

She sucks on the cigarette, exhales toward the ceiling, places the filter back between his lips. He swears he can taste her on it.

"I'll tell him that," she says.

"I want to talk to him this time. No middleman, not like it was with Jamieson. I want to deal with him directly."

She shakes her head slightly. He knew she would.

"We bought a service," the soldier says, recalling her own phrasing. "It didn't execute."

"You knew there was an element of risk. You embraced that when you told me what Jamieson and the others wanted to buy."

"It didn't execute." He puts the cigarette out in the ashtray, feels the sharp point of heat of the cinder dying on the glass against his skin. He moves the ashtray to the nightstand, and when he rolls back, she is exactly as she was before. "We're no better off than when we started."

"I've seen the news, baby. We both know that's not true."

"It's not enough. It's not what we wanted."

She shrugs, and it's as elegant as every other movement she makes. He wonders, not for the first time, what she was before she was this. He used to think she was as American as he, but over time he has revised that theory. There's an Eastern European touch to her beauty, to the dark hair and dark eyes and almost too-fair skin. When he's tried to look into who she really is — carefully, very, very carefully — all the answers come back entirely plausible, the banal lies of espionage that he has come to recognize from thirty years of service. When he's asked her, her response has always been the same.

"I am what you need me to be."

She's been a lot of things for him. She's been an ardent and eager and skilled lover. She's been a woman who has made him feel adored and strong and potent. She's been a comfort, laughing at the right time at the right jokes, asking the right questions when he needed to talk about himself. She's been a confessor, listening to secrets he has no right to tell anyone else. She's been the gateway. When the soldier and Jamieson and the others concluded what they needed to do to save their country, she heard the edge of conspiracy in his voice, and she offered the way to the means. It was she who told the soldier she knew a man who knew a man who could provide the terror they wanted. It was she who put Jamieson and the Uzbek in the same place at the same time.

She's been all these things, but right now, he needs her to be something else. Right now, he needs her to be a rope, he needs her to keep him from drowning. Right now, the soldier needs her to tell him that what he's done, what they've done, cannot come back to harm them, and that there is still a way forward.

She moves against him, lays her head against his chest. One hand finds his, laces fingers.

"Tell me what you want," she says. "Tell me what you're offering. I'll speak to him, and I'll tell you what he says."

A sudden, sharp anger bursts in him. He resents her patience, resents what feels like condescension from this woman so much younger than he, who makes him hard despite himself, who has secrets he cannot uncover. He grips her wrists and rolls atop her, pins her arms over her head, and the way she yields only makes him that much more frustrated and aroused. She's looking up at him unafraid, that same expression, as if anything he might do to her now is what she wants him to do, or, worse, what she expects from him, that he is entirely predictable to her. She pushes against his grip, but only just. She opens her legs.

"We want what we paid for," the soldier says.

She arches, receiving him, makes a sound that thrills him.

"Yes," she says.

"You tell him that. You tell him that."

"Yes."

"You tell him...oh...goddamn it..."

"Yes."

"...damn you, goddamn you, woman..."

"Yes."

"...tell him..."

"Yes."

"...we want..."

"Yes."

"…we want the war we paid for!"

After a time, his hands leave her wrists, and she wraps her arms around him, and the silence returns, the air conditioner, the ticking of the clock, the racing of his pulse. Her lips brush his ear.

"He'll want something in return."

Chapter Two

BELL IS THE penetrator, first through the door, Chaindragger nuts-to-ass on him. Steelriver follows tight on Chain's heels, sweeping up at the back, making sure nothing comes up on their six.

They enter noisy and hard, hydrocharge blasting hinges from door frame, wood and brick splinters that shower the hardwood floor of the entry hall. Steelriver sends the first flashbang in its wake, the grenade's detonation turned from deafening to dull behind their ear protection, and then they're out of the night and into a new darkness, NVG compensating with all the ambient light it can steal. Outside in the back, Cardboard opens up on the house with his grenade launcher, dropping more bangers onto the roof, through the windows, peppering the building with noise in an attempt to sow mayhem and confusion, all while maintaining his overwatch.

They know their positions and their duty the way they know their names, ranks, and serial numbers. The flight into country was spent going over the terrain, a JSOC windfall of intelligence gathered from who knows where, examining blueprints, memorizing faces on digital displays. Then the gear prep, each man attending his loadout, then finally sneaking what sleep they could. Now they have sacrificed stealth for speed, a heavily armed footrace to claim an unwilling prize.

Down the hall, Bell counting steps not quite subconsciously, taking in details with the same ingrained assess-and-discard, moving to target. Door, left, he passes without pause, leaves it to Chaindragger to clear. Hears the next grenade's dulled thump, feels the vibration as he drives ever forward. In Bell's mind's eye, the floor plan is a cross between some high-tech heads-up display and, oddly, a treasure map, parchment-aged and ragged-edged. It's one of his mnemonics, some part of the boy's adventure fantasy that has endured through his nearly forty years. It may be the only childhood illusion he has left.

Just short of the end of the hall, the shock-entry is beginning to wear off. Between the blasts from Cardboard's rain, Bell can now hear muffled shouting, the alarm rising in near hysteria, voices yelling in Russian and Uzbek. He imagines the clatter and scramble of hasty movement and breaking panic. Bell's seventeenth step brings him to an intersection, and he throws his first 9-bang, corners as it detonates, his carbine high and ready. A man staggers into view, disoriented from the roughly 180 decibels that have deafened him, the white flash that has blinded him, a weapon in hand. He blinks, useless, in Bell's direction, and Bell puts two suppressed shots into him without breaking stride. The man drops. At his back, Chaindragger fires again, new target, one Bell has skipped. They keep moving.

They have been inside for six seconds.

Following the route, the map in Bell's mind never wavering, the absurd *X* marking the imaginary spot on the floor above. Behind him, far enough back that it must be Steelriver, he registers more shots, suppressor muffled, the sound of a body collapsing, deadweight. Passes another door, and Chaindragger hits it, pops the banger while hugging the wall, follows the blast with a pivot and a burst of gunfire, then resumes, stacked tight on Bell.

Still counting his paces, and Bell has reached the bottom of the staircase, sweeps his barrel upward, tracing his line of ascent. He hates stairs; stairs are dangerous, and to prove him right he sights movement, fires twice, and is rewarded with an ownerless assault rifle clattering down the stairs toward him. Bell notes the gun is an AK, the same way he notes that Steelriver has turned, giving their back full cover. More shots, these unsuppressed, and that means it's not one of Bell's doing the shooting but rather the opposition, and then it cuts off as abruptly and brutally as it began. An instant of silence, and then a voice dulled by ear protection begins screaming in pain and fear, then that, too, is lost as another of Cardboard's grenades detonates, the bombardment continuing.

Eleven seconds.

Bell throws his second banger of the op, lofting it up the stairs to the landing, and another grenade arcs after the first, this thrown by Chaindragger. Each detonates within an instant of one another, concussion vibration they can feel in their torsos, light flaring, the NVG filters compensating a fraction of an instant behind the blasts. The explosion is still ringing through the house as Bell ascends, reaches the top, the treasure-map *X* looming closer, the room that the blueprints identified as the master suite. Two men here, still reeling, one wide-eyed and dumbstruck, the other flat on the floor, hands covering his ears. Bell takes the one in his quadrant, Chain shoots the second. The door to the room they want is dead ahead, and Bell moves to it with the confidence of a man who knows that no one is going to take his back by surprise. He knocks the goggles up out of his eyes, back to his helmet, and Chaindragger follows suit, waiting the word.

Bell gives the go sign, and they're crashing through the second door.

It has taken seventeen seconds.

For the master bedroom of a master criminal, the room is remarkably restrained, something Bell registers without realizing he's doing so, the same way he also concludes that this makes perfect sense. This man they've come for, this Uzbek, has been anything but ostentatious, even in the face of crimes that are both audacious and extravagant. It has been seventy-two hours since Bell and this same team — with the exception of Steelriver — prevented a terrorist takeover of one of the biggest theme parks in the world. It has been less than seventy-two hours since Bell himself stopped the detonation of a dirty bomb in that same park, a device that, upon recovery, had been constructed to appear as though it were manufactured and supplied by the Islamic Republic of Iran.

This is the home, this is the bedroom, of the man Bell and his masters believe to be responsible for these things.

This is the home of Vosil Tohir.

Briefed on the flight into Tashkent, again in the SUV speeding from the staging point at the airfield to this house, Bell wondered what this man, this Uzbek, would be like. His audacity notwithstanding, the takeover of the WilsonVille theme park had been expertly done, cleared of fifty thousand guests in a matter of minutes, then held for hours before Bell, Chaindragger, Cardboard, and the currently absent and convalescing Bonebreaker had managed to shake the Uzbek's men loose. Bell still feels the aches and pains earned that day, physical and emotional; the soreness in his lacerated palm still knitting itself back together; the betrayal in the eyes of his daughter, Athena.

When all was said and done, only then did the trail lead to Vosil Tohir.

Putting the name to the man in turn put the man in a place, and that is why four very deniable shooters, trained by the United States Army, are here, in Tashkent, in Uzbekistan. They have come for Vosil Tohir.

Because Vosil Tohir has a lot of explaining to do.

Eighteen seconds.

Two figures in the blue darkness, the bed between them and Bell, a man and a woman. The man is kicking open a door that was *not* on the blueprints, and Bell knows it was an aftermarket addition. Vosil Tohir has a bolt-hole, and he is almost through it. Bell sees this in an instant, just as he sees that both are half dressed and both have go bags in one hand and a weapon in the other.

The mission is to take Vosil Tohir alive. The gun he is raising at them is therefore problematic; the gun that the woman is raising less so.

Chaindragger's carbine spits, a single suppressed shot, and the man seems to pirouette before collapsing on his side. Bell, through the window of the EOTech sight on his rifle, already has his reticule on the woman's face, his finger is about to slap the trigger, and it is then he registers what she is shouting at him, sees her hands rising, empty, weapon and bag falling to the floor.

"Biplane! Biplane!"

Bell stops himself from killing her.

"Biplane." The woman is breathless. "The word of the day is *biplane*."

Bell takes two uncounted steps forward, face-to-face with the woman. He hears the sound of metal sliding over the floor as Chaindragger kicks the dropped guns away, hears the man on the floor's chopped breathing as he struggles to keep from vocalizing the pain that comes with a bullet shattering the hip. Bell, who has been shot four times in his almost twenty years of service, can imagine quite easily how much it hurts. He feels just a moment's sympathy.

The woman doesn't move, but she doesn't look away, meeting Bell's gaze. She stands straight, proud; closer, Bell sees that she is beautiful, which he expected, but unafraid, which he did not. Her hands are still raised, but her elbows are bent, giving her surrender an insolence.

A flash of light, a brief moment of illumination as Chaindragger checks the man on the floor against the digital copy on his smartphone, the same photograph all the shooters carry. The sound of a zip tie being ratcheted around the target's wrists.

"Verified," Chaindragger tells Bell.

"Biplane." When she says it this time, the corner of her mouth turns to smirk.

Bell punches her in the solar plexus.

Twenty-five seconds.

Chapter Three

THE SOLDIER HASN'T been sleeping well, and that's why he's awake when his phone rings, the special one, the one that ties him to everything and everyone under his command back at the Pentagon. He's sitting in the living room of his home outside Chevy Chase, Maryland, in the almost dark, just the light from the dining room bleeding all over him. He's been staring into the cold dead pit of his fireplace in August. If it were winter, he'd have something burning and take comfort in the dance of the flames, but it's not winter, it's summer, and even with the air-conditioning cranked he couldn't justify lighting a fire, because that would be stupid, wouldn't it? Until a while ago he'd been working on his laptop, but now it's forgotten, awake but screen-locked, a black monitor displaying the ubiquitous star field that hides all the top secrets within. He's thinking about work but he's not, because he's thinking about that woman in the West End that he cannot get enough of, that he cannot ever get enough of, and he's thinking of the man who has mastered her and who isn't him.

He hates that man. Sincerely, deeply, utterly, purely hates him. He would kill him with his hands, something that he did once to the enemy many many years ago, a moment and a sensation he has never forgotten. Different from taking a life with a gun and a thousand times removed from drone strikes or overseen ops in the far corners of the world. He remembers that battle, that desperation and savagery, and the wound in his left leg awakens with sympathy, aching again. He fought for his life, and he won, and poets and writers and better men than he have tried to put into words what that moment is like, the triumph of survival, the ecstasy and elation of victory, the sorrow that follows. The soldier used to wonder if all who survive feel the same way. Then he decided it didn't matter.

When he thinks of that man, though, the man he hates, it all comes back. That man with no name, and with no name no identity, no country, no motive, no reason. That man whom he has never seen and thus has imagined; younger than the soldier, and more handsome, and always well dressed, like those fey male models that used to be all the fashion. That man, the soldier has decided, wears glasses. That man, who maybe had Jamieson killed, maybe was trying to tie off a loose end, to keep his precious anonymity and his terrible secrets.

That man whom the soldier has come to think of as the Architect, because it fits, because calling that man a cocksucking goatfucker is too much of a mouthful, even if he never says it aloud, and because he's an officer who wears stars, and officers who wear stars don't use words like that in polite company. That man, as reported by the Bravo-Interdict operator code-named Blackfriars via her control, Captain Abigail Heath, and who has been designated target: Echo. So he is called Echo on paper, but still, in the soldier's mind, he is the Architect.

Joke's on you, the soldier thinks. *We're closer than you know.*

Just not close enough. Not yet.

Then the phone rings, and the soldier learns how wrong he is.

He stabs the button on his phone with the angry haste that comes when silence is disturbed. The soldier's wife is asleep upstairs, and even though he knows it won't, he's afraid the sound will wake her. He answers it angry, because when he gets a phone call he isn't expecting at five of five in the morning, something has gone very wrong indeed.

"Brock," he says.

It's Heath. "I'm sorry to disturb you at home, sir," she says. "Blackfriars is about to be blown."

For a moment, the soldier genuinely cannot speak, suffers the extraordinary feeling of being punched in the gut through words alone. He's a rational man, but this feels like witchcraft, as if the Architect, wherever he skulks and hides, has reached across miles and matter and pulled the prize straight from the soldier's mind. His thoughts jumble, trying to remember, but he's sure he's never so much as whispered a word of Blackfriars, never even mentioned the name to the woman in the West End. She had everything he could give her, but he never gave her that.

He registers the tense Heath has used, says, "About to be?" He hears the stress in his voice as he speaks, wonders if Heath can hear it, too.

"Conops for an Indigo capture op in Tashkent, targeting Heatdish, just crossed my desk," Heath says. She's speaking quickly, and the soldier realizes that any stress in his voice must sound like harmony to what he's hearing in hers. "They were boots-on-the-ground as of seventeen minutes ago. They have to have the jackpot by now unless they were stopped at the breach."

Heatdish is the code name used for Blackfriars's primary target, the man she's been working, an Uzbeki national named Vosil Tohir. It is Vosil Tohir who ties everyone in Brock's deceptions together, from the woman in the West End to Jamieson to the events at the theme park in California. It is Blackfriars who leads to Heatdish, who leads, finally, to the Architect, and until this moment, Brock has held faith that he is the only one aware of this connection.

"Jackpot is Heatdish, confirmed?"

"By the conops, yes, sir." Heath pauses for a fraction, it's barely there, but it's what the soldier is thinking, too, and he hears it. "Sir, if it's a parakeet op, they'll kill Blackfriars before she can identify herself."

"Get Ruiz."

"Yes, sir."

Heath puts him on hold, and the soldier gets to his feet, wedging his phone between ear and shoulder. He takes his laptop with him, moves it to the dining room table, and the motion awakens the screen, and the machine demands to know who he is. He types his passphrase, then his password, then his second password in quick succession, turns to the bottles of liquor on the sideboard, shifts the phone to his other shoulder, his other ear. Pours himself a glass of whiskey and brings it back to the laptop. He never told the woman in the West End about Blackfriars. He never gave that up, he's more certain than ever.

So this is something else. The price of asymmetrical warfare fought with a Special Forces sword and shield. Everything happens fast, sometimes too damn fast to track all the elements.

Heath comes back. "Sir, I have Colonel Ruiz."

"Patch."

There's a hiss, and then all three of them are sharing a line.

"General Brock," Ruiz says. "What can I do for you, sir?"

"Danny, what's this about you running an op in Tashkent?" the soldier, Brigadier General Emmet Brock, asks. "Why didn't I see a concept of operations before this went green?"

"Begging your pardon, sir, but I wasn't aware Indigo operations needed your approval."

"They fucking well do when I've got an operator in theater. Jesus Christ, Danny, where the fuck did this even come from? Your men go through the door, they'll drop her on the way to target. I'm ordering you to abort."

"I can't do that, sir."

"I am anxious to hear why not, Colonel."

"They're on egress to exfil staging," Ruiz says. "It's done."

Heath swears, certain her agent is dead, and the soldier, Brock, wants to swear, too, but for different reasons. Blackfriars dead means his best reach for the Architect is now gone.

"You have communications with your unit?"

"Due for a sitrep from them in...four minutes."

"Captain Heath," Brock says. "You will stay in contact with Colonel Ruiz, and you will inform me immediately on the disposition of the operation. Colonel, the captain is Blackfriars's handler. You'll need her to verify that your men just killed one of our operators."

Brock hangs up before either Ruiz or Heath can acknowledge him. He drops the phone on the table beside his laptop and his whiskey, takes the glass and brings it to his lips, anxious to drink, but stops. Blackfriars had been the reach to the Architect, but if the operation has been a success, there's still hope, maybe even a better hope for reaching the man. Maybe the Indigo shooters have killed Blackfriars, but it doesn't really matter, because Blackfriars became irrelevant the moment they went through the door. If they have Heatdish, if they have Vosil Tohir, that's a tradeup.

He thinks about the woman in the West End again, the woman he knows as Jordan Webber-Hayden. She put Jamieson and Tohir together, albeit indirectly. When Brock asked her about Tohir, about this contact Jamieson was dealing with, she'd claimed ignorance. He'd never mentioned his name to her, hadn't wanted to reveal how much he knew for fear of it getting back to the Architect. Now he has to wonder what she might know.

He sits down at the table, brings up the encryption and link to his files, opens the one for Blackfriars. A message informs him that the file is currently being viewed by another user, Heath, Abigail Anne, Captain, and he sees the tracking string of alphanumeric code that proves she's real and authorized. Worried about her girl. The file says that Blackfriars is still "active," but Brock's certain that's wishful thinking.

He thinks about Jordan again, in her West End condominium, the irony of his relationship with her. He works to do to others what she has done to him. All the things he doesn't know about her, all the things he's allowed to continue because he cannot stand the thought of not having her anymore. All the things he's never asked, never *really* asked, content with her evasions and her lies because he literally fucking hurts, the way his leg still sometimes hurts, at the thought of losing her. Thinking that maybe, if Heatdish, if Tohir, doesn't give him what he needs, maybe it's time to entertain the unthinkable.

Maybe it's time to ask Jordan Webber-Hayden questions in a way she can't refuse to answer them anymore.

His phone rings again.

"Brock, go."

"She's out." Heath exhales relief in his ear. "She's alive, she's with them, and she's out."

"And Heatdish?"

"Wounded but stable. They're coming back through Hurlburt. I'd like permission to fly down and be there for her reintegration."

"That's negative. You know protocol, Captain. Leave it to Counter-intelligence. You can do her debrief at Belvoir."

"Yes, sir."

"Anything else?"

"No, sir. We got lucky the Indigo who found her held his fire."

"Yes, we did," Brock says, and he hangs up, wondering if it was skill or luck that saved Blackfriars's life.

Or maybe the shooter was just slow.

Chapter Four

BRICKYARD NEEDS HER NAME.

Bell turns to the woman, hands zip-tied at the small of her back, kneeling on the concrete bed of the hangar, hair mussed and hiding her face, with Steelriver standing guard over her. She's barely half dressed, had managed to get herself into a pair of black jeans and some kind of sheer black tank, or perhaps she was already in them when they crashed the bedroom but hadn't made it as far as shoes, socks, or a shirt. The top doesn't cover as much as promise more, the kind of thing women wear because men want them to, and Bell can see scars on her, one recent, one long since healed; a scoring along her shoulder that might have been made by a bullet's touch, the other visible just above the right hip, where an inch or so of flesh was torn away. Her hair is as black as the tank pretends to be, and neither is as black as her mood. Dark brown eyes glare at Bell from behind the curtain of her hair when he relays the question.

"Blackfriars. The word of the day," she adds, "is *biplane.*"

"Your name," he repeats.

"Blackfriars. Biplane. Fuck you."

Bell brings the sat phone back to his ear, gives Brickyard that answer. Far away in the TOC, in the tactical operations center, Bell imagines Colonel Daniel Ruiz looking expectantly at the duty officer as he or she runs this new information through the computers. While he waits for the comeback he crosses to Vosil Tohir, now laid out on a stretcher. Chaindragger is guarding while Cardboard finishes putting a line into the man's arm. Tohir is unconscious, and Bell suspects he didn't go there easily or without a chemical escort.

"Stable," Cardboard tells him, looking up. "He's going to be hurting when he wakes up."

"Ready to move in two," Bell says.

Both men nod.

"Warlock," Brickyard says in Bell's ear. "Confirm presence of Blackfriars—Nessuno, Petra Graziella, chief warrant officer two, United States Army, in your AO, attached Bravo-Interdict. Cannot confirm proof of life at this time. Grade provisional as friendly. Will update as information becomes available."

Bell looks back to the woman, who, Ruiz says, has quite probably been telling them the truth. The black mood makes the smile she shoots him positively poisonous. Bell's heard Bravo-Interdict mentioned before. He's heard the nickname, too.

Bitches Incorporated.

"Cut her loose and bring her back," Brickyard says. "Your ride should be wheels-down now."

"Affirm," Bell says, and kills the call. Outside the hangar, he can hear the approaching whine of the Learjet. He stuffs the phone away, motions Steelriver from his post, and points him to the doors of the hangar for overwatch. The other soldier moves without a word, and Bell frees his knife, thumbs the blade to out-and-locked while moving behind CW2 Petra Graziella Nessuno, called Blackfriars. She tracks his every move until she's sure of what he's doing, does it without a sense of satisfaction or even impatience, and when the zip-tie binding is cut, she's back to her feet almost immediately. She rubs her wrists, kicks out her legs, easing the ache in her knees, restoring circulation.

"I gave you the word of the day." There's no accusation.

"You gave me tomorrow's word of the day."

"It *is* tomorrow. You shifted time zones."

Bell hears Cardboard chuckle.

"Board." Bell doesn't look at him. "Give the chief your shirt."

Combat climb to thirty-eight thousand feet before they've leveled off and are streaking west. Tohir strapped down, still in his chemically assisted slumber, lying across the bench on the port side of the cabin. Cardboard, known as Sergeant Freddie Cooper, without his shirt but still wearing his jacket, now zipped half shut, sits opposite the prisoner, watching him, occasionally leaning forward to check the dressing on the wound or to adjust the flow from the IV. They're closest to the cockpit, and when Cardboard isn't attending the package, he sips water from a plastic bottle, lost in his own thoughts. It's his way after action, Bell knows; they've served together for more than a decade, they know the scent of each other's tears. After the fight, Cardboard always goes inside.

Chaindragger and Steelriver are parked on the benches midcabin, and if Chaindragger wants to follow Cardboard's example, nothing's doing. Steelriver keeps peppering him with questions as the younger man attempts to read a book on his tablet. Steelriver is spacing the questions out for maximum annoyance effect, testing the other man's patience.

Of the four Indigo shooters, Chaindragger — Isaiah Rincon — is the youngest, assigned to Bell's team for just under a year now. Twenty-six years old, Afro-Caribbean, slight and serious, he's got nothing to prove to Bell or, frankly, to anyone else. But Steelriver, Master Sergeant Tom O'Day, is a substitute on their team, pulled to fill in for another of Bell's shooters who's currently convalescing from the cracked ribs his vest gave him in trade for saving his life. Normally Steelriver heads up his own team, and that gives him certain privileges. One of those is to heckle the new guy, even if the new guy is only new to him.

"So what's that you're doing?"

"Reading."

"And what're you reading?"

Chaindragger never looks up. "A book."

O'Day shoots a grin at Bell, then asks Chaindragger, "Any dirty parts?"

"Nope."

"So what's it about?"

"The corruption of American politics as predicted by Eisenhower."

Long pause this time. "Say again?"

"How it is we've become the bitch of the military-industrial complex."

Pause, not quite as long as the last. "And why the fuck would a lean, mean door kicker like yourself be reading something like that?"

"Know your enemy."

And so on.

Bell gives his attention to the small collection of objects recovered from Tohir's person. They've been tagged and labeled and stowed in Ziploc bags. There's a knife, not unlike the one he himself is carrying, taken from the man's pocket; a very nice Patek Philippe watch, taken from the man's wrist; a metal cigarette lighter from another pocket that shows scratches and wear but no insignia or design. There's a wad of bills, euros and dollars among them, retrieved from the man's Skivvies. There's a smartphone from another pocket, and, despite the temptation, Bell leaves that thing alone. The techs will go to town on it, and if there's security keeping the device protected, they'll go to town on that, too. No sense risking a data wipe.

Blackfriars, who is really Nessuno, emerges from the shitter, where she disappeared shortly after takeoff, almost half an hour ago. She grabs a bottle of water for herself from a galley cabinet, then drops into the leather-upholstered seat opposite Bell. She's a big girl, maybe five ten, but Freddie's shirt is still large on her. Her compromise has been to knot one edge of the hem above her scarred hip and to roll the sleeves up to her shoulders. Before, in the house and again in the hangar, there was no personalization to the skin she was showing. Now that her body is more concealed, Bell finds himself oddly more aware of it. She is soldier-fit, and there's a fading flush on her cheeks. He watches her for a moment too long, and she catches him at it.

"Why wasn't I warned you were coming?" Again, no accusation, but she's looking directly at Bell, and the gaze has strength.

"Same reason we didn't know you'd be there. Someone didn't see fit to share."

"He's mine." She indicates the items spread out on the small table between them, each in its bag. "I've been working him for sixteen months. All this is mine."

"We can sort it when we're back home."

She weighs Bell's decision not to argue. Takes a drink from her bottle.

"Sixteen months," Bell says.

"And a year to get into position, to earn his trust."

Her eyes are not so much brown as amber, a touch of red, like rust. There's no emotion in them for Bell to read, just as there was no inflection in her words. He doesn't want to imagine what is required to earn the trust of Vosil Tohir. But more than two years on an operation, that raises questions for him, and he makes a mental note to bracket Ruiz and see if an explanation or two might not be forthcoming.

"Two years. Over in less than a minute," she says, like she's in his head. Her voice is oddly monotone.

"Tohir wasn't the primary target?"

Nessuno shakes her head slightly, answering and refusing at once. No, Vosil Tohir wasn't her primary target, and no, she will not be telling him who was. There is no smile, no frown.

"Someone owes you an apology."

"It's standard operating procedure, right?" she says. "SOP, I was an unknown, a potential threat. I'd have punched me in the gut, too."

There is no smile, and Bell can't tell if she's joking, but he grins anyway. "You were the source of our intel."

"Possibly. Above my pay grade."

"Above mine."

"That so?" She indicates Freddie with her chin, then tilts her head back slightly, toward Isaiah and Tom O'Day. "I get to know who you are?"

"Warlock," Bell says. "Cardboard, Chaindragger, Steelriver."

"Ah." She takes another drink from her bottle. "What does that make me?"

"A breath of fresh air," O'Day says, having given up on harassing Chaindragger and now half leaning over the back of his seat to face them. He's giving Nessuno a smile that Bell imagines she gets an awful lot.

"Where do we touch down?" she asks.

"Ramstein to refuel, continuing to Hurlburt. Still sorting out the delivery. You're on for the duration."

"That on orders?"

"That is on orders, Chief."

She shows no reaction at all, no displeasure, no emotion, and Bell thinks she must be very good at her job. Now that she's stepping back into the light from her cover for the first time in more than two years, he wonders how long it will be before she doesn't second-guess her every action and reaction. Bell has done undercover work himself, but only on short-term assignments, the longest just over four months, and always in service of a very directed op. His last placement, at the WilsonVille theme park, lasted just shy of two months, a preemptive move that failed in its initial goal but succeeded in its ultimate one. For Bell, that was a plenty long time to be under, and it hadn't been in a hostile theater. What the chief has done he can accept without pause. How she has done it is beyond his imagining.

Bravo-Interdict is another of the many secrets that make up the Joint

Special Operations Command, like SOAR and DEVGRU and all the rest. Whereas the Special Operations Aviation Regiment provides operational aircraft alongside the Air Force Tactical Equipment Group — this Learjet and its crew no doubt among them — and DEVGRU has its cadre of navy-trained shooters, Bravo-Interdict stands by itself. Not strictly shooters, though all of them know where to point the business end of a gun, but rather an intelligence unit that places its operators covertly, sometimes under very deep cover indeed. Indigo, Delta, and DEVGRU all do the same to a lesser extent. The differences are that this is Bravo-Interdict's mandate, and Bravo-Interdict's operators are all female.

Y chromosomes need not apply.

Politicians and the brass can argue about putting women on the front line all they like, but the fact is, war is and always has been driven by necessity. You use what you've got, the same way you go to war with the army you have, not the army you want. JSOC has been placing women *behind* the front lines for years now, and anyone who thinks that work has been bleach-clean and flower-print dresses is demonstrating a remarkable and willful naïveté. That CW2 Petra Nessuno was in Vosil Tohir's bed when they hit the house and not in the clear means that either someone back home fucked up or she was working on a very long leash.

What she was doing in that bed Bell fully knows and doesn't really care. The army gets the body, and to imply a moral difference between sleeping with someone and shooting that person in the face to achieve the mission's objective is academic. The goal is the same. The goal is to successfully complete the mission. The goal is victory.

For the first time, Bell lets himself consider how close he came to killing the woman opposite him, and that opens the gates. The adrenaline crashes. Tension unlocks. Muscles relax. The trembling starts in his hands, and he keeps them below the line of the table, tries to relax his palms against his thighs, waiting for the reaction to pass. This is normal, a physiological response, one he has experienced too many times to count; it is the reason Cardboard goes inside after an op and why Chaindragger buries himself in a book and why Steelriver won't shut up. Bell knew it was coming, but Nessuno's presence makes it all the more fierce. She is still watching him, and Bell moves his eyes from her to the man strapped down on the couch, one who, he knows, cannot, at least for the moment, return the gaze.

It occurs to him that the chief was in the shitter for a long time. He didn't hear her vomiting. Maybe he's engaging in transference. Or maybe one of the things Bravo-Interdict teaches its operators is how to throw up in silence.

When he looks back to her, she's staring out the window at black sky. The water bottle in her hand is empty, crushed. The knuckles on the holding hand are white from her grip.

The Learjet tires kiss the tarmac at Ramstein, come to a stop long enough for a ground crew to connect hoses and force-feed fuel, for the air crew to swap. Once they're flying again Bell switches seats with Cardboard. He checks Vosil Tohir's vitals, replaces the bag on the IV with a fresh one. Pulse, respiration, blood pressure all look good. Bell concludes that their prize is stable and will survive the journey intact and thus their mission will be deemed a success. Steelriver, Cardboard, and Chaindragger are all being smart soldiers, stealing sleep, but Nessuno, like Bell, remains awake, still pondering the unseen out her window. Bell glances at her every so often, but is careful to not do so too much or for too long.

Fatigue settles along with the silence, the constant thrum of the engines. It's been a hard handful of days that culminated with breaking through Vosil Tohir's door. Bell lacerated his right palm on a piece of broken glass four days earlier, took cuts across his lower back at the same time. Muscles in his left shoulder, strained in a nearly fatal fall, join the chorus of injuries. He has bruises along his left side, stitches on his left forearm closing a slash from a knife, innumerable scrapes and scratches, and for most of them he cannot remember the moment of acquisition. He was punched in the nose, and when he holds a tissue to it and blows he ends up with dried kernels of blood in his snot. How he was spared a break he can't imagine. He hurts.

He knows his mind is drifting, tries to rope it back, and looks to Nessuno again, still showing her profile. He doesn't see her. Instead, he sees Athena, his daughter, and the other hurt reawakens, one he's had to put out of his mind to do the job at hand. She must feel him looking because she meets his eyes, and he sees her confusion and her anger and her loss. The deaf have a focus to make a sniper weep, and Athena is boring through him like she's digging for a core sample in an ice sheet. Her hands move, quick, angry, signing to him, and he cannot understand what she's trying to say. Carmine droplets mar his daughter's fair skin, a fine mist that settles on her cheek. It's the blood of the woman who saved her life, a CIA operative named Shoshana Nuri. Bell thinks his daughter looks more like her mother each time he sees her. He's afraid she looks at him now the way Amy does, as something unfeeling and monstrous.

"Coffee."

Nessuno is on the couch beside him, indicating two mugs resting on the tray she's unfolded.

"I figured black," she says.

Bell grunts assent, straightens against the couch, runs a hand over his eyes. It's the lacerated palm; he catches a lingering whiff of antiseptic and nothing pungent underneath, and the dressing doesn't seem to have slipped. Runs his other hand through his dark hair, leans back, sitting like a human once more. He takes the mug closest to him and inhales the unmistakable scent of instant. It tastes like thin charcoal. She drinks hers, and together they watch Vosil Tohir's chest rise and fall in gentle rhythm.

"You were staring at me."

"Apologies, Chief."

"You were sleeping with your eyes open."

This is news to Bell. There's nothing in her tone to indicate she's joking. There's been no change in her tone at all.

"Trade secret," he says. "Was I?"

"At first. They closed eventually."

"I was seeing my daughter."

Nessuno turns her head to study him. There's more rust than amber now, a trick of the cabin lighting. "Strong resemblance?"

"None whatsoever." He stops himself from adding "except that you both are beautiful." He suspects it is the last thing the chief wants to hear, true or not. "I must have been dreaming."

"You're married."

"For almost twenty years. Ended about nine months ago." Bell goes back to watching Tohir, the movement of his slumbering breast. He can feel Nessuno still staring at him, and it reminds him of Athena, and he wonders if that weren't the fuel for his brief fugue.

"You must've been young."

"Eighteen. Got married just after advanced individual training."

Nessuno maybe nods. "Long time to be married."

"I missed most of the last decade."

She maybe nods again, joins him once more in watching Tohir sleep.

"You have people waiting?" Bell asks her.

She maybe shakes her head.

"Nobody?"

"It's not ten years, but it's long enough."

"Can't be easy."

"You come back, it's like having been at deep ocean depths." Nothing in her voice has changed, though she's picking her words with obvious care. She holds her mug of instant in both hands, and Bell can see the color draining from her fingers as her grip tightens. "You have to come back up slowly or you get the bends. Decompression. I can feel it now. I keep looking at him, afraid he'll wake up and see me on this plane, with all of you, and then he'll know I lied to him. He'll know I betrayed him. I'll be blown, and he'll kill me. It's not rational. It's over now. But I keep feeling it."

"He's not going to wake up before we land."

"I know. It's not rational, I said. I'm not rational. I think I've got the bends."

Bell smiles. "You're going to be okay, Chief."

"Why do you say that?"

"Because right now you know you're not."

She considers that for a long time before asking, "I hope that's true. I hope that's all it takes. What about you?"

Bell can't find it in himself to answer at first. He's thinking about Athena again, all that his daughter saw, all that his daughter must've felt. He thinks about how she must be struggling to process the murders she witnessed and the pain she experienced, all the helplessness and confusion and fear. He thinks about her courage and her brilliance. He thinks about the WilsonVille theme park, with its many magical characters and many magical stories, and how all of them end happily ever after.

"I don't know," Bell says.

Chapter Five

SHE HAD WANTED to be a dancer. She'd been pretty good, too. Once. But she was poor, from a desperately poor family, and that poverty brought the worst out in those around her in word and deed. If it hadn't been for her Lover, she would never have escaped, and if it hadn't been for her genes, her Lover would never have discovered her at all. She was smart, and she was lovely, and while she was still too young, certain men took a fancy to her. It was with one of those men her Lover had seen her, and it was from those men her Lover had taken her, and she had been gratefully, gladly his ever since.

Sometimes, against all protocol, she would dance. Late at night and alone, without the soldier or any of the others who so often came to call, her iPod strapped to her upper arm and her noise-canceling headphones over her ears, she would be the prima ballerina she'd dreamed of becoming, the shining star held aloft. She would lose herself in imagination, falling back into childhood fantasy and out of this life. She would blend steps and styles, and in the end, she would always see her Lover, the man who had made her. Her fantasy would focus, and memory would reinvent details, and the imagined audience would disappear — the stage, the lights, all of it — would vanish, and she would be in her expensive condo in Washington, D.C.'s, West End, dancing just for him. He would see again her devotion, and know how much she loved him, and she would feel once more how much he loved her.

There was very little in her life that she believed without restraint or suspicion. The men and women who came to her, that she had carefully seduced—and that was the only word for it, she knew—she viewed with an ever-present caution. The nature of her relationship with each and every one of them was the same, changed only in the details. The soldier, the sailor, the financier, the lawmaker, the expert, the analyst, it didn't matter. The frame of any affair is deceit, after all. She would've understood that anyway, even if her Lover hadn't made it clear.

"They are targets, Zoya," her Lover told her. "They will want you because you are forbidden. They will want you because they should *not* want you, and your task will be to use that desire, without their knowing, to bring them close, and once they take that step into your arms, you will be everything they need you to be. If you do that, if you give them that, they will come back again and again and again."

"So I am to be a prostitute," she said, unwilling to keep the bitterness from her voice. She was sixteen at the time and already had lost her illusions.

He took her chin in his hand. He kissed her lips gently.

"You think that is how I see you, Zoyenka? That I could think so little of you? No. You are an artist, body and soul."

She had needed to believe him, had needed the validation, but in the way that all lies told by lovers ultimately ring hollow, it had been his actions more than his words that proved him right. He spent money, so much money, on her. So many classes, so many instructors, traveling from one city to another as her Lover directed, sent to meet this man or this woman. At every door, greeted as if she were expected, as if whoever this teacher was, they were delighted by her presence, by the opportunity to share knowledge with her. She would go days or weeks or even a month or more without hearing from him, only to be surprised by a message passed along by her tutor du jour that her Lover was at the Portobello, or the Cipriani, or the Kempinski, or wherever, and that he was waiting to see her.

"Show me what you've learned," he would say, and, nervously, she would. When she did it well, displayed some new facet to her Art, his delight would shine, and her heart would sing. When she fumbled, misspoke, or in some other way faltered, he would chide her, tell her that art was a journey, not a destination, that what she did would require a lifetime of work. She was so smart; he made a point of telling her this again and again. He assured her that her mind far more than her body was what had captured him. As she learned to display her wit, she learned she could make him laugh, and he told her she was the only one to do that, and that he loved her for it all the more.

"Beauty is made common," he said one night in Copenhagen. "Beauty can be bought off the shelf in Zurich or London or New York; everywhere you look, it's on sale. And sex, you know already. Sex is easy, there for the taking. You keep your beauty uncommon, Zoyenka. Let it be your own. Your beauty is gravity, and it will draw others into your orbit just as it has drawn me. But who you *are* will capture and keep them."

"You're not jealous, *dorogoy?* Of the things that I will do with them? The ways they will touch me?"

"I am terribly jealous," her Lover said, his honesty delighting her. "Already I am, and I will always be. Jealous that others are with you when I cannot be. Jealous that I spend so much of my life away from you already, and not with you. I would be with you always, Zoya, all day, every day, if I could. But we are remaking the world, and if the sacrifice required means I must suffer without you, if I must suffer another's hands upon you until the work is done, then that is my burden, and I shall carry it. And I will take heart that you are with me, that we are working together, and that one day, we will have our victory, and our reward."

They would part, and she would return to her studies, to mastering her Art, and sometimes she would think that if any other man spoke to her like that, spoke about remaking the world, she would've thought him insane. But her Lover was the most rational, thoughtful man she had ever known, and she suspected it was genius rather than madness she saw in him. Surely it took genius to do what he did, to live so invisibly and yet to have such power, and as her studies advanced with her years, she became more and more certain of this.

When he had first found her, he had been a man others feared. Now, a decade gone, he had become a ghost and a god, a guiding, invisible hand that could move her across dozens of borders under dozens of names and she would never once earn a second glance in her passing. He was a secret to be whispered into the ears of men like the soldier in the breathless moments postclimax, a name that could shatter the world at a command. She knew this. She knew what had happened in California, the terrorists and the theme park, and she knew it had been her Lover who had made it happen on behalf of the soldier and his friends.

It had been a decade since he had discovered her, changed her, claimed her. It had been ten years since he had brought her to life, and given her his love, and she never, not for a moment, doubted the sincerity of his devotion to her. He had done for her everything he had promised and more. Never once had a door been barred, let alone closed. Never once, since he found her, had she wanted for anything.

Except him.

This is what made her moments of doubt so much worse. In the beginning, they had been few and far between, but as time wore on, as the distance between her and her Lover seemed to expand, they came more frequently. They would steal in upon her, always when she was alone, always when she was passive, waiting between rendezvous for one lover or the next. She would be idling, browsing in a bookstore or playing tourist along the Mall or gazing at the displays at the Smithsonian or at Air and Space, or she would be in the cool chill of a movie theater while voices boomed from speakers on every side.

Then she would feel the desire to simply abandon everything. To get up and walk out and drop the things that made her Jordan Webber-Hayden in the nearest trash can and to just keep walking until everything was left behind; every pretense, every artifice, every deception, divesting herself of all of it.

She could do it. She knew she could. She knew how; her Lover had made certain of that. He had given her the training and the skills to make such a disappearance not only viable but also relatively simple. A quick stop by one of the handful of caches that dotted the area around D.C. and she could pick up cash, fake ID — everything was there in carefully loaded go bags. Everything from a change of name to a change of clothes. She could leave it all, with only unanswered questions in her wake and a handful of lovers who would wonder what happened, where she went, but who would never dare search for her for fear of revealing their own indiscretions.

She could do it. Escape this life and become anyone she wanted. Escape this life and pretend to be normal, to have what she saw all around her, a life without fear, a life without lies.

All it would take is betrayal. The betrayal of him. The betrayal of his trust. The betrayal of every promise for their future together.

If she could have her Lover again, she was sure her doubts would vanish, that these thoughts would no longer prey upon her. Just a moment to be with him, to hear his voice, to feel his arms around her and not the arms of these others, these men and women who whispered that they loved her. These men and women to whom she whispered back, telling them the lies they wanted to believe.

She could do it, if she would betray him.

She hated herself for even considering such a thing.

The morning after the soldier's visit, she rises late and goes downstairs to the condo's fitness center to swim her laps. She does this every day except Sunday, varying the length of her swim to keep it fresh to her body, sometimes twenty minutes, sometimes forty minutes, and, once every other week, a full hour. This is a lesson from her first tutor, an Italian who looked barely past forty and assured Zoya that she was almost seventy, who asserted that she'd never had so much as a nip or a tuck, who claimed to have been setting honey traps since the Cold War. Fitness, the woman had taught her, more than diet. The body is made to move, and moving the body keeps it happy, and happiness is always beautiful. Swimming is the best movement. Weights are for sculpting; swimming is to provide something to sculpt. So Zoya works with weights three days a week, mostly her legs and core, only rarely her arms, because the swimming is good for that, too.

Going from the pool back upstairs, a smile and sincere good morning to Mr. Kamen in the elevator as he steps out and she steps in, hair dripping from the pool, towel snugged about her waist.

"Jordan, you're all wet!"

"It happens every time I see you, Stephen."

He laughs and wishes her a good day, and she grins as he goes. Stephen Kamen is gay, in his fifties, and works down on K Street, and they both enjoy the joke. She figured him out early, the way she studied every tenant in the building to the best of her ability. That had been a lesson from her third instructor, the nervous American who had lived too many years spying in Moscow, who would switch midsentence from English to Russian and back again and not realize he'd done it. Learn the terrain, he'd taught her; learn the people, the places, the patterns, and watch them for even the slightest change.

Back in her apartment, she showers, dresses in jeans and a plain white T-shirt, makes herself a breakfast of yogurt with sliced peaches and a cup of green tea. She washes up, then she takes her laptop, the one her Lover had made just for her, puts it in her messenger bag, sets the alarm by the door, locks up, and heads out. She rides the elevator down to the parking lot with Theresa Irwin (forty-two, attorney, married to Ian, forty-one, attorney at the same firm, no children), small talk about the humidity and wondering when the weather is going to break and did you know D.C. was built on a swamp? Tell me about it.

She takes her car, a new Jetta, nothing ostentatious, past the Kennedy Center and almost across the Potomac, making her checks before reversing direction northeast. This she learned from the American, and the Frenchwoman, and the Spaniard, otherwise known as instructors three, five, and six. Ultimately she ends up in Georgetown, finds a place to park, and takes her time walking to the Saxbys on O Street. She orders another green tea and finds a seat at a sticky-topped table where no one can peek over her shoulder, where she looks like every other summertime student working on a laptop.

Dorogoy, will you speak to me?

Camera.

She switches the laptop's camera on, resettles herself so she is framed. She smiles, hoping against hope that he will return the favor, that she will get to see him, though she never does. Sometimes, she wonders if it's even he at the other end of their conversations, but she cannot imagine who else it could possibly be. Even so, it feels unfair, that her Lover can see her while he denies her the same. She understands why, of course. His secret is greater than hers. Even now, after all this time, she has no name for him other than *dorogoy* — my love.

Good.
Begin.

She types quickly.

B visited. They feel they are owed. He says Jamieson is dead.

There is a brief pause, and she is surprised by the response.

I did not know that.
They got what they paid for.

He was anxious. He wants what was promised.

Did he say anything more?

I don't understand.

Did he mention Tashkent?

He did not.

She stares at the screen, the empty messenger box, unsure if she should add anything else, resisting the urge to ask. It's unlike her Lover to pause during these conversations. These communications, encrypted though they are, bring risk, and she knows as well as he does that speed is crucial. But still, no response comes, nothing, and she takes a sip of her tea and glances about the coffee shop again, feeling a spur of anxiety, of warning. The memory of so many lessons, of the nervous American who told her to always trust her instincts. It's those instincts that make her type:

Is there a problem?

He still doesn't answer. The clock on the menu bar of her laptop marks a minute passing, then another, and she's feeling a tightness in her stomach, a nervousness she hasn't experienced in years, not since she first arrived in the United States with papers saying her name is Jordan Webber-Hayden and with the background to match. Not since she moved into the condo in the West End and those first, terrifying months of being careful, oh so very careful, that no one who shouldn't had noted her arrival. Not since she drew her first asset, the attorney from Justice, that careful dance that had to never once look like a dance at all. The first of many men and women who could surrender secrets that she would pass to her Lover, or could provide a service that he required, or simply be used, one day, for profit or gain.

> Meet him. Tell him this, exactly:
> I have the contingency. I will execute the contingency on my timeline. It will take seven days.

She nods, but now the words are appearing quickly.

> I want three things in return. I will not move forward until all are fulfilled.
> One: Tohir cannot be allowed to talk.
> Two: Correlation between those responsible for the counteroperation in California and the capture operation in Tashkent.
> If there is correlation, information on individuals involved.

Three?

> Three will depend on the answer to the two.

She waits, but nothing more appears. She reads over his words again, and the name Tohir means nothing to her at all. She understands what her Lover is demanding. It doesn't bother her in the slightest. Whoever Tohir is, whatever he has done, he is an enemy of her Lover and therefore an enemy of hers. His death is undoubtedly well deserved. It's the second and third conditions she finds confusing, and that does nothing to settle her nerves. She knows that what happened in California was resolved through use of force, that specialists went into the theme park and killed the terrorists. This draws a line from them to him, and the horrible thought strikes her that the reason for her Lover's pause is that they are now after him, too.

Are you safe?

> Tohir has made me vulnerable.
> I am not safe.
> Neither are you.

She stares at the screen.

> I love you.

The connection terminates.

Chapter Six

THERE'S A SUGAR maple in the front yard of the house on Edinborough Drive in Burlington, afternoon shade that falls across the front porch of the house, and it shelters it from the August heat. Half a kilometer from Appletree Bay, on Lake Champlain, and it's humid, but nothing like what Bell left behind on the Gulf of Mexico in the predawn. He's showered and changed since leaving Hurlburt, now wearing old 501s and a black T-shirt and a black windbreaker. He has a small duffel slung from his shoulder, the violet head of a stuffed dragon peering out. He flew in commercial, picked the stuffed animal up at the airport before grabbing his rental car, and he's still wondering if it was a good idea, if Athena will think it too childish. Wondering if any of this is a good idea, in fact, hearing his steps ring on the wooden porch as he stops at the front door. He called from Boston to tell Amy he was coming but didn't get an answer, left a message instead. She hasn't called back. She's never liked surprises.

The front door is a dull ivory and weathered by the Vermont winters, and Bell has steeled himself to knock when he hears the animal coming, looks to see a Rottweiler bounding around from the east side of the house. He's a big beast, even for the breed, and comes to a sudden stop at the sight of him, and together they share this moment of surprise. Broad skull and neck a little longer than average, black fur broken with patches of brown like the leather on a loved baseball glove. A dark red nylon collar is around his neck, tags visible but illegible from this distance.

He waits for the growl, but none comes. The dog makes its way to the foot of the porch, forepaws mounting the step, looking up at him.

"I'm Jad," Bell says.

The Rottweiler seems to accept that, comes closer. Bell lifts his right hand slightly, and the dog moves in to sniff at him, then lick his fingers. Bell uses his left hand to stroke the animal's neck, then scratch behind his ears. The heavy skull pushes up against his hand in approval. Bell drops to his haunches, putting the two of them at eye level, then proceeds to rub the dog's coarse coat with vigor. He also takes this opportunity for a closer look at the tags. The name is Leaf. The phone number is for Amy's mobile.

"Leaf," Bell says. "Hello."

Leaf flops on his side on the porch, making the boards creak. He looks at Bell hopefully.

"Yeah, you're a ferocious beast." Bell grins, rubbing the dog's chin and belly. Leaf lolls. "Nothing gets past your perimeter, huh?"

The door behind him opens, and Bell swears he can feel the tension. Leaf lifts his head to look as Bell does, and they see Amy standing there. She's wearing cutoffs and a T-shirt that's been made to look older than it really is, faded blue with classic Wonder Woman on it and the words AMAZON PRINCESS.

"I called." Bell tries not to sound defensive.

"I know."

She pats her thighs with her palms, and the dog rolls onto his feet, rises from beneath Bell's hands and moves to Amy. Bell stands and faces her, feels the awkwardness and everything that comes with it. He's looking at the only woman he's ever loved, and she will always be beautiful in his eyes. There was distance between them before the divorce, but the gulf seemed to stabilize once the separation became legal. Then came the Hollyoakes School for the Deaf's visit to WilsonVille, and everything else that followed, and six days later he thinks that she maybe hates him now. He feels that, and he feels his affection for her still.

Amy runs a hand along Leaf's back, and the dog nudges past her thigh and into the house.

"You didn't call back," Bell says.

"No, I didn't."

"If you didn't want me to come…"

Her lower lip juts out as she exhales, the sigh enough to make her bangs flutter slightly. "I don't know what I want. I couldn't decide."

"How's Athena doing?"

"Not well. She's been spending a lot of time at Joel's. He had to have surgery."

Bell remembers Joel, a classmate and maybe more of his daughter's. The young man had been injured at the park. "He's recovering?"

Amy nods once. She's just looking at him, her expression neutral except at her eyes, where the slight lines of age have deepened. Bell thinks that once, he would've known exactly what she was thinking.

"How are you doing?" he asks.

She looks past him, at the trees between them and Appletree Bay.

"Not that well, either," Amy says.

She turns around and heads inside, but she leaves the door open, so Bell thinks he's at least welcome that far. He follows her down the hall, past pictures of her parents and Athena and other faces he recognizes but cannot immediately place. There's only one picture of them together, from a different age, she in her cheerleader outfit and he dressed to play ball. He remembers the game, fall of his senior year, against Jefferson, their hated rival. He remembers winning that game and being self-aware enough to think he was the all-American male cliché, a Springsteen song, the football player with the cheerleader sweetheart.

He should've listened more carefully to those songs back then, Bell thinks. He'd have known it would've never worked out.

The hall ends at a large, open kitchen, split in half by a cooking island on the left. Leaf is waiting for them, lapping water from a stainless steel bowl. The dog stops long enough to acknowledge their arrival before noisily resuming. Perhaps inspired by this, Amy goes to the fridge and pulls out a pitcher of iced tea, pours two glasses without a word. She leaves Bell's on the counter for him to take.

"How long do you have?" Amy asks. "I mean, we have plans for dinner."

"So I should leave before dinner."

"Or you can eat alone."

Bell gestures back down the hall. "I'm not in love with this place."

"It was a bargain, Jad, especially for what I can afford. Athena loves it here."

He tries to explain. "I don't like the sight lines. There's no good cover."

She stares at him.

"You still have the shotgun?"

"Jad."

"I don't want anything to happen to either of you, that's all."

"What, you mean like being taken hostage with your daughter's class at fucking WilsonVille, is that what you mean?"

"I told you not to come."

"But you didn't say *why,* Jad!"

"I didn't know why, Amy. I told you what I could when I could."

She shakes her head, beyond frustrated with him. Looks out the window over the kitchen sink, into a backyard that's big and fenced with tall, thick trees, and Bell doesn't like the looks of those, either. He keeps that to himself.

"And what aren't you telling me now?" she asks. "In my house all of two minutes, you're asking where the shotgun is, you're telling me you don't like my front hall? What aren't you telling me?"

"I don't want anything to happen to you."

"Because something *might*?"

"Something always might."

"No, no, you don't get to do that, Jad! Fuck you, fuck your security and your secrets, just tell me!"

He hesitates. Leaf has left his water bowl and now moved to post up at Amy's left leg, watching him. Bell appreciates that, at least.

"We don't know who was responsible, and we don't know how much they know."

"You're saying they might know about you. What you did."

"Yes."

"That you killed all those men."

"Yes."

"And that they might come after Athena and me to get at you? To hurt you?"

"Yes."

"You're paranoid, and you're trying to make me paranoid. You killed them all. You, and Freddie, and Jorge, and Isaiah, you did your jobs, you killed the bad guys, you splashed the Tangos, however the fuck you put it. They're all dead. How could they know who I am? How could they know who you are?"

Bell just shakes his head. There are too many ways, even if there shouldn't be any ways at all.

The look she gives him overflows with contempt, and she's about to voice as much, but instead is signing when she speaks, looking past him. "Look who's here."

Athena stands on the other side of the kitchen, beside the square dining table. She nods, staring at her father, feeling the tension between her parents. Bell opens his arms to her, and his daughter moves into the hug without hesitation, but slowly, without a smile. He feels her arms close around him, her face pressing into his chest. She's taller every time he sees her, he thinks. It has barely been a week, and he's sure she's put on another quarter of an inch. He puts his nose in her hair at the top of her head, closes his eyes, squeezing her gently in return. She smells like apples.

She holds on to him for the better part of a minute before letting go, gazes up at him. Her expression is grave, and he feels like he's being measured in those gray eyes. Then she tracks along the strap at his shoulder to the duffel he's still wearing, and she sees the dragon's head poking out. She pulls the stuffed animal free, raises an eyebrow at him. *Really?*

He signs, *Saw it in the airport thought of you.*

She gnaws on her lip, a mannerism that makes her look all the more like her mother, and the resemblance between Amy then and Athena now is so striking Bell feels it in his breast. She manages a small smile, then sets the dragon on the counter beside the untouched iced teas.

Did not know you were coming.

Sorry, Bell says. *Called no answer.*

Staying? The question is asked more in her face than in her sign.

Only a couple of hours.

Where?

Going to visit Uncle Jorge.

Want you to stay.

Bell shakes his head.

The small smile fades.

Want to go for a walk? Bell asks.

Athena nods.

"Go," Amy says.

Bell thinks it sounds like an order.

They walk without talking, along Edinborough, then south, roughly in the direction of the water, following the Island Line Trail until they're into Leddy Park. It's cool in the shade, and they take their time, and Bell doesn't know what to say, so he says nothing. He's beginning to think Athena's adopted the same tactic when she veers onto a side trail and takes a couple quick steps to get ahead of him. She pivots so she's walking backwards, her hands flying.

You should have come back with Mom and me you left us alone.

I know, Bell signs. *I did not want to leave you alone I wanted to be with you.*

Always job I do not like your job now I know your job Dad.

She's still walking backwards, glaring at him, and Bell feels a nervous spur that she'll trip over something, that she'll fall. The same feeling when she was learning to walk and he and Amy tried to baby-proof the house in Arizona, fitting foam cushions to every sharp corner they found. It's the same feeling he had when he would watch her run to meet him after he returned from deployment, or as he was coming up the driveway, or at any number of other moments. He thinks that this is the nature of being a parent; always trying to protect your children from the inevitable fall.

Maybe watch where you are walking? Bell signs.

The glare ratchets up to include scorn, and Athena throws her hands up in the air, pivots without stopping, her steps brisk. He has to hurry to move abreast of her, then catches her eyes long enough to sign again.

Angry at me.

She lets her look say it all. There's a bench made from recycled plastic painted to look like green wooden planks. She springs toward it, onto the seat so she stands half a foot taller than he does, looks over his head as she signs.

I see the blood out of her mouth.

Bell nods.

That woman died she saved my life she has no name.

Her name was Shoshana Nuri, Bell answers, spelling it out. *Very brave.*

Athena's jaw clenches, and her eyes narrow, and Bell can see she's fighting tears.

Mom says Joel feels better.

She ignores the change of subject, ignores what he's signed. *I see the blood out her mouth I see Mr. Howe's broken head I feel that man touch me.*

It's that last one that cuts deepest. None of the hostages was assaulted, Bell knows this, just as he knows that the threat of rape was implicit against his daughter and ex-wife and the other female students from Hollyoakes. He's never been held against his will himself, not outside of Survival, Evasion, Resistance, and Escape training. SERE tries to run as close as possible to the real thing, and it does a mighty good job of it, too; Bell has no fond memories of his experiences. Instilling helplessness is what a captor does, and unwanted hands on your person is just another means to accomplish that. But it's not the same, and it's another thing entirely for women for all the obvious reasons.

Bell finds himself thinking about Chief Petra Nessuno, wondering where she is now.

Nightmares? he asks his daughter.

Athena nods slowly. If she clenches her jaw any tighter, Bell thinks, she'll shatter her molars.

You tell your mother?

Her brow furrows for an instant, her lips compressing to white lines, forcing the blood from them. She shakes her head.

She has nightmares too I think.

Bell exhales, looks down the narrow trail, feels like an ass for not granting Amy what he so readily gave Athena. His own sleep is not so much that of the just as that of the exhausted, and he rarely can recall his dreams. It's always been that way for him; nightmares, when they do come, when he can remember them upon waking, consistently revolve around the mundane. Less about bloodshed directly than about bloodshed through his mistakes, failings as a soldier, failing his squad. Most often, when he remembers his bad dreams, they center on his daughter and his ex-wife.

Nightmares go away if you talk about them, Bell signs. *You should talk about them.*

Athena shrugs, signs quickly. *Just did.*

Maybe talk about them with Mom.

She blinks at him slowly. *Mom worries.*

I worry.

She takes a moment, then signs, *Always am careful.*

Tell me.

She gives him a look that is pure teenager, the look that says she knows this already, and doesn't want to repeat the obvious for the thousandth time.

Tell me, Bell signs.

Know who is around know where to go know how to get out know where to hide know where to get help.

He smiles. *Good memory.*

Shotgun in closet with towels.

Mom says shotgun in basement.

She glances down at her feet on the faux planks, then back to him. The sign is fast. *Moved it.*

Loaded?

A look that says duh, and then she signs, *Expensive bat.*

Bell laughs softly. She's quoting him.

Not safe tell Mom.

Athena nods.

She will worry less if you share with her, Bell says.

You talk to her?

She does not want to talk to me I think.

Athena considers that, then nods again, agreeing. Bell offers her the hug and she hops down from her perch into it, and he wraps her tightly again in his arms. He doesn't think he'll be able to let go when the time comes.

"I love you," he whispers into her hair. She can't hear him, but she feels him speaking.

"I love you, too, Daddy," she says.

* * *

The airport in Hailey, Idaho, is just long enough to accommodate a private jet, which is, of course, one of the factors that recommended the place. The National Guard barracks nearby is another. The fact that it's a small community occasionally favored by the rich and famous as a getaway is a third, because that brings with it a fourth; it is a community that values privacy, that has taught itself not to stare, that's small enough to be close but isn't so isolated as to be closed. Those who come and go draw only a modest amount of attention.

Bell steps off the plane just after 2200 local, crosses the tarmac, and proceeds on through the small terminal into the parking lot and the night beyond. He finds the F-150 exactly where it should be, double-checks the plates to be sure, then uses the wireless key from the packet the duty sergeant gave him before he boarded the plane at the Air National Guard base back in Burlington to open the pickup. He tosses his duffel on the seat beside him, starts the vehicle, and checks the sat nav. There's a destination programmed, and he keys it, then follows directions along near-empty streets until he's parking in front of a house he's never visited before that is now, he's been told, his. He climbs out, locks up, and for a moment pauses, just to take everything in, to take stock. It's a quiet street, only six other houses, each of them with plenty of elbow room along the property lines. Lights in two of the six, more pickups and SUVs parked outside. The sky has the faded darkness and abundance of stars you can only get when away from the urban light dome, and the air smells of grass and pine and summer.

He's got a set of keys from the same packet, and one of them opens the door to the house. He knocks the door closed behind him with the heel of his boot, throws the lock, finds the switch. Still with the duffel on his shoulder, he spends the next fifteen minutes or so on a walk-through, peering into each room, opening and closing cupboards and pantries and closets. There're three bedrooms, two baths, a finished basement, and a kitchen that looks to have been recently renovated. Whoever handled the decorating and furnishing kept things modest, regional, and almost impersonal. If you didn't look too closely, you could believe that someone was already living here.

In the master bedroom, Bell unpacks his duffel, a process that takes him almost no time at all. There are already clothes in the dresser, and he knows they'll fit. He takes the .45 in its holster from his hip, empties his pockets, then strips down and steps into the bathroom for a quick shower. The soap is Ivory. The shampoo is something called American Crew, and he's amused by that. There's even deodorant in the medicine cabinet, a Speed Stick.

He's getting dressed when the loneliness hits him, the thoughts he's kept at bay now breaking through. This was supposed to be his last house, for Amy and Athena and him. This was the house where he'd have told them that they could unpack all the boxes. This was the house, the community, where Athena could make friends she would keep, stay until she left for college, to come back to on holidays. His house.

His alone.

"Beer's in the fridge, bourbon's on the counter, vodka's in the freezer," Sergeant Jorge Velez, the fourth man on Bell's team, call sign Bone-breaker, calls out to Bell.

"So we have three of the four food groups, then."

"Isaiah's bringing pizza," Freddie Cooper says. "So we've actually got all four covered."

Bell heads to the kitchen and the fridge, finds a bottle, and snaps off the cap. Jorge's house is similar to Bell's, similar layout, just smaller, a one-hundred-and-some-odd-meter straight shot from one backyard to the other. Freddie's home is two down from Jorge's, the biggest of the three; he's somehow managed to maintain his marriage, and he's got two kids as proof. Isaiah lives down the block from Bell, at the corner, another two-bedroom, like Jorge's.

Bell comes back to the living room, where Jorge's seated on the couch, leaning against the arm to favor his uninjured ribs. Freddie's taken the easy chair, and both men are focused on a soccer game on the television, what Bell concludes must be a rebroadcast, judging by the late hour.

"Dig your digs?" Jorge asks.

"High speed," Bell says.

"Nice thing about being off rotation. I got to redecorate."

Bell looks around and concludes that the only real redecorating Jorge has done was to bring in a larger television, a sound system, and a gaming console. "Yeah, you've definitely put your stamp on it."

"I've got broken ribs. I have to work slow."

"He's malingering," Freddie says. "Trying to get sympathy from the local fillies."

"I don't need sympathy to get the local fillies." Jorge taps his chest with his palm. He's shorter than Bell and Freddie, but still taller than Isaiah, long in the leg and lean, a dancer's body. If he had the personality to be hunting hookups he'd have no problem finding them, but in all the time Bell has known him, Jorge's gone on all of two dates. With his friends and his comrades, when he's on the job, he's deep in the give-and-take. Outside of those spheres, Bell — along with Freddie and Isaiah — knows Jorge to be painfully shy.

Isaiah arrives with pizza, two boxes, and their contents are rapidly decimated, and more beer is just as quickly consumed. The soccer game ends, and talking heads replace them, and Jorge turns the television off in annoyance. Conversation bounces from topic to topic, but centers at first on this community, on Hailey. Freddie's been here the longest, just under a year, time enough to settle his family, and then Jorge was placed next, just six months ago. Isaiah got his keys two weeks before moving to join Bell on the operation in California and, like Bell, had been placed undercover, which means he's had no chance to establish himself.

"Sticking out like a sore thumb," Isaiah says. "Black guy in white town."

"The eyefucking stops pretty quick," Jorge tells him.

"You're not black."

"I sure as shit ain't white."

"True dat."

"We'll put you behind the counter at the store," Freddie says. "Keep the customers away."

"What do we sell?" Bell asks.

"Repurposed and recovered antique wood products." Jorge raises his beer in respect. "We are like Jesus. We are carpenters."

"Tradesmen," Freddie says.

"You seen the website, Top?" Isaiah asks Bell. "Apparently we've got an armoire we're selling for fifty grand."

Bell laughs. "We line it with gold?"

Isaiah wipes his palms on the thighs of his jeans, holds them up to illustrate the grandeur of the armoire in question. "This is an antique hand-carved country French armoire from the Auvergne region, circa 1770, now restored in loving detail from the fixtures to the beveled mirror. We have spared no expense in returning it to its former glory, scouring the globe to find just the right sources in our quest to return it to its pristine condition."

Bell looks at Freddie. "You can't put him at the counter; he'll sell the damn thing, and then where will we be?"

"I'm sure the colonel could supply us with one if we really needed it."

"And take it out of our pay," Jorge says.

The business, the cover, is called Saw and Plane, chosen — Bell assumes — because it's so vague as to be useless. Part antiques resale, part restoration, it's a business that quite reasonably is maintained by four men who, naturally, travel often in support of their work. It's the kind of boutique specialty affair that justifies prices that beggar belief, a business that nonetheless is entirely plausible. It's the kind of cover that Ruiz would give his First Team operators to allow them to hide in plain sight, here in central Idaho, with convenient transport available at a moment's notice. Here, in theory, all of them are secure, safe, and hidden. Here Freddie doesn't have to worry about his wife, Melinda, or his daughters, Bettie and Georgia, and their safety and security. If Melinda is keeping a loaded shotgun in with the towels, it's because she wants to, not because she might need it.

Freddie maybe knows what Bell is thinking, because he says, "How's the family?"

The instinctive response is the cordial lie, that they're fine, but Bell doesn't say that, because he doesn't need to, not here, not with these men. "Rattled."

"Amy's made of steel," Jorge says. "She'll bounce back. So will Athena."

"It's not just what happened to them," Bell says after a moment. "It's all of it. You stack the divorce on top of it…Amy understood what we do, but she always kept her head down, and it's not like we ever talked about it, not like she ever knew the details. She can't forgive me, she thinks it's my fault, that I should've told her what would happen."

"Nobody knew what would happen," Isaiah says. "That's why we were there in the first place."

"But the fact is she's right. They should never have been there. I should've put Ruiz on her, had him shut the whole trip down." Bell empties the bottle in his hand, uses his thumbnail to pick at the peeling label. "But instead I gambled that it would be safe, and it was a bad bet, and I lost."

"They lived through it," Freddie says.

"Nuri didn't," Bell says.

Isaiah and Freddie leave just after one, each of them back to his own home, and after they're gone, Jorge says, "So."

"So?"

"Bitches Incorporated."

Bell gives him a dark look. "Somebody's been talking out of turn."

Jorge shrugs. "Just because I wasn't on the op doesn't mean I'm not on the team. Unless you're saying O'Day's got my job now."

"Not by my word."

"Good to hear. Freddie says she was in his bed when you hit jackpot."

"Freddie wasn't in the room."

"So you're saying she wasn't in his bed?"

"Sergeant, we are not talking about this."

"I didn't think they existed. Bitches Incorporated, I mean."

"They exist."

Jorge thinks about that. "Damn. I thought we were hard-core."

"Yeah," Bell says. "Me, too."

Chapter Seven

———————————

"I THINK YOU should get laid." Heath pours more Maker's Mark into the glass in front of Nessuno. "That's probably against doctor's advice, but then again, I think doctors are mostly full of shit. I think you should get laid, sleep late, read a dozen books, eat out at restaurants that serve your favorite foods, see every movie you've missed, spend some of that money you've saved up on things you don't need but you certainly deserve, and then get laid again. So there you go."

Nessuno takes the drink, holding it from the top by her fingertips, tented, and she can feel the slight chill from the ice beneath her palm. The cubes knock together in near silence.

"Or get drunk," Heath says. "Blind falling down throwing-up until you think you'll turn inside out drunk. You talk to your parents yet?"

"I talked to my parents." The answer comes flat, and Nessuno tries to remedy that, adding, "They want me to come home for a bit."

"So maybe you should listen to your parents." Heath finishes refilling her own glass, sets the bottle down before picking up her drink and leaning back against the couch. The bottle is more than half empty. It was full when they started. They're sitting in the living room of Heath's small home in Montgomery Village, Maryland, and it's past midnight.

"Maybe I should."

"Chicago in August. Might be nice."

"Have you been to Chicago in August?"

Heath raises her drink in mock toast, takes a swallow. Nessuno rocks her glass from side to side, slightly, watching the plane of alcohol shift, then brings it to her lips and finishes most of the pour in two swallows. She's not tasting the bourbon so much as feeling it, the scorching race of alcohol through her breast. She looks out the window to her left again, out over the front yard of the comfortable house, into a neighborhood that is silent and still. It's been more than thirty minutes since she's seen anything moving outside. Not even a car since then. It all feels deceptively safe and reassuring.

"The verbal debrief will hold," Heath says. "I'll stall the brass, you can take your time with the written. Seriously, take the time you need to get your head straight."

Nessuno tilts the glass, finds that it's empty.

"We need more ice," Heath says, rising and heading for the kitchen.

The Lear taxis straight into one of Hurlburt's hangars upon landing, and the doors close immediately behind them. The one called Steelriver is first down the stairs, with Nessuno coming second to last in the group of shooters, Warlock behind her. She's seen predawn creeping into the sky as they touched down, but once she's out of the light of the plane and into the hangar, everything here is sharp and bright, high halogens that bathe the cavernous interior blue-white and bounce a glare off the polished floor.

There are eleven men waiting, all in civvies. Nessuno casts her eyes over them in quick survey, trying to recognize faces and, failing that, duties. A black Chevy Blazer has been parked maybe ten meters away, and its motor is running, one man in a suit standing beside it and another visible behind the wheel. Something about them shouts federal to her rather than military. The others are all from the army, though, she's sure of that, even if she's not sure who they are or what they're here to do. Maybe a couple of MPs, she figures, and one or two counterintelligence agents. The shooters have humped their gear bags off the plane, and they drop them at their feet. Warlock peels off immediately for a quick consult with a stone-faced Latino whom Nessuno puts in his midforties. They start exchanging quick, quiet words that she cannot and does not try to overhear.

She's tired, still shaky, and there's a pressure behind her eyes that's either the start of one hell of a headache or the demand of tears or both. The headache she can deal with, the way she dealt with the shakes and the vomiting, but she doesn't want tears, not here, not now. She knows they're coming, and she's willing to accept them later without complaint, the same way she saw Warlock accept his adrenaline crash. The price of doing business. But she will neither accept nor allow water from her eyes in front of these men.

The flight crew disembarks, and Nessuno watches them make a silent beeline for the rear of the hangar, never once looking back. They don't know, and they know better than to want to know. Four of the waiting group go up the stairs, disappear inside the plane, come out again in just over a minute. They're carrying Tohir, strapped to a stretcher. He's still unconscious. They load him immediately into the back of the Blazer. The one in the suit watches without comment. Nessuno wonders how Tohir will be parceled up, if it'll be DIA or FBI or perhaps some other arm of Justice that takes possession. The man is a criminal as much as a terrorist. She wonders if someone, somewhere, imagines a trial.

It doesn't matter. In the end, everyone will get a piece of him.

She doesn't care.

Right now, she tells herself that she never wants to see Vosil Tohir's face again.

Someone opens the hangar doors, and she watches the Blazer roll away, speeding up and then turning out of sight. When she turns back, the stone-faced man is in front of her, offering his hand.

"Colonel Daniel Ruiz," he says. "Welcome home, Chief."

"Thank you, sir."

Ruiz shakes her hand as though he means what he says, then indicates two of the remaining men. The older of them is black, wearing blue jeans and a Red Sox sweatshirt, head shaved and glossy enough to kick light. The other looks a bit younger, midtwenties, perhaps, white, shorter, also blue jeans but no jacket, and he's made no attempt to hide the SIG riding at his hip or the cuffs in their case on his belt. He's got a haircut that hasn't quite forgotten regulation but is doing its best.

"These are Sergeants Danso and Harrington," Ruiz says. "You'll need to go with them."

"Yes, sir."

"Mind if I sit in?" Warlock asks.

The older sergeant, Danso, shrugs. "You missing the CI action, Jad?"

"I just want to make sure you haven't lost a step, Han."

"No objection. Chief?"

"No objection."

There are more words, Ruiz telling the shooters where they need to be and when. The one called Cardboard offers her his hand.

"Keep the shirt," he says.

She falls in with Danso on one side and Harrington on the other, Warlock walking a little behind, begins crossing the hangar, following the path of the flight crew. They're trying to keep it soft, but she can't escape the feeling of being guarded, of being watched.

"I was hoping you'd ask for it back," she hears Steelriver say.

Heath comes back with more ice. She's five years older than Nessuno, has crossed over into her thirties, blond hair cut short and neat, and a Laura Ingalls Wilder face that makes the people who meet her think words like *sweet* and *innocent,* an illusion that's shattered the moment she opens her mouth and begins to swear in a way that would make the entirety of the marine corps blush. Right now, she's not doing a very good job of hiding her concern.

Nessuno holds out her glass for ice.

"You need to reintegrate," Heath says.

Nessuno takes the bottle, refills her drink. "I thought that was what we're doing."

"No, we're getting drunk. This is off-the-record shitface time."

"Unofficial."

"Fuck official. I saw your medical, did I tell you? You're clean."

"You said."

"Did I? The bourbon must be working." Heath takes her seat on the couch again, tucking her feet beneath her. She swallows some of her drink. "So tell me."

"What?"

Heath indicates Nessuno with the glass in her hand, gesturing vaguely at her shoulder. "Scarring along the shoulder, consistent with bullet track or similar projectile injury whatever the fuck that means and which, I note, you failed to offer an adequate explanation of how you came to have such a mark when questioned by the examining physician for such and shit I *am* drunk. You know how I know I'm drunk?"

"Run-on sentences."

"Run-on sentences," Heath says.

"You always talk in run-on sentences, ma'am."

"Call me ma'am again and I'll club you with this bottle. Tell me."

Nessuno shrugs. "He didn't do it, if that's what you're asking."

"That was kind of what I was asking, yes."

"I didn't duck fast enough."

"I thought Tohir didn't use you like that."

"Nice."

Heath winces. "Not what I meant."

Nessuno actually grins, is surprised by how good it feels. It passes fast. "There was a deal—heroin—and he wanted me to go with him and look like arm candy. They were selling to some Italians."

"December." Heath nods. "I remember the report."

"So Tohir wanted me there to look good, but also to listen in on what was being said in Italian because his Italian is shit. We finish up, and I'm being a pretty hostess and clearing the drinks, and I overhear one of these guys saying they're going to fuck us over. So I told Tohir."

"And?"

"Bullets were employed." She says each word clearly, aware that she, too, is now quite drunk. She looks into her glass. There's a fingernail's depth of bourbon remaining, but she thinks it's less, because of the displacement from the ice.

"You left that part out."

"What were you going to do, ma'am? Come take me home? Kiss it all better?" Nessuno empties her glass and sets it down, harder than she intends to, and it knocks loudly on the surface of the coffee table. "Yeah, I'm drunk, too."

"You fucking well better be, you just called me ma'am again. And you killed the fucking bottle. That bottle was full when we started, Chief."

Nessuno is staring at the empty glass, the ice cubes slowly melting. The wave of sudden self-pity she feels is followed by a surge of anger that she suspects is directed, more than anything, at herself but that she points at Heath instead.

"That's not my fucking name," Nessuno says.

They end up in a briefing room attached to the hangar, with Nessuno seated at one side of a long table and Danso and Harrington opposite. Warlock stands. On the table is a pitcher of water, three plastic cups in a stack, a cardboard box about the right size for shoes, and a thick envelope, catalog size, stamped with declarations of secrecy and warnings of exactly how much trouble your ass will be in if you open it and aren't authorized to do so. There's a routing sequence on the envelope, and four signatures, arranged by date, ending with the most recent. Reading upside down, she's pretty sure the last signature is H. DANSO. The first one, she knows, is A. HEATH. There's also a small monitor-like unit that resembles nothing so much as a View-Master, except it's molded ballistic black plastic and probably costs a hundred times as much as the toy.

"We're going to ask you some questions, Chief," Danso says, breaking the seal on Nessuno's proof-of-life envelope without ceremony and pulling a sheaf of papers free. He hands the envelope off to Harrington, who empties the rest of the contents on the table, a set of eight-by-ten photographs, and begins laying them out in front of her.

"CI?" Nessuno asks.

She knows the answer already, knows she's asking only to buy herself time, though she's had the entirety of the flight in to get her head straight. It hasn't been enough, and while she knows absolutely that nothing in what she has said so far, in anything that she has done, has betrayed the fact, she is scared. She is as afraid as she ever was in the past sixteen months, as frightened here in Florida as she was in Tashkent, or Vienna, or Moscow, that she will be revealed as an impostor, as a fraud, as a spy. She knows, absolutely, that she shouldn't feel these things. She knows that she is home, that she is safe.

But she cannot make herself stop feeling what she feels, and that, in turn, makes her feel all the more adrift.

"We are counterintel, that is correct." Danso pats his pockets for a moment, and Harrington stops moving the photos around long enough to shake his head and produce a ballpoint, handing it over. Danso clicks the pen alive, begins running down the first sheet, and Warlock takes the opportunity to reach in for the pitcher and pour. He sets one of the cups in front of her, takes another for himself. She's oddly touched by the act, tries to find a smile to give him, but by then he's already backed off, and Danso is ready to begin.

"What's your name?" Danso asks.

"Nessuno," she says. "Petra Graziella."

"Rank?"

"CWO Two."

"DOB?"

She needs a moment before she can tell him.

"And where were you born?"

This comes a little faster. "Philly, Thomas Jefferson University Hospital."

"Your father's name?"

She tells him.

"Your mother's maiden name?"

She tells him, feeling marginally more confident. All the answers are there, waiting in the back of her mind. Covered in dust, hidden in corners, but there. She just needs to stay calm, she thinks, and it'll all come back.

"Your mother's place of birth?"

"Palermo."

"Name of your first DI?"

"Sergeant Mendoza."

"Where did you have your first kiss?"

"Wrigley Field." Feeling more confident now. Nessuno can practically see the game in her mind's eye, remember it like yesterday, the view from her seat on the first-base line. She can smell the beer, taste the peanuts. "Cubs were playing the Pirates."

"How old were you?"

"I was eleven."

Danso, who has been making tick marks on the sheet, looks up at her. "How old were you?"

She blinks, guard instantly in place, rising on instinct. No change in her expression, no darting eyes, no shift in her posture, all the things she knows to keep her lies looking like the truth. Outside, what she is showing Danso and Harrington and Warlock looks like nothing at all, she knows. Just a pause, just a woman taking a moment to reconsider.

But inside, a piece of her is writhing, fighting rising panic. Remembering Tohir, when he asked her the same question, his arms around her, flushed from their lovemaking. He'd told her that the first time he'd had sex he was eleven, and she'd said something about him starting early. He thought himself a good lover, his performance had mattered to him. She remembers what she said, how she'd told him that he was probably fucking before she'd even kissed a boy for the first time, and he had laughed and buried his face against her neck and told her he loved her foul mouth.

"I was eleven," Nessuno says again, and the part of her that watches during these moments, that looks to both her performance and its reception, relaxes. "Maybe twelve. I'm sorry, I don't remember."

Danso holds his gaze on her a moment longer, and she gives him nothing in return. He goes back to his sheet. Harrington, still silent, hasn't looked away from her once, and she thinks that he is the more dangerous of the two, that he is the one she needs to worry about convincing right now.

"Name of your favorite pet," Danso asks.

Not good, she thinks. There's nothing there; she can't remember the cat's name. She can see the cat, curled on the foot of her bed; she can see the powder-blue comforter beneath it, the lace edge of one of the throw pillows. But there's no name, and she feels them watching her, waiting, and this time she knows she must say something before her silence condemns her.

"She was a tabby," Nessuno says. "I don't…Daphne. Her name was Daphne."

The questions keep coming, another two dozen that range from the banal to the invasive. She answers as best she can. From the corner of her eye, she can see Warlock standing aside, leaning against the wall. Unlike Danso and Harrington, he doesn't seem to be looking at her, but she isn't willing to bank on that.

Danso makes another mark, then indicates the photographs spread out between them with the pen. "From my right, please identity these."

She looks at the photos. "That's my uncle Nicholas, at my baptism. That one is first grade, class photo."

Harrington speaks for the first time. "Indicate, please, where you are in the photograph."

Nessuno puts her finger on a dark-haired girl in a blue jumper in the second row.

Harrington indicates the blond woman standing beside the third row. "Who is this?"

"Miss Johnson."

Danso makes another mark. "Continue."

She does, identifying pictures of friends and family. Her best friend from fourth grade, Carla Quinones; her field hockey team from high school, with Coach Linden and Tina the Terrible; the facade of her parents' restaurant in Chicago, in Six Corners; friends and family celebrating after her first communion; her fourteenth birthday party, with all the guests as she blows out the candles; her junior prom, with Alexander Buckman, wearing that neon-blue tux, and she in a dress she thought was wonderful and that now looks absurd and dated. All these questions, and looking at her hair in that picture makes her want to blush.

When she finishes with the photographs, Harrington gathers them up again, slips them back into the envelope.

"Last one," Danso says. "Who is Elisabetta Villanova?"

Nessuno answers without thinking and without hesitation. This question is easy. This answer holds no doubt. There is no need to plumb memory.

"Me," she says.

They make it through half of another bottle, this of Bulleit rye, before both of them are far too drunk to continue. Nessuno tries to argue for taking a cab back to her hotel, but Heath is having none of it. This argument ultimately collapses on both sides, less because of persuasion than because the pauses between declarations stretch longer and longer, and the next thing Nessuno knows she's awake, wincing, her back and hips aching from having slept in this damn chair for God knows how long. Heath is still asleep, sprawled on the couch, snoring with her mouth open.

Nessuno makes her way to the kitchen and pours water into her body, enough to make the throbbing headache retreat, if only slightly. Her mouth feels like paste, and she's still drunk. She searches around through kitchen drawers, finds a notepad and a pencil, scribbles a message. She leaves it tucked beneath the bottle on the coffee table, where Heath will see it when she wakes. Then she calls a cab to take her back to her hotel. Heath is still snoring when she leaves.

She's got a room at the Courtyard by Marriott in Gaithersburg, because that is the kind of place that an army CW2 with a pay grade of W-2 and is pulling down just over 42K a year before taxes stays. It is exactly the kind of place that Petra Nessuno stays, and she hates it, because Elisabetta Villanova slummed it when she had to but lived large when she could.

She has lost count of the number of hotels she has slept in over the past two years.

When she first met Tohir, it was in a suite at the Baltschug Kempinski, in Moscow. Elisabetta Villanova was many things, and one of them was an art and antiquities dealer. She'd been brought in by a third party who had Tohir's trust to evaluate a painting, *The Cheaters* by Jan Miense Molenaer. The painting had been stolen from the Netherlands the year before, and Tohir claimed to be selling it for a "friend" who'd had no idea it had been stolen. He'd hoped Signora Villanova could help arrange the sale, perhaps for a private buyer. For the right price, she'd told him, it would be her pleasure.

She left that first meeting without ever learning his name, but she knew she had made an impression. Before they'd parted company, he had asked about her nationality (American), her passports (U.S. and Italy), the number of languages she spoke (nine, but only five fluently).

All things, she knew, that would make her very useful to a man engaged in transnational crime.

She had been correct. Over the next four months, he contacted her twice more; once to broker the sale of a stolen Picasso, then a set of Babylonian coins stolen during the fall of Baghdad. With Heath's assistance back home, Elisabetta Villanova was able to move them all, and they both knew that each one of these jobs was a test, a means for him to evaluate her, to check on her history, her identity, her story. Was Elisabetta Villanova for real? Was she to be trusted?

It had been at their second face-to-face meeting when she finally learned his name. Another hotel, the Dukes, in London, and Tohir had invited her to meet him there at the bar. She'd been staying at the Athenaeum when the invitation came, and she knew then that he had been having her watched, which was just what she and Heath had expected. Tohir had thanked her for her help, bought her a drink that was very, very strong, and then invited her upstairs. They had sex for the first time in a room overlooking the street, the curtains open, sunlight painting them as they collapsed together atop the bed.

Nessuno passes a television in the lobby, shrill punditry talking about WilsonVille and terrorism right here at home. Stories about what happened in California still live above the fold on the complimentary copies of *USA Today*. There were American flags flying everywhere during the cab ride here. When Nessuno had passed the warning to Heath, she hadn't known much, just that something was planned; likely target, a theme park. The intelligence had seemed pitiful to her even then, and it seems somewhat miraculous to her now that it was of any use at all. When she looks at the flags, listens to the news, she thinks she should feel something more than what she does. The part of her that is trying so hard to remember Petra Nessuno feels only a distant sadness, a disconnect. Elisabetta Villanova feels nothing but scorn.

Her new cell phone says it's eleven minutes past seven in the morning when she reaches her room, and the clock on the nightstand disagrees by only two minutes. Nessuno hates the room even more than she hates the hotel, cheap furniture and art on the wall that's bought by the yard. She checks the bed, and the bottom sheet is not fitted and does not cover the end of the mattress. She thinks about changing into workout clothes and trying to sweat out the rest of the drunk with a run or weights, starts to get changed to do just that, and then finds herself sitting on the floor in her underwear.

Here it comes, she thinks.

The tears are sudden and fat. She sits there, just like that, until she's run dry, and for a little while longer, too. She cries silently, trying to purge a toxic mix of self-loathing and self-pity and relief and anxiety, stored over twenty-eight months filled with every striation and nuance of fear. Feeling the rough carpet beneath her skin, clawing at it with her fingernails until she's pulling threads.

When it's over, she rises, goes to the bathroom and washes her face and drinks more water, watching her reflection as she does so. Her face, hers alone, and that is how she feels at this moment: very alone. She wonders if that wasn't why Heath was so insistent that she get laid. Or maybe it's Heath's way of telling her to take her body back. Or maybe Heath just thinks sex is the answer to everything. Right now, Nessuno can't see sex as anything other than just another tool in the toolbox.

She leaves the bathroom, opens the door to the hall long enough to hang the DO NOT DISTURB, then closes the door and locks it. She pulls the blackout curtains until only one line of sunlight stabs the darkness, then strips off the rest of her clothes and climbs into the bed. She tells herself that when she wakes up, she won't have to be afraid, or confused, or adrift, or anything. She tells herself that these are the bends, and they will pass.

She tells herself that when she wakes up, she'll be alone, and safe, and Elisabetta Villanova will be a memory.

*   *   *

Harrington uses the device that isn't a View-Master to scan and check her retinas against their records. It's a HIIDE, a type of handheld interagency identity detection equipment, and Nessuno has seen — even used — one before, but never a model like this. One more thing that's gotten an upgrade while she's away. Harrington presses a couple of buttons on the monitor side, then shows the results to Danso, who nods. He sets the unit down and smiles at her for the first time, sliding the cardboard box across to her.

"You're all clear, Chief," Harrington says. "Your RP."

She lifts the lid off her reintegration pack, the box in which she sealed her life away more than two years ago, takes a moment to look before removing the items one by one. Her CAC, the common access card that serves as her military ID, that says she is Petra Nessuno, CW2. Her wallet, with credit cards, her driver's license, all of them agreeing with the name on her CAC, all of them kept current courtesy of Heath and others in BI. There's three hundred and eleven dollars in the wallet. Her Saint Nicholas medal on its gold chain. Her cell phone, battery long, long dead, and now looking antiquated as hell, all the more so in comparison to the latest-generation smartphone Elisabetta Villanova left behind in Tohir's bedroom. Her knife, a Mel Pardue folding stiletto, silver fittings and fluted mother-of-pearl scales with a pearl-inlay thumb stud. She puts the Saint Nicholas medal around her neck first.

"We have your orders, Chief," Danso says. "Report Fort Belvoir, building one-oh-eight, room three hundred, thirteen hundred hours tomorrow for debrief by Captain Heath. Transport at your discretion."

"Fort Belvoir, building one-oh-eight, room three hundred, thirteen hundred," Nessuno repeats, now stowing her wallet, her knife, in her pockets. She doesn't know what to do with the cell phone, finds herself holding it in one hand. She'll need a new one. Danso and Harrington have already cleaned up the photographs and papers, the HIIDE back in its case, and they're on their feet. She rises reflexively with them. Both men offer her a hand, one after the other.

"Welcome back to the world," Harrington says.

They leave, Danso exchanging a nod and a grin with Warlock, and Nessuno finds herself just standing there, dead cell phone in her hand.

"Not the homecoming you imagined?" Warlock asks.

"No."

"It never is." He gives her an easy smile, and then, he, too, offers her his hand. "I'm Jad. Nice to meet you, Petra."

The phone wakes her, not the one on the nightstand but the secured mobile that Heath gave her after the debriefing at Belvoir. It doesn't ring so much as whine, and the sound lances her dreams and jolts her awake in a guilty panic. She was dreaming of Tohir, and that only compounds the disorientation, the darkness of the room, the sheets in a tangle around her. She is in Tashkent, certain she's been blown, that Tohir is holding her down and that every one of her fears has come to pass.

The phone cries for her attention again, and that's what brings her back. She frees an arm, fumbles for the device, puts it to her ear as she thumbs the connection. It takes another moment before she can remember which name she should use.

"Nessuno, go," she says. Her voice sounds like something crawled into her mouth and expired in her larynx.

"Get showered, get dressed, get down to the lobby," Heath says. "I'm taking you to the house."

"You said—"

"I fucking know what I said, all right? Your presence is required at the house. They want you listening in."

Nessuno is sitting up now. The air conditioner has been running all along, and it turns the sweat on her skin cold.

"Why?"

"Fuck." Heath leans on the *f*, an expression of her frustration. "They've got a million whys, Chief. They want to verify what he's saying. They want an expert present. They want the operator who was next to him for a year and knows him better than anyone to listen to his bull-shit and if it comes to it to look him in the eye and call him a liar. It doesn't matter why. I said no, they said fuck you, Captain, this comes from the shiny on-high, and now I'm on my way to your hotel and you will be in the lobby and waiting for me when I arrive."

Nessuno closes her eyes.

"Understood."

She's expecting Heath to kill the connection then and there, but there's a pause.

"I'm sorry, Chief," Heath says. "I tried."

"Understood."

The call ends.

Nessuno throws the phone across the room, into the mirror over the desk. The mirror shatters, and she appreciates the weak satisfaction that provides. She takes another moment, pushes hair off her forehead, then untangles herself from the sheets. The Saint Nicholas medal bounces against her chest as she moves, and she puts the fingertips of one hand to it as she heads for the bathroom, the shower, and what will come next.

Praying for Saint Nicholas to protect Elisabetta Villanova and Petra Nessuno both from Vosil Tohir.

Chapter Eight

THE HOUSE IS outside of Leesburg, some thirty miles west of D.C., twenty from Gaithersburg. The driveway drops from the county road abruptly, past a screen of trees and around a slow bend that Bell knows is crammed with surveillance, human and electronic both, despite the fact that he doesn't see anyone or anything. Four cars parked out front, two of them nose out, and both of those are big Ford Expeditions, black. Nose in is another Ford, a Taurus, painted the kind of tan that anyone who has ever changed a diaper can recognize immediately—and anyone who works in government can recognize it, too, but for entirely different reasons. The last car is a new Honda Civic, black, parked a few yards off to the side, as if intimidated by the presence of so much Detroit steel. It's the only vehicle that would look inconspicuous, except for the company it's keeping.

Bell thinks that there are too many fucking cars parked out front for a place full of people trying to keep a secret.

He swings his ride around, parks farther off to the side, nose also pointed out. He's been given the keys to a Mustang convertible, but he's driven top up, despite the glorious Virginia summer's day. When he exits the car, he bashes his head against the door frame. He rubs the bump and uses that as an excuse to eyeball the area for a second time. The trees provide a nice screen from the road, but closer to the house they've been cut back, clearing the sight lines. The house itself is at least one hundred years old, beaten red clapboard and capped redbrick chimney, the curtains drawn in almost every window he can see. He's not seeing motion or cameras, and he thinks the place looks like exactly what it is. The difference between hiding in plain sight in Hailey and hiding in plain sight here is almost painful to behold.

He makes his way over gravel that crunches beneath his sneakers to the door. He's knocked once and is about to knock again when it's opened by a wrinkle-faced old man with hair that's passed silver and graduated straight to white. Bell, who stands over six feet, positively towers above the face looking up at him. The old man has both hands out of sight, and only one is on the doorknob, Bell knows.

"Steve send you?" the man says. The challenge phrase comes out with a smoker's rasp.

"Sorry I'm running late," Bell says. "Had to change a flat."

The old man eyeballs him, weighing the confirmation, then grunts and steps back, and Bell steps forward into an entry hall where two men are lowering their weapons, one an MP7A1, the other a Benelli shotgun. Both are dressed plainclothes, T-shirts and blue jeans and hair long enough for Bell to know they've been at undercover work at least six months. One starts a muted conversation over his earpiece, never taking his eyes off Bell. The white-haired old man ignores everything and everyone, resumes his post on a wooden stool near the door. A small black-and-white video monitor rests at his elbow, showing a split view of the approach to the house, covering the exit from the county road and the drive. There's another shotgun in easy reach.

The one on the earpiece asks, "Carrying?"

"Yeah."

"No weapons in with him."

"He try anything?" Bell asks.

He gets two shrugs in response, and the other guard points down the hall. "You go that way."

Bell goes that way until he finds himself in a kitchen not that different from the one where his ex-wife served him iced tea less than seventy-two hours earlier. Another three men and the guns that go with them are here, the men in variants of the undercover garb he's already seen in the hall, mostly running to jeans and tees, all of them Caucasian, and not a face that looks over thirty. Bell gets nods of acknowledgment rather than greeting, feels them sizing him up and evaluating. He doesn't know them, and it's anyone's guess where they're from, but Bell thinks probably DSS or the like rather than FBI or CIA. If a special deputy AG has been assigned to Tohir's case they could even be federal marshals.

"There's coffee," one of them says, using his chin to indicate the coffeemaker on the counter. "It's not entirely horrible."

Bell laughs, goes to the sink and finds a dirty mug, which he proceeds to wash, then fill. There's a window, and through it he can see yet another undercover, this one female, pretending to play with a German shepherd in the backyard. He wonders how far out the bubble stretches, just how dug in the defenses actually are. Inconspicuous or not, if anybody comes for Vosil Tohir, they're going to have one hell of a time reaching him.

"Jad."

He looks, and Steelriver is standing in the doorway off to his right, the entry to a hall running perpendicular to the one where Bell entered.

"Hey, Tom."

Steelriver motions for Bell to follow him. Bell finishes his not-entirely-awful coffee before setting the mug back in the sink. They start back down the hall.

"Brought me in to give the play-by-play on the capture," Steelriver says.

"They put you in the room?"

"Nah, but I got to watch the first couple rounds via the monitors. He's not going down easily."

"Who's lead?"

"Some guy from the Company," Steelriver says. "At least, he's got the ball today. Name's Wallford. That's if you believe it when someone from CIA gives you a name."

"I may know him."

"Which would explain why he wants you in there."

"He try anything?"

"Heatdish? Not yet, but I wouldn't put it past him. He wasn't out from surgery and recovered enough to start talking in earnest until yesterday afternoon, and he's been restless ever since. Like he's putting himself through his own physical therapy."

"But he is talking?"

"Oh, he's talking, but whether he's saying anything, that's something else entirely."

They make a turn, passing another undercover, armed like all the rest, then they come to a stop at the end of the hall, a closed door. Bell takes the moment to pull the keys to his rental out of his pocket and drop them into Steelriver's hand, who jangles them once in his palm.

"You got me a Mustang."

"It was nothing."

"The classic ones are better. This ain't bad, though." Steelriver jangles the keys once more, then claps Bell on his shoulder. "Keep your eye on that motherfucker. He's going to try something."

Bell knocks twice on the door, then opens it into what was once a spacious living or sitting room and is now the command-and-control for the safe house. Monitors have bred and multiplied in the space, including three flat-screen displays mounted on the far wall and easily another dozen of varying shapes and sizes elsewhere in the room. Images of the house's exterior, the approaches; some of the cameras static, some of them scanning; all the pictures relayed in high def. He can see To-hir on one of the small screens, in what looks like a bedroom. Another monitor appears to be dedicated to radio traffic, and the whole apparatus is staffed by three more of the ubiquitous undercover agents, and all of them brimming with youth. Bell is starting to feel old.

The three on the monitors don't spare him a glance, but the remaining three, standing in a cluster at the center of the room, watch him enter. Of them, Bell recognizes Wallford, but it's the presence of Petra Nessuno that surprises him. He hadn't thought he'd see her again, ever, and the fact that she's here throws him for a moment.

"Chief," he says.

She looks at him with those dark eyes that betray nothing. "Master Sergeant."

The other one's a woman, blond, with gravel-gray eyes, who gives him an eyeball and a slight nod before going back to the black three-ring binder she's got balanced, open, in one hand. Nessuno's gaze holds on Bell for a second longer, and then she, too, turns her attention to the paperwork. The room has the peculiar funk that comes from too many electronics and too many bodies and not enough fresh air. There are two empty pizza boxes open and discarded on the floor, and the trash can on this side of the monitor table is overflowing with empty bottles of water and Mountain Dew.

"Jad, nice catch." Jerome Wallford is offering his hand, and Bell takes it. "Good to see you again. Thanks for coming in. So I understand you've met the chief. This is Captain Heath."

The blonde grunts. "Hey."

"Captain."

"You know why you're here?" Wallford asks. He's got a young, pleasant face, a whip-lean body that makes the suit he's wearing seem sized wrong, too long at the sleeves, too short at the cuffs. The same grin that Bell remembers from when they last met. It's the grin that comes with an in joke, and every time Bell sees it, he thinks that Wallford's the only one who gets the punch line.

"California."

"That's where it starts." Wallford spreads his hands. "This is the line, right? Lee Jamieson, now, sadly, deceased, paid a lot of money to some-one to finance a terrorist attack on American soil, i.e., the WilsonVille assault. There are a thousand questions still unanswered, and some of them are damn frightening. We know Heatdish was involved, but if he wasn't the mastermind behind it all, we need to know who is. That's just for starters."

Nessuno looks up from the binder at the two of them. "I'm not sure he knows."

"He's not top of the chain?" Bell asks.

"No, though I think he was very close to it. We never got an ID, any-thing, not even a nickname for the one at the top. We ended up giving him the code-name Echo."

"How high up was he?"

"Tohir? I can't say. Criminal enterprise and terrorism blur here. I mean, Tohir was a criminal; it was only ever about the money to him, never politics. He ran everything on a cell structure, like he was running agents. And I'm certain we were being run the same way, from higher up."

"All that time, you never got anything more?" Wallford asks.

Heath shoots a look that would be complete only with the addition of death beams, but Nessuno either misses it or doesn't care.

"I asked him three separate times," Nessuno says. "Once point-blank, just flat out asked, 'Who do we work for? Is this a government or some-thing else?' He got angry. He told me not even he knew that, that he didn't *want* to know that, and that I shouldn't want to know that, ei-ther. 'We work for the devil,' he said. 'We work for God. We work for money.' He told me to never ask him again."

Something in the way she says it tells Bell it hadn't been a pleasant conversation, but aside from her frown there's been nothing in her face and nothing in her voice that he can read.

"Did you know about the WilsonVille plot?" Bell asks. "The thing in California?"

Nessuno glances to Heath before answering. The other woman has lowered the binder, still open, and she moves her head just enough that Nessuno, if not Bell himself, sees her nod.

"I knew enough to send up the balloon about a strike on American soil, and that it'd be a theme park or similar," Nessuno says. "I knew about an operation in Iran to acquire the plutonium. That was bought, not stolen. Tohir arranged the buy, got it from one of the scientists working at the facility in Chalus. This was last November; we had a meet in Paris at La Trémoille to arrange it."

"Wait — you were there?" Bell asks.

"My value to Tohir was primarily as a translator. Tohir didn't like that, by the way; he thought the plutonium overcomplicated things. He said it would've been easier and more effective to use cesium or strontium, which is what made me think they planned to use the material in a dirty bomb. I tried following up on that, but the best I got was that it was 'what the customer ordered.'"

Bell looks at Wallford, and Wallford gives him the in-joke grin. "I know, right? Confirms what we already know, that the attack was supposed to look like the work of Iran or an Iran proxy."

"Who bought it?" Nessuno asks.

"We've got some ideas," says Wallford. "Captain?"

"What?" Heath snaps the word off like she's trying to break its back.

"Anything you want to add?"

"I'm still going through the transcript. Wish to God you'd waited until we were here to get started."

"First couple interviews were only background; this one's the sell." Wallford produces an earbud, offers it to Bell. "We're going to put the chief in your ear. You'll be her mouth."

Bell fits the earbud while Wallford moves to the monitor table, uses a radio there to order Tohir moved for interrogation. The flat screens on the wall come to life with a flicker, three angles on a single room with a bare table and a couple of chairs set around it. He sees Nessuno's attention shift from the binder to the screens, then Heath's, and then they're all watching in a silence that's broken only by the whir of electronics and the measured voices of the men on the monitors.

Then the light in the room on the screens shifts, brightens for a moment before dropping to its previous level, and one of the undercovers that Bell met in the kitchen is there, helping Tohir to a seat. He looks tired, stubble growth on his cheeks, and once in the chair he winces and shifts, trying to accommodate his wounded hip. His clothes are clean.

"Time to meet the mastermind," Wallford says.

They're taking the stairs down to the cellar when Bell asks, "You going to put her in the room?"

"Which one?" Wallford asks.

"You know which one."

"Might. Tohir sees the chief sitting opposite him, no telling what that'll shake loose."

"I think she's seen enough of him," Bell says.

"She's seen *all* of him, from what I understand."

Bell stops short, and Wallford, ahead of him, stops, too. They're at the foot of the stairs, and the other two undercovers from the kitchen are standing dead ahead of them, flanking a new door in a new wall, the construction so recent Bell can smell it. A snarl of cables runs from a bundle along one of the support beams overhead, feeding into the newly constructed interrogation room.

"That was a joke, Master Sergeant," Wallford says.

"I know what it was. You do what she did, then you talk."

Wallford frowns at him. He's carrying a black leather portfolio, which he now switches from beneath his arm into his hands. "You're sweet on her, is that it?"

"What I am is sympathetic to sacrifice. Don't diminish it."

"We're a united front when we get inside."

"Are we inside?"

"Point taken. We good?"

Bell reaches around to his right hip, draws his .45 from the pancake holster riding there, ignoring Wallford's rapidly rising eyebrows. Bell drops the magazine, pops the ready round, then offers the whole package to the undercover standing on the hinge side of the door. The man takes it without a word.

"Good to go," says Bell.

"So how's the hip?" Wallford asks.

Vosil Tohir sits on the other side of a dull gray metal table, a rectangle of industrial design affixed to the floor of the newly built interrogation room by hasps, which are in turn locked down by bolts bored into the concrete. The table, Bell observes, goes with the room. White acoustic tile on the walls and the ceiling, recessed lighting, and two cameras that he can see. The lights all cant away from the entrance, directed at the subject on the other side of the table, and if Tohir weren't wearing glasses, it would be effective intimidation. As it is, the glare off his lenses does an effective job of concealing his eyes, and the result is a zero-sum game.

"No better than the last time you asked," Tohir says. His chin moves, indicates Bell. "Who is this?"

Wallford drops his leather portfolio on the table, pulls one of the two chairs on this side out, metal scraping on the concrete floor. Bell takes the other seat.

"Just another one of your fans, Vosil," Wallford says. He doesn't look at the man, instead concentrates on drawing out his preparations, runs the zipper around the portfolio slowly. He slides a ballpoint from where it's held in a loop along the spine, twists it slowly to deploy its point. Flips a page on the pad, begins scribbling.

Bell waits, hands in his lap, watching Tohir, and Tohir sighs, settles his gaze on Bell, returning it. He looks different from the way he did on the plane, in the hangar in Tashkent, the disparity between his face in repose and now not. A handsome face, more European than Asian, but worn with fatigue and, Bell suspects, some pain. If Chain had shattered his hip, there's no way Vosil Tohir would be sitting anywhere anytime soon, let alone here and now. Bell thinks Tohir got lucky.

There's a *click-click* in Bell's ear, and then Nessuno's voice, the signal so clear that he suffers the momentary disorientation of believing she is at his shoulder, whispering to him. *"Move your right hand to indicate five by five."*

Bell sets his right palm on the table, shifts it a few centimeters.

"Confirm reading me five by," Nessuno says.

"A fan," Tohir says. He's still looking at Bell. "Do you want an autograph?"

Bell doesn't answer, doesn't smile, doesn't respond. He figures he's in the room to play the heavy. With all that in mind, though, Bell doesn't think he much likes Vosil Tohir. There's an arrogance to him, remarkable given the circumstances. Or maybe it's that Nessuno is in his ear, and he's been thinking about her more than he thinks he should be doing.

"I'm going to cut to the chase here, Vosil," Wallford says, finally looking up from his open portfolio. He's wearing his grin. We're all friends here, except, of course, we're not.

"Oh, please do."

"We want who you work for."

Tohir adjusts his glasses. "Without dinner and a movie first? You think you can just ask me to bend over and I'll do it, just like that? Speaking of which, where's Elisabet?"

"Who's Elisabet?"

Even with the light kicking off Tohir's glasses, Bell sees him roll his eyes. "You know the answer to that better than I. Who's Elisabet? She's the woman I loved. She's the woman I trusted. She's the woman who was with me when I was taken and who did not, I note, get shot because she knew the right word to say to your people. Which means she is one of your people. Which means she's a liar. Which means she's a whore."

The voice in Bell's ear is silent.

"She's in custody," Wallford says.

"Is that true? I don't think that's true, Jerry." Tohir spreads his hands, palms up, on the table, looks from Wallford to Bell. "That would not make a lot of sense. She's here, isn't she? She would be here, that makes more sense. Watching us? Just to observe this interrogation?"

"You're maybe a little paranoid," Wallford says.

Tohir shakes his head, then lifts his chin to face one of the obvious cameras. The movement makes him wince. He raises a hand in greeting, then drops it, and this time puts his attention on Bell.

"She would be here, that makes sense. To verify what I say. To confirm. But can you trust her? Really? I mean, she is an excellent liar. She fooled me, and — not to commend myself or seem arrogant — that's not an easy thing to do. She fooled me for a long time. She did everything required to fool me. She killed two men, did you know that? One of them, he had to have been an American agent. Did you know that? Never mind that she gave me her body whenever and wherever I wanted it. She's a woman, after all; it's what they do. But it makes you wonder, doesn't it? How can you trust a woman like that?"

Bell doesn't answer, and neither does Nessuno.

"We're not here to talk about this Elisabet person, Vosil," Wallford says.

"No, you're not." Tohir glares at Wallford. "But I have something I want to say to her. Just in case she's listening. Just in case she reads the transcript or watches the video. A message." He turns back to the same camera as before. "Elisabet, I know what you did to me. You better hope he kills me, because if I live, I will find you, and I will kill you. It will be like it was in Prague, but slower. A thousand times slower."

"What happened in Prague?" Bell asks.

"Ask her," Tohir says.

"Are you finished?" Wallford leans forward. "Really, are you finished now, Vosil? Or should I ask one of the guys to get you a ruler so you can see if your dick is still as short as it was when we started?"

"No," Bell says. "I want to hear about Prague."

"You don't," Nessuno says. *"It's not relevant."*

Tohir looks hard at Bell, as if trying to determine who he is and why he's here. "She was tested in Prague. She had to prove herself to me. She passed."

Wallford taps the table with his pen. "Who do you work for, Vosil?"

Tohir just shakes his head. "I've lost track of time. How long has it been since you took me from Tashkent? Since you broke down my door and murdered my men?"

"Call it seventy-two hours, give or take."

"And this safe house, this place where we are right now, it's in the United States? That's too fucking long, Jerry. He knows I'm gone by now, he knows what happened, and he almost certainly knows it was you who took me. Which means he's looking to find me."

"What do you mean, he knows who it was who took you?" Bell asks.

"Your government. He has to know. You are military? Were you one of the shooters?"

Bell shakes his head.

Tohir frowns, then it smooths, and he sighs. "It does make things easier, now, doesn't it?"

"Easier how?"

"I've been giving this a lot of thought, as you might imagine. When I've been conscious, I should say. There are things I require. Things I want. You give me those things, you promise me those things, and we can deal."

"You're coming to the table empty," Wallford says. "Give us something we can use, a name, something, then we can work a deal."

"He doesn't know the name," Nessuno says. There's frustration in her voice, and Bell wonders at its source. Every interrogation is a give-and-take, and if there's impatience on her part, he imagines it as out of

character. He suffers no confusion; Elisabet is Nessuno. Until this moment, he's taken everything Tohir has said about her with enough salt to kill a snail; it's what he's expected of the man, to sow confusion and to raise doubt. She had to know it was coming as well as he. *"If he knew the name, I would've gotten it. You're wasting time."*

"Not yet," Tohir tells Wallford. "I have what you want; you have to give me what *I* want first. It's very simple."

"He doesn't know," Nessuno hisses, but Bell is already speaking even as she says it.

"But you can't, can you?" Bell says. "You can't give us what you don't have, and you don't know his name."

Tohir slowly draws his gaze back to Bell. "She told you that?"

Bell gets up. "This is bullshit, you know it, I know it. He's scared and he's caught and he's got dick. He'll sell his mother, his children, to get out of this room. He's got nothing."

"He's scared," Nessuno murmurs. *"He always tried to hide it, but Echo terrified him."*

"Let's go," Bell tells Wallford.

Wallford sighs, leans back in his chair to make it scrape again on the concrete floor. He rotates his pen, moves to replace it in the portfolio.

"Wait," Tohir says.

"For what? To listen to you puff yourself up? To listen to a deal when you've got nothing to deal with?" He ignores Tohir, adds to Wallford, "He's wasting our fucking time."

"Is that true, Vosil? Is this just you playing make-believe?"

Tohir grimaces, and Bell could believe it's the man's hip giving him pain but for the fact that he hasn't moved. "You are right, I cannot give you what you really want. I cannot give you his name. I cannot tell you where to find him. But I am willing to offer other things. I am willing to offer you what I have, but I cannot do it for free. I cannot — it means my life, do you understand? It means my life, and I wish to keep it. But I can give you other things, important things."

Wallford waits, then looks to Bell, and Bell takes his seat again.

"Then get fucking started," he says.

"You must promise me things first," Tohir says. "You must promise me that I will be moved, that I will be safe. You must do this at once. There isn't much time, not for any of us."

"He can reach you here?"

"You have no idea his reach. You have no idea what he is capable of, who he controls, who he has made his own either through deception or coercion or reward." There is, for a moment, a new note in Vosil Tohir's voice, and Bell hears it, hears the truth in what Nessuno has said. The man is not simply scared. His fear is mortal, and complete.

"We can protect you," Wallford says.

"Sincerely, Jerry, really, fuck you. Fuck you in the face. Why aren't you listening to me?"

"We can —"

"How many people know I am here?" Tohir, agitated, slams his hand on the table. "How many? Do you even know, Jerry? This guy — you, new guy, yours is a new face. How many new faces are in this house right now, at this very moment? How many people know I am here, people in Langley and Bethesda and D.C.? How many, Jerry?"

Wallford hesitates.

"You don't know, do you? You don't even fucking know. You've already lost count. That is why you cannot protect me."

"We know how to keep a secret," Wallford says.

Tohir laughs, bitterly amused. "No, you don't. Your head of CIA couldn't keep it secret that he was fucking his biographer. You have contractors hiding in Russian airports, selling their secrets to China. You don't know how to keep a secret, not one of you does. Elisabet, *she* knew how to keep a secret. Ask her how to do it, you stupid fuck. Listen to me, you *must* move me, you must do it now."

"He scares you that much?" Bell asks. "This guy, this name you don't even know?"

"He fucking terrifies me, new guy. He should terrify you, too, but you're too stupid, too blind, to understand. You'd shit yourself now, right here, if you knew what I knew."

"There are no secrets," Nessuno murmurs.

"There are no secrets," Bell says.

"Yes! Yes, this, exactly this!" Tohir nods, points, leans forward, wincing yet again. "The man you want, the man who controlled me, I met him only once face-to-face, it was years ago, years ago. Do you understand now what I am telling you? Are you getting this?"

"I understand."

"He could've changed his face, he could've fucking changed his gender for all I know. He could be in this house, he could be you."

"Not me."

"Which is what he would say, is it not? The only reason I dare believe you is that I know how he works, that he will not dirty his hands if he can at all help it. That is why he needed me. What he does better than anyone else, better than you snakes at CIA, is make others dirty their hands for him."

"How?" Wallford asks.

"The same fucking way you do; don't be naive. Christ. He has two powers, Jerry. He has reach, and he has information, and with those two things he can make almost anyone do almost anything. It is no different from what you do, what your government does, what everyone around the world strives to do. He buys what he can, and if it is not for sale, he takes it, either through extortion or force or both."

"If he has an agent, a sleeper, someone who knows where you are, and you can tell us —"

"I would have already! Jesus Christ, don't you hear me, Jerry? I don't know who he has, I only know that he *does,* and I know it as surely as I know you fuckers shot me, as surely as I know Elisabet lied to me. You must move me, you must move me at once. Someplace secure, someplace hidden. Put me in chains, drug me, whatever you require, but you must limit the people who know. You must learn to keep a secret. Only the people you can trust most, and even then, you must be certain."

Bell shakes his head. "If he has all this reach, why are you even here? Why didn't you know we were coming? If he has all this reach, why don't you already have a bullet in your head?"

"New guy." Tohir looks at him with patent disappointment. "It's coming. This is what I'm saying, listen, fuck you, listen to me! He doesn't want to free me. He doesn't have a choice now. He knows you have me and he knows I am talking to you right now, because he knows it is my only option. I still breathe because he hasn't done it *yet*. Why do you have me at all? Because you got fucking lucky. You had Elisabet, and she gave me to you, and that's all. You got lucky. Your good fortune and my bad. But that is not enough; it will run out. It is running out even now. He will find me and he will kill me. He'll kill everyone here if he has to."

"That doesn't sound smart," Bell says. "That sounds insane."

"No, not insane. Pragmatic."

"And if we just leave you here?" Wallford asks.

"Don't insult me, don't bluff with me. I have told you I am willing to trade. You want what I have."

"We may not actually need you."

"You do. You have nothing without me."

"We have Chalus," Bell says. "We have La Trémoille."

"Yes, because the lying cunt told you, of course. And you know how I take my coffee and that I enjoyed fucking her ass and that I have an aversion to avocado. You know some names I deal with, even some names I've used. You know lots of little things, and all of it equals nothing, because it is all in the past, and the past is gone. I see the future."

"Then give us a prediction."

"I'll give you a prophecy, how about that, new guy? I'll give you a prophecy, and once you get me fucking out of this fucking not-safe house, I'll give you more. How about that?"

"We're listening."

"The theme park, WilsonVille, it was the primary job, but there was a contingency in place. The same thing, but different."

"Explain."

"No. No, that is all I give right now. You stopped the thing in California because Elisabet knew enough to warn you. And after this you will go to her and you will ask her what else she knows, and she will tell you she knows nothing, and you will not know whether to believe her or not. But in this, she will be telling the truth, she will not know. But I know, and I can warn you."

"That's not enough," Wallford says. "We need a proof, Vosil."

"July twenty-eighth, Lufthansa one-six-nine-seven, Prague to Munich, connecting with Lufthansa four-ten, Munich to Kennedy. You are looking for a passenger by the name of Zein."

"And why are we looking for him?"

"No; you answer that yourself. Then you move me, you make me disappear, you take me someplace truly safe, someplace nobody knows about. Someplace secure. You do that, I will give you more, I will give you the rest, every detail of the operation, the timetable, all of it. But I would do it quickly, Jerry. I'd put it at the top of your to-do list, I'd do it right fucking now."

"Zein," Wallford says, noting it down. "Is that a surname or —"

"No. We're done. My hip hurts. And you're wasting time."

Chapter Nine

NESSUNO FEELS THE foam peel from her ears as she lifts the headphones free, sets them down on the long table in front of her. On the flat screens, three views of Vosil Tohir as he's cuffed up again and escorted out of the makeshift interrogation room by two of the undercovers. She focuses on their faces, the way she's focused on every face throughout the safe house since she and Heath arrived. She doesn't recognize any of them, not from Tashkent, not from Vienna, not from Moscow, not from Cairo, not from London, not from any of the places she traveled with Tohir on "business." She stares at the flat screens and, doing this, she doesn't have to look at the others in the room, the ones who've heard everything Tohir has said, just as she has. She tells herself it doesn't matter what they think, that she served her country, that she did what was required to earn his trust.

She thinks all this, but she cannot keep herself from remembering Poland, almost a year and a half prior. She cannot keep from remembering the sounds and the smells and the sights of the farmhouse outside of Prague, the bitterly cold predawn, when Tohir tested Elisabetta Villanova for the final time. He had put a gun in her hand and told her to kill two men kept inside, two broken, beaten, tortured men. The first known to Elisabetta, the same man who had put her and Tohir together so many months prior in a hotel in Moscow over a stolen painting. Elisabetta had never seen the second man before in her life.

CW2 Petra Nessuno, if asked, could not say the same thing.

Heath is already on one of the secure telephones at the monitor station, demanding the passenger manifests for Lufthansa flights 1697 and 410 this past July 28, for anything in the system on the surname Zein. She's not swearing, which makes Nessuno think she's dealing interagency, perhaps, or more likely with someone who outranks her.

Wallford and Bell are still on the flat screens, Wallford writing in his leather portfolio, Bell pulling the earbud free. She's gratified by the partnership, by how easily he took her commentary and cues during the course of the interrogation, made them his own to redirect and prod Tohir. All the same, she has to wonder at his presence here. He's a shooter, not a thinker, not a planner, and his appearance at the safe house surprised her. She thinks he looks weary as he rises and turns past one of the cameras. Weary and worried, perhaps.

All her time with him, Tohir had demonstrated caution, deliberation, was ever the pragmatist. It was, she had concluded, one of the reasons why Echo trusted him, why Tohir had been so useful. It was one of the reasons, she knew, that Tohir had grown to trust her as well. While Tohir's respect for — if not fear of — Echo had always been evident, it had also always been well controlled. That had been slipping from the first moments of the interrogation, had erupted near its end. For that reason, if none other, Nessuno knows that he's telling the truth, that the lead he's offered is good. To bargain it must be, and Vosil Tohir needs this bargain.

It occurs to her that if Echo can find Tohir here, it's just as likely that Echo can find her as well.

Heath hangs up. "It's going to take a bit. Zein isn't exactly an uncommon name. Sounds German."

"Might be Yemeni."

"And it doesn't ring any bells for you?"

"Not that I can recall. You've already got everything I have on his Yemeni dealings."

Heath looks at her for a moment longer, just long enough for Nessuno to wonder about the seeds of suspicion Tohir was working so diligently to plant. She matches the gaze, doesn't flinch, back-brain conscious of her own expression, of what she's showing her handler.

"You think it's legit?" Heath asks. "You think we're going to get hit again?"

"Count on it," Nessuno says.

Wallford crawls into a phone as soon as he and Bell are back in the room, and for a few minutes there's nothing to do but verify the transcript of the interrogation and double-check that all security is still in place and doing exactly what it should. Tohir is back in his room and under guard once more, and Bell leaves to go walkabout, saying he'll double-check the perimeter. Nessuno turns her attention back to the paperwork, the previous interview transcripts, the background data and briefs that have been compiled. The binders are multiplying. She adds her own notes, punches the new pages and fits them to the rings, then hands everything over to Heath.

She does this, concentrating on the work, aware the whole time of the eyes stealing in her direction, and for an instant she feels such a spur of anger she wants to whirl and confront the room. To shout at them, to say, *If there is an accusation, make it. If there's a polygraph, hook me up and let's get started.* But even as she thinks this, she feels Elisabetta's manner settling on her again, feels her posture shift just that much, just enough to cock her hip, to brush her hair aside. There is nothing to see in her, just a body men find beautiful, a manner that is self-assured, self-confident, professional. Show no hesitation, Elisabetta reminds her. Show no fear.

Show no guilt.

By the time Bell has returned it's become clear that they're done for the day. Wallford hasn't indicated one way or another if he's going to move Tohir, but Nessuno thinks it's a done deal. Tohir opened the door, and if Wallford wants what the man is offering, then Wallford will have to walk through. Every couple of minutes his phone rings and he goes off to one of the far corners to speak before coming back, looking less and less cheerful than before.

"Are we done here?" Nessuno finally asks. She directs it to Heath, who is currently bent over one of the laptops, but Wallford answers before she can.

"You can roll."

He stares a moment too long, and she sees him weighing what Tohir has said about her. She wonders if she should worry about him, if she should try to work him, to put him at ease, but this is not the time or the place. She wants to believe that everyone can see this for what it is, their prisoner playing power games, trying to turn the tables.

Wallford looks at Bell, then back to her. "Take the master sergeant with you; he's making me nervous."

Heath gives Nessuno her car keys, so she climbs behind the wheel of the black Civic, waits for Bell to buckle up beside her. He's tall enough that he has to slide the seat all the way back, and it still doesn't look like he's got enough room. It was easy to lose track of time inside the house, but as they turn onto the road it's already dusk. Nessuno heads them the wrong way, into Leesburg and then stair-stepping them through town, and neither of them speaks, the head checks on automatic, and while they do this, she's trying to get a sense of Bell, trying to read him. He's barely looked at her since coming up from interrogation, and this is different. She suspected his attraction to her on the flight, aboard the Lear, was all the more sure of it when she saw his reaction to seeing her for the first time today. She resents Tohir for poisoning that well, and now she has time to slowly fuel the resentment she's feeling, to argue with herself. She knows it's not valid. She knows she's being paranoid.

Once she's satisfied they're clean, she whips the Honda into one last abrupt U-turn before pointing the nose onto the Harry Byrd Highway and back toward the capital.

"The same thing but different," she says.

"That's what the man said."

"So he has knowledge of an imminent terror attack on American soil, that's what he's offering."

"He's playing games," Bell says. "He played games the whole time."

"You don't believe him?"

"Do you?"

"About that, yes."

"He was offering anything to get out of that room. Hell, he offered you up."

"That why you're here?" She makes a point of not looking at him, still with eyes on the road, eyes on the mirrors, and she's pleased that she asks it without any of the rancor she's feeling. Heath would be proud.

"You think I bought that line?"

It's a redirect, turning the question back to her, and she gives Elisabetta's answer. "He was spewing a lot of poison, and you can't fault his logic, can you? Some of it must have made it into your ears, that CIA man's ears. Whoever's going to end up reading that transcript at DIA and in Bethesda and who knows where. They don't know me any better than you know me. I'd have doubts."

She glances at him, the hint of a smile; it's an Elisabetta move, but it comes as easily as the words.

"Give yourself a little credit even if you don't give it to us, Chief. I say again, Heatdish was offering anything he could to get a leg up. You were the cheap shot. Easiest mind game in the world to play."

The Honda eats another mile, both of them silent.

"So what do you think?" she asks, finally.

"I try not to."

"Shooter answer."

"Easier that way. I go through the door and try not to worry about why. I leave it to you brainy types to figure out what's really going on."

She almost laughs. "You think I'm management?"

"Wouldn't dare insult you like that, Chief."

"Then don't play the dumb grunt line on me."

"I think that Zein will lead to more questions, and that'll bring Wallford back to the table with Tohir, and Tohir will try to bargain for more."

"Everything Tohir was involved with came down to only one thing the whole time I was beside him," Nessuno says. "Just one thing. Money. No politics, no religion, no philosophy except long daddy green. That's all it was ever about. If Echo has an agenda beyond that, it's a mystery to me. These are criminals who've monetized terrorism."

"So they're both."

"Exactly. But if Echo's selling a service, who's buying it?"

Bell is silent for several seconds, and when he speaks again, Nessuno expects a theory, a guess, speculation, something, but he surprises her.

"I don't believe in much," he says. "I believe in loyalty. I believe in honor. I believe in this country, for all its many, many flaws. I'm a patriot to my peril, I suppose. I believe deeply in duty, and in self-sacrifice in the pursuit of something greater. Maybe because of that I can understand the mind of a *jihadi,* or of the enemy, or I can at least try to. I believe in myself. That's the framing."

"God?" she asks.

"How's it go? There's no such thing as an atheist in a foxhole?"

"And outside a foxhole?"

"Too dark to read?"

She laughs again.

"I don't know," Bell says quietly. "You travel the world, you see a lot of things, and some of them defy rational explanation. I believe in spirituality, how's that?"

"But personally?"

"Personally? If there is a God, he, she, or it has a lot of explaining to do."

She checks the mirrors again. The last daylight has gone, and everything is headlights now. The Saint Nicholas medal shifts against her skin when she moves, making her aware of it once more.

"Where am I taking you?" she asks.

"I just need a room for the night."

"Someplace with a bed and bathtub's all right?"

"And a deck of cards to play some solitaire, yeah. What about you?"

"I don't want to be alone," Nessuno says.

The management at the Courtyard by Marriott in Gaithersburg did not take kindly to the damage to the mirror in her room. Nessuno gathers her things, settles her bill, and then she and Bell take the Civic south again, back into D.C. and down Massachusetts Avenue until they find the Hotel Palomar on P Street. It's expensive, and definitely above their combined pay grades, but Nessuno thinks that the salary she hasn't spent for two years might as well go to something she'll enjoy. They valet the car and Bell takes his duffel and she takes hers and she beats him to the front desk by a step. She sends him to find a table at the hotel restaurant, Urbana, where she joins him five minutes later. It's western Mediterranean fare, and goes with the style of the hotel, the food self-important and expensive and good. They share a bottle of wine and talk about anything they can think of that isn't work, and she's not surprised he played football, though he is surprised that she wanted to be a nun.

"Every good Catholic girl wants to be a nun at some point," Nessuno says.

"You were a good Catholic girl?"

"I was a very catholic Catholic girl. That's why I never became a nun."

They finish their meal and linger over coffee, and when the check comes, she's quicker.

"Stop doing that."

"I want to."

"I can get a room of my own," Bell says.

"Do you want to get a room of your own?"

He doesn't look away, silent for several seconds. There's a melancholy in his eyes, and it makes him all the more attractive to her.

"You still have the bends," he says.

She gets up from the table. "Like you don't?"

She heads for the lobby, the elevator, and their room without looking to see if he'll follow.

He does.

Another hotel room.

They start awkwardly, almost clumsily, each of them undressing without pretense or modesty or expectation, standing opposite one another. They've left the lights off, the curtains open, and the city glow shows her his body, his scars. She likes his shoulders, his arms, the slope of his hips. His legs are long and strong, like the rest of him, which is what she imagined when she had allowed herself to imagine them like this. She moves first, closing the space between them, meeting his mouth with her own, tastes him tentatively, then again, and he kisses her in return just as gently.

"Is this Petra?" he asks. "Or Elisabetta?"

"Elisabetta is better in bed." She grins.

"That's not what I mean."

She touches his face, traces the concern at his mouth. She takes hold of his hands, places them on her hips, moves them along her body.

"It's all right," she says. "I've had the shot. I'm not going to get knocked up."

"Don't mean that, either. I mean you."

"I'm not crazy, Jad. You know I'm not crazy. This isn't multiple personality disorder or schizophrenia or Stockholm syndrome or sex addiction. Just us. It's just us."

One of his hands slips from hers, draws a line between her breasts.

Touches the Saint Nicholas medal on its chain. Looks her in the eyes.

"It's all right," she says again.

She kisses him once more, and this time, he answers. She can feel a passion in him warring with restraint, and she seizes it, draws upon it, returns it. His hands move, a caress, then a hold, then a grip that delights her. He lifts her, and she wraps herself around him, the stubble at his throat scraping her cheek. He sets her on the bed, lays her down, moves along her body, exploring, touching, and she pulls at him, hands at his arms, at his shoulders, at his hips.

When he goes down on her, she claws at his back, tears at the bedclothes, cries out with the sudden intensity of the pleasure. It's something Vosil Tohir never did, something he thought demeaning, servile, unmanning, and unbecoming; the source of his pleasure and hers was to be found in his cock, no place else. Bell's pleasure is in her, and it takes her by surprise, and it delights her. She wonders if this is what Heath imagined, this shift from object to identity. When she thinks she can bear it no more, she pushes him away, rolls to climb him. She tastes herself in his mouth. He is hard, and she is eager, and she does not look away, meeting his eyes as she guides him inside, as she mounts him. This, too, is welcome, and wonderful, and never what Tohir would allow; he was always on top, and so often behind, and while his hands could be gentle, they would always announce possession.

She bends to him, kisses him, riding him. His hands rise, and she almost flinches, imagining he is reaching for her throat, but instead they find her shoulders, describe a descent along her arms. Fingers lacing with hers, as if to steady her, and now the Saint Nicholas medal is swaying, rocking between them, and she feels him beginning to lose himself, and she wants to go with him, wants to climax as one. Her forehead touches his, her grip on him tightening, the sudden burst of urgency and that tremendous pulse building inside her until she can barely manage the word.

"Now," she tells him.

*   *   *

They lie together in the darkness, and she stays in his arms, postcoital, still coasting in shared pleasure. She moves first, slipping from his embrace, separating; yet another difference between the two men, Tohir always so anxious to rebuild the barriers eroded by their intimacy. Nessuno expects Bell to drop off into sleep after they separate, but instead he rolls on his side, his hand drawing lines on her flank.

"Tell me about Poland," Bell says.

"You don't want me to tell you how to keep a secret?" It's Elisabetta talking now, far more than Petra Nessuno, playful, teasing. The smile comes unbidden, the satisfaction of having shared this bed.

"I know how to keep a secret."

She laughs softly. "Not like he was talking about you don't."

"Sure I do. The way Heatdish keeps a secret? He kills everyone who knows it. That's posturing."

"Not how he saw it."

"You're still here."

"You know how to kill a moment." It's another evasion, another Elisabetta quip, and Nessuno feels herself struggling for equilibrium between two covers, between this person she wants to be here and now and the person she has had to be for so terribly long. She knows somewhere in the middle ground there's a truth, the amalgam, but it's out of reach, like the taillights ahead of them on the drive back from Leesburg, visible at steady distance but somehow impossible to close the gap.

He moves hair out of her eyes, tucks it behind her ear. Even in the darkness, she can make out his face, his expression, the concentration.

"This is your idea of pillow talk?" she asks.

He kisses her, softer than before.

"We had a lead, this Italian named Pallazzini," she says. "I—Elisabetta, I mean—met him in Dubai. He was moving antiquities, stolen art, like that. He'd done very well with the fall of Baghdad."

"Seems like a number of folks did."

She snorts, hates herself for doing it. Elisabetta never snorts; she laughs or she doesn't, but she never lets herself sound like a pig.

"Pallazzini led to Heatdish?" Bell asks.

Nessuno nods, wets her lips. She's finding this harder to talk about than she imagined, but now that she's offered it, she cannot turn back. She needs Elisabetta's voice, her distance, her remove. It was Elisabetta who did these things, she tells herself, not Petra.

"I knew Tohir was a mover," she says. "When Pallazzini brought me to meet him, it wasn't obvious, he wasn't flashy — he was never flashy — but I knew it. I mean, he didn't even give me his name at that first meeting. And I was fucking brilliant, I have to tell you. I was gorgeous, and I was sexy, and I was smart, and I made sure he saw all of it, and it worked. Moved the first piece — it was a painting — flawlessly."

"With a little help, I'm sure."

This time, she doesn't snort. It's a gentle laugh, exactly what it needs to be.

"Just a little," she says. "He contacted me twice after that over the next few months, had me move two more pieces. I did those flawlessly, too."

"And all the time, he's checking you out."

"Oh, yes. The full exam, tit to toe. Had me followed. My finances were a mess, credit maxed, straining the limits of my lifestyle. Everything to make me look ideal but not too ideal. I was living in Rome, and I'm almost positive he had the place searched on two different occasions while I was away."

"You were living in Rome?"

"I was. What's the matter, you don't like Rome?"

"I like Rome fine. Go on."

She shifts, lays her head against his breast, and Bell lies back. It's easier this way; she doesn't have to look at him.

"I ended up in London on, quote, business, unquote, and he contacted me there. Everything prior had been intermediaries, but this time he wanted to meet in person. We met, and he told me he had more work if I was willing. I was willing. I spent the next couple months acting as courier, sometimes as translator, sometimes as arm candy. By that point we were lovers."

She hesitates, waiting for Bell to make some comment, some acknowledgment that he's heard. She can hear his heart beat in his chest, steady, regular.

"After a few more months, we met up in Prague. Beautiful hotel, like this one, but classic. We had dinner, went back to the room, made love. The middle of the night he pulls me out of bed, says we're going for a drive. His manner was different, he was…anxious, I couldn't read him. All the alarms were going off. I had Petra's voice in my head, just screaming warnings at me."

"He tested you," Bell says.

"Final exam," Nessuno says. "We ended up at a farmhouse about two hours out of town. The kind of middle of nowhere where you know nothing good ever happens."

"And there were two men."

"There were two men. And Tohir told me that he wanted me to be beside him, because he loved me, and we could do great things together. But he had to be certain, there could be no doubt. That if I were to go further with him, he had to be sure. The first one, it was Pallazzini, of course. They'd beaten him, not as bad as some I'd seen, but he'd been worked over. Vosil put the gun in my hand, and I did it, I killed him. He thought that was the hard one, you know? Because he knew I knew Pallazzini, he thought we'd been lovers, too. We hadn't, but he believed it. He thought that was the anguish."

Bell, beneath her, makes no move, makes no sound.

"The other one, he couldn't have known," she says. "They'd tortured him. The full works, he was missing teeth, fingers, they'd savaged one eye."

"You knew him," Bell says.

"Tohir couldn't have known. If he had known, he'd have killed me, too. He couldn't have known. But Petra Nessuno knew him, this second one. They really *had* been lovers, you see? He was…they'd done language training together. It was just dumb fate. And he recognized me, even that far gone, I could see it in his last eye."

Bell's hand moves, climbs along her back, settles, palm broad and warm, and she realizes she is shaking. The words, for her, for Elisabetta, are hard to break free.

"He was going to say my name," she says.

The phone wakes them both while it's still dark, and there's a moment of confusion before she realizes it's his and not hers demanding the attention. She pulls hair out of her face and sees the clock saying it's eighteen minutes past three in the morning. She can't hear what's being said on the other end of the line, but she doesn't need to; everything in his body shifts as the last shreds of his sleep vanish.

"Five minutes," he says. He gives the hotel's address.

Nessuno reaches for the lamp, switches it on, flinches. He's out of bed and pulling on his clothes already. She watches the way he moves, watches him dress, sees again the scars both old and new that she discovered on him the night before.

"We're moving him," he says, putting his gun back on his hip.

Nessuno nods.

He picks up his phone again, and she thinks he's going for the door next and will leave without another word, but he turns back toward her, climbs back on the bed on his knees. She sits up, and he takes her face in his hands, big palms cool against her skin. He kisses her, and despite having only three minutes left, he does it slowly, and it is sweet and earnest. She thinks he is as reluctant to let go as she is.

"I'd like to see you again," Bell tells her. "I very much want to see you again."

Then he's out of sight, and she hears the door open, then close and latch. She puts a hand to her mouth, trying to somehow preserve the press of his lips. She can feel herself grinning, feel a rising spur of joy in her breast. She wants to laugh, instead just shakes her head. She climbs out of the bed long enough to go secure the locks before returning to climb back undercover, switch off the bedside lamp, and lie down again to sleep.

When she wakes there's bright sunlight, the feel of late morning. She drifts in its warmth, stretches for the cool corners of the sheets. When she buries her face in the other pillows, she can smell hints of Bell, and she smiles again. Her phone rings, and she doesn't need to remember which name should answer.

"Nessuno, go."

"Tohir's dead," Heath says.

Chapter Ten

THE CAR HAD been waiting for Bell outside the hotel, but still, he is last to arrive, everyone else already seated. Their gear, what little required for the op, is laid out on two tables at the side of the room, and the room itself is remarkably anonymous, even for this kind of work. They're in an office in one of D.C.'s many federal buildings, repurposed for this briefing.

Bell turns to Jorge and says, "Ribs?"

"Won't be needing them," Jorge says.

Bell holds his friend's gaze for a second, tries to see how much he's lying. Jorge should still be down for rest, but he's here, and so is O'Day, which means Ruiz is drawing extra cards for his hand, so to speak. If Jorge is back on rotation, then O'Day should be with his team, but he isn't, and Bell turns back to face Ruiz, trying not to wonder exactly what they're in for.

"The mission is to transport the asset." Ruiz hits a button and a projector throws a map onto the wall behind him. "The mission is to transport the asset."

Bell tries to focus on what Ruiz is saying, on the map and the op, and finds it uncharacteristically difficult. He's seeing the route they're to take, hearing the words Ruiz is saying, and he knows he's taking it all in, but he also knows he's not all here, that he's not entirely in the moment as he needs to be. A piece of him has been left behind, is still in a hotel room across town, with a woman he's afraid he's taken advantage of, a woman he'd prefer to be with right now. He's feeling guilty, and he is afraid he has behaved dishonorably. What he is feeling for Petra Nessuno is more than simple physical attraction. It's the first time since Amy that he can remember feeling this way about anyone. He is suspicious of his own motives, and this is made worse because he is suspicious of Nessuno's as well.

Her loyalty is not a question to him, despite everything Tohir said. If she is a traitor, if she has been turned, then Bell and the rest of the team never would have gone to Tashkent. That's simple logic, and if Bell can see it, he is certain that others, higher on the chain, can too. He's a shooter, not a planner, after all, and if his analysis checks, surely theirs will. It's not a question of loyalty.

It's a question of reliability.

There had been moments when it was clear to Bell that she did not know who she was or, perhaps more precisely, who she was supposed to be. Nothing overt, just a subtle shift in manner, the moments when she'd seem to tense, then relax, when she seemed to come alive with a smile, a look in her eye. Talking about living in Rome, not as cover but as her home. There had been two women with him in the car, at dinner, in the hotel. She had known it, too. She had said as much.

He doesn't know which of those women he's left in the bed at the hotel, which of them had brought him up to the room to begin with. He wants to believe it doesn't matter, that the two form a whole. He wants to believe that Petra or Elisabetta, it makes no difference, but he can't. He cannot rely upon her, and that means he cannot rely on what he is feeling, and that makes him believe his attraction to her is all the more suspect.

The colonel is wrapping it up. Ruiz gives good briefings; the man's sat through his own stack of them, after all, and he's been delivering them for years now.

"Gear, keys, and paper on the table," Ruiz says.

They get up as one, gather their things.

"Where's the target?" Bell asks.

"In the trunk," Ruiz says.

Bell drives, with Steelriver riding shotgun beside him, and neither has anything to say to the other. It's not uncomfortable, but it's not companionable, and Bell thinks that maybe he and O'Day are pondering the same things, because yes, this op is about moving Tohir safely, but it's about something else, too, that much is clear to Bell. Maybe O'Day is thinking the same things, or maybe he's worried about Jorge's ribs, or maybe he's just tired.

Eight minutes past five brings them to Leesburg, and Bell stops the car in the deepest darkness he can find, sits with the engine idling and all the lights off for two minutes, then Cardboard pulls in beside them, gives Bell a significant nod. They're off coms for this part, as directed by Ruiz.

"Good," Bell tells O'Day.

Steelriver climbs out of the vehicle without a word, and Bell pulls the release for the trunk as Cardboard is climbing out of his car. O'Day and Freddie meet at the back of the car, and in less than a minute they've got their passenger buckled up and in the backseat, all of it done in silence. Freddie closes the trunk, climbs back behind the wheel of his own car, and O'Day buckles up beside Bell once again. Bell checks his watch, waits until the faintly luminescent second hand sweeps past twelve, bringing them to 0511. He puts the car in gear, pulls out, and with Freddie following puts them onto Edwards Ferry Road, heading east.

Traffic is sparse, but Bell keeps the car just below the speed limit anyway, at least until they hit the Leesburg Bypass. Then they're turning north, and he accelerates, Cardboard following suit three car lengths behind. The Leesburg Bypass becomes the James Monroe Highway, State Route 15, and the town vanishes behind them and the road collapses to two lanes only, and Bell is now doing fifty-five. Cardboard holds his distance.

"Three minutes," O'Day says.

Bell thinks he sounds bored.

Trees cluster along the side of the road, then fade, reveal flat planes of farmland, the occasional shape of a dark home. The smell of summer fields mixes with the scent beginning to fill the inside of the car, a distinct odor that Bell is more familiar with than he cares to admit. Trees spring up once more, fall away once more, and they're passing a cluster of commercial businesses dressed in residential clothes. They pass an antiques store.

"There's the church," O'Day says.

Bell slows, makes the left onto an even narrower two-lane road, now on State Route 663. He feels the adrenaline dump, makes the conscious effort to keep his grip on the wheel from tightening. The road cuts through more farmland on either side, makes a sharp dogleg right, correcting north once more. Cardboard's headlights close up, maybe a length and a half back. Bell checks his speed as they slip past yet another farmhouse, this one bigger, hay bales wrapped in white plastic, now tinged rose with the rising sun. They're heading into a new cluster of trees, thick on both sides once more, and Bell sees the crossroads ahead, the steeple of yet another church just beyond. The trees continue along the left-hand side past the crossroads, as if offering the church some modesty, but along the right-hand side there's nothing but open field and, almost invisible in the light, a tree line marking the edge of that property to the north. Bell checks his speed once more, taps his brakes.

He doesn't see the shot, but he feels it instantly through the car, feels the vehicle gag and shudder. The sound the engine makes is horrific, thousands of smoothly machined revolutions per minute abruptly violated. The car tries to slew left, already slowing, and Bell has to fight to correct it, braking at the same time. O'Day rocks forward against his belt, but behind them, the target stays securely held in his seat.

The second shot punches through the windshield, safety glass cracking and the high-speed whip of the round as it passes by. Bell feels the air compress against his skin, displaced, hears the bursting from the body behind him. He doesn't move, fights to keep from moving, from flinching, hands on the wheel, and then the third shot comes, and then the fourth, the fifth, the sixth, and he can't see a muzzle flash, but he knows the rounds are being sent from more than three hundred meters away, from that tree line at the edge of the field. The windshield is in tatters, falling in chunks, and two more rounds pass between Bell and O'Day, and now the rolling report reaches them, the distant echo of eight .50-caliber shots fired in less than two seconds, and then that fades.

There's the sound of something liquid settling behind Bell, and the sound of the car hissing, and there's nothing else. In the rearview mirror, Bell can see Cardboard's car where it's skidded to a stop, perhaps twenty feet behind them, see Board just now emerging from the vehicle, submachine gun in hand.

Bell pulls his own MP7 from where it's been riding by his leg, looks at O'Day.

"Well," Bell says. "That was exciting."

Chapter Eleven

IN SEVENTEEN YEARS with the Loudoun County sheriff's department, Deputy Martin Loughridge had never, not once, seen anything like it.

Which is not to say he'd never seen a corpse before, or even corpses made that way through violent means. It wasn't to say he hadn't rolled up on his fair share of MVAs in the past, either, seen the damage a drunk driver could do, seen the fates of teenagers who'd thought their seat belts were only an option. He still carried memories of the three-car accident he'd been first on the scene to, four dead, including a little girl all of three.

That had been heartbreak.

This was akin to horror.

He'd been pouring himself coffee from his Thermos, just seated in his ride outside the Old Lucketts Store, window rolled down and facing south, toward the community center, waiting for dawn and the end of the shift. Summer nights and kids staying out late, and there'd been some recent vandalism reported in the area, so he'd finished his latest circuit and figured he'd take his break here, just keep an eye on things. In another hour, the hamlet would begin to rouse itself, and shortly thereafter he'd roll back to base and clock out to allow the morning shift to come on and deal with the commuters, the fender benders. Like most nights in his patrol sector, Loughridge's was a preventative presence rather than a reactive one.

"Unit twelve, we've got a report of gunshots out by Christ Church on Stumptown Road."

He shifted his coffee, almost spilling it, took the handset. "Responding."

"Ten-four."

He rolled without siren but with his lights, took it fast, heading west out of Lucketts, trying to keep an open mind. He wasn't worried, and he wasn't particularly anxious, because he wasn't expecting to find anything. Reports of gunfire were more common than people thought, especially in the summer, when a string of firecrackers could be mistaken for the sound of a weapon by those who couldn't tell the difference. And there was nothing, but nothing, out by Christ Church except, well, Christ Church and a couple of farms. Long, broad stretches of fields broken by stands of trees, exactly the kind of place kids would end up when they stayed out too late and got up to some mischief.

So it was mischief he was expecting when his cruiser flattened out of the bend, coming down the very easy slope of Stumptown Road toward the intersection with 663. Then his lights hit the cars in the middle of the road, and he saw the figures and the damage. The car in the front was a Ford, its windshield all but missing, a puddle of radiator fluid and the last wisps of smoke or steam rising from its front end. Where his headlights hit it, he could see a hole the size of a man's fist through the car's grille.

There were three men that he could see, one of them on his knees, doing something on the ground, the two others standing over him, and they were holding weapons, they were holding fucking submachine guns. Loughridge stomped his brakes, sent his remaining coffee sloshing, and stared at them for a second as they seemed to stare back. Then he grabbed the radio.

"This is unit twelve, intersection of Stumptown and six sixty-three. I have an MVA and three armed suspects. Need backup."

"Marty, what?"

"Three of them, they've got submachine guns."

Then he was out of his car and drawing his own weapon. Abstractly, he knew it wasn't a very smart thing to do, to match his Glock against two, maybe three, submachine guns, but after the fact he understood it had been intuition telling him he'd be safe. The two on their feet, yes, they'd had their weapons to hand, but neither had made a move other than to watch his approach, and some part of him understood that he was safe with them.

"Loudoun County sheriff's department," Loughridge said behind his weapon. "Hold it right there. Drop your weapons."

The one closest to him, the taller of the two standing, raised one empty hand and with his other set his submachine gun on the furrowed hood of the Ford. Loughridge took another half dozen steps forward, and as he did he cleared enough angle on the Ford to see what the third man, the one he thought had been kneeling or praying, was actually doing.

That was when he nearly threw up.

The third one was doing CPR on a fourth, and there clearly wasn't any point. The body was literally missing pieces. Large pieces. That the man kneeling on the ground had even been attempting CPR was nothing less than folly, because it looked like there were chunks of head missing. The blood was everywhere, shining black in the dawn, dripping from the open rear door of the Ford. When Loughridge looked in the car, he felt his gorge rise again. Gore and bone had been blown against the seat and the shattered rear window as if by a hurricane. Specks of meat mixed with tufts of upholstery. The scent was overwhelming. A trail ran from the backseat to the asphalt, showing where the body had been moved from the vehicle to the ground in an attempt to resuscitate him. Loughridge thought more of the body remained in the car than had been taken outside of it.

The tall man, the one who'd set aside his submachine gun, spoke.

"My name is Jacoby," he said. "United States Army. This is a military operation that's been compromised. I have contacted my command, and military police are en route."

Loughridge looked at him, dumbfounded. He could hear sirens, faint, the approach of the nearest unit responding. It would be Hollister, in sector 11.

"The situation," Jacoby said, "is under control."

Loughridge found his voice. "I need to see some ID."

"This is a military operation that has been compromised," Jacoby repeated. "There are MPs en route."

"I need to see some ID."

Jacoby reached into his coat, removed a billfold, opened it one-handed, and offered it to Loughridge, who took it, holstering his weapon. He brought out his Mini Maglite and flashed it on the card, and it confirmed what Jacoby was saying, his name, that he was a sergeant, that he was military intelligence. Loughridge handed it back.

"I need to see their IDs."

"No, Officer," Jacoby said. "You don't."

"I'm sorry?"

"You don't need to know that."

"This is a crime scene, sir. You're out of your jurisdiction. I'm taking you into custody. You, move away from the body."

The one who'd been doing CPR slowed, then stopped his efforts, looked up at Jacoby. Blood smeared his front, covered his hands. He was slender, blond, whereas Jacoby's hair was black. The third one, the shortest, just ignored him. They were all dressed pretty much alike, Loughridge realized. Windbreakers, jeans, different shirts, of course. They didn't really look military, though, their haircuts all outside the high and tight, and the one who'd been doing CPR actually had a ponytail.

"I'm taking you into custody," Loughridge said. "You're all under arrest."

Jacoby seemed to give this some thought. Then he shrugged, and the other two set their submachine guns aside and all of them moved to stand by the Ford.

Loughridge steeled himself, took another look at the body, then back to Jacoby.

"Who's he?"

"You don't need to know that, either," Jacoby said.

Hollister arrived within a minute, and then Dole two minutes later, from sector 9, and they put cuffs on the three men and put one of them each in the back of their cruisers. None of them resisted, and none of them said anything except Jacoby, and that was during the pat down.

"We are armed, Officer."

They sure as hell were, too, and all high-speed stuff. Each of them with a .45 — the short one was also carrying a SIG — and each of them with a knife, a real knife, not a for-show combat thing, but Mel Pardue blades, and they looked genuine, not like licensed replicas. Jacoby was the only one carrying ID of any sort at all.

"What the fuck do you think happened here?" Dole asked after they'd gotten all of them secured in the cars.

"I think somebody murdered the hell out of whoever it was they were transporting," Loughridge said.

"Spook stuff," Hollister said.

"Spook stuff," Dole agreed.

Loughridge checked over his shoulder, looking to his car, to where Jacoby had been placed on the rear bench. The man was just sitting there, watching them, and there was nothing to find in his expression. There wasn't any malice, there wasn't any regret, there wasn't even any anxiety.

"I don't think they're military intelligence," Loughridge said. "I think they're something else."

From there, it turned pure clusterfuck as far as Loughridge was concerned. Another three units arrived over the next five minutes, and

Loughridge, being first on the scene, was now responsible for securing said scene. They'd just gotten started measuring the skid marks and trying to fix the angles when Lieutenant Lucas showed up, leading the parade of detectives and technicians who would be spending the next six hours or so of their lives here. The chatter over their radios became nearly constant.

"They say they're with military intelligence," Loughridge told Lucas, showing him Jacoby's badge and ID. The badge said that Jacoby was a special agent.

"Yeah, well, they're not on a base and there's nothing special about him." Lucas stormed to the cruiser, opened the door. "You Jacoby? That's you?"

"That's correct."

"These other guys, they're with you?"

"That's correct."

"And the dead guy? Who's the dead guy?"

Loughridge found himself mouthing the words as Jacoby said them. Lucas, predictably, exploded.

"The fuck you are telling me I don't need to know that? Who the fuck do you think you are?"

"I'm with army intelligence. There's been an incident. MPs are en route."

"They have no jurisdiction."

"I can give you a number to call —"

"You can give me answers. These your men? Who're these other guys?"

"You don't need to know that."

Lucas spun around, pointed at Loughridge. "Take them in. You take them all in, you book them on suspicion of murder."

"Yes, sir."

"The fuck he thinks he is, telling me what I need to know and what I don't need to know. Military intelligence. Fucking contradiction in terms. What's that called? A contradiction in terms."

"An oxymoron."

"That's right, fucking oxymoron. You run these oxymorons in, you charge them and put them in separate fucking cells, and then we'll see what they think I need to know and what I don't."

Loughridge led the procession, Jacoby in the back, with Hollister and the short one, then Dole and the tall, ponytailed one, following, heading south into Leesburg. Jacoby just sat there, in the backseat in his cuffs, eyes closed, head tilted back. By the time they were halfway there, Loughridge was sure the man wasn't faking it.

He really was asleep.

You're not military intelligence, Loughridge thought.

It was after eight by the time all three were booked and processed and put into their separate cells for holding. The last Loughridge saw of Jacoby was as he was being escorted down the hall, past the security door. Then it clanged closed, and that was that, and Loughridge went to get changed out of his uniform and to call his wife, to explain why he was late. She was very understanding, the way she always was, and Loughridge once again found himself thinking how lucky he was to have found her, that she had consented to marry him.

He got home and had a light snack, then showered, changed into his pajamas, and spent an hour reading the novel he was working his way through. It was a thriller, about a CIA-trained killer who had gone rogue to hunt down terrorists and who could apparently take multiple rounds without ever being hit in the vitals. Bullets didn't seem to slow him down. In fact, they seemed to speed him up. Loughridge found himself wondering what kind of bullet could do the damage he'd seen that morning. Something big, he knew. Something that could kill a car as easily as a man. Fifty-caliber, probably.

He was tired, but now he was curious, and he couldn't get the image of the dead man out of his mind. It was changing, though, becoming less painful, less obscene. He went into the sewing room that also served as his home office, booted up the desktop, then did a Google search for .50-caliber sniper rifles. The very first hit was for the Barrett M82, and Wikipedia told him that it was an antimateriel weapon and in service with the military. There were a couple of YouTube videos, people test-firing the gun, and in one of them, a man fired off a whole clip in less than two seconds. He learned that it had an effective range of two thousand yards and could punch through half an inch of steel at the end of its trip.

Loughridge yawned, shut down his computer, and headed for bed. His last thought before drifting off was that there was no way — no way — those guys were from military intelligence.

Dole and Hollister were already in when Loughridge showed up for work at eleven that night.

"Get this," Dole said. "Those three guys?"

"From this morning?"

Hollister nodded.

"About an hour after you left, guy comes in from the army, full uniform, wearing eagles."

"A colonel," Hollister said.

"A colonel, he comes in, he's got three MPs with him, he walks up to Rivera at the desk, and he says he needs the guys we brought in released into their custody."

"For real," Hollister said.

"So Rivera calls Lucas, and Lucas blows a fuse at the colonel. Swearing up and down, insulting him, making a big stink about jurisdiction and how the military has no leg to stand on here, like that. And the colonel just takes it, doesn't say anything except pull out his cell phone and dial a number, and then as soon as Lucas has to stop and catch his breath, this guy just hands him the phone. So Lucas takes it, right? And he starts in on the phone and then he stops, and Rivera swears he just loses all his color. He doesn't say anything. Just listens for, like, five seconds."

"And?" Loughridge asked.

"And then," Dole said, "he apologizes. He *apologizes*. You believe that?"

Loughridge shook his head. "Who was he talking to? Who was on the phone?"

"No fucking clue. Lucas just hands the phone back to the colonel, he turns to Rivera, and he tells him to give the colonel anything he wants. Then he goes back into his office and stays in there for the rest of the shift."

"And the three guys? Jacoby and those guys?"

"The MPs cuff them, and they all walk out with the colonel leading ten minutes later." Dole grinned. "What do you think about that?"

"Yeah," Loughridge said. "Yeah, you know what?"

"What?"

He opened his mouth to speak, then shut it again. He thought about four men in two cars driving deserted back roads in the predawn of a summer morning. He thought about an antimateriel rifle that could go from full to empty in less than two seconds and maybe faster if the sniper using it really knew what he was doing. He thought about .50-caliber rounds that could turn a man from alive into Jell-O.

He thought about Jacoby, the man's patience and manners and manner, too. Jacoby, not Loughridge, not Lucas, not any of them, had been in control of the whole situation the entire time.

He thought about the one thing Jacoby kept repeating.

Dole and Hollister were waiting.

"Never mind," Loughridge said.

Chapter Twelve

BROCK GETS THE news during the early morning brief at the Pentagon, and even though the operation is referred to by code name and the asset in question referred to as just that, an "asset," he knows they're talking about Tohir, and he finds himself both angered and relieved at the same time. Angered because, as far as he's concerned, the Architect has gotten impatient and was unwilling to wait for Brock to do what he has been asked to do, and angered all the more because this means the Architect has his own assets on the ground capable of performing the assassination. Relieved because it means Brock won't have to arrange it, a problem he's been wrestling with for the past three days and that has stymied him more than he cares to admit. If it had been anything else, he could've tasked an operator to it, maybe even dressed it up as a proper action, but as it stood he'd been looking at options outside of his purview, and he hadn't yet found any he liked.

So yes, it is a relief, but it is also troubling. Never mind the fact that he can't be sure yet that it *is* Tohir who's been killed. Details are sketchy at the briefing; he learns there's been a compromised operation outside of Leesburg, and that the detail responsible for the movement was detained by the Loudoun County sheriff's department and is now under arrest at Fort Detrick, ostensibly for dereliction of duty. He learns that the whole thing has been an unmitigated disaster, and that there is going to be hell to pay. That's the extent of it, but it isn't enough.

Brock needs to be sure.

Calling Danny Ruiz is out of the question; he has no oversight of Task Force Indigo, just as Ruiz has no reason to interact with Bravo-Interdict. Direct contact just to ask what happened would be so inappropriate as to beg suspicion, something Brock is careful to avoid. This leads him to Heath, and that makes more and more sense as he considers it; part one, Heatdish was their asset, they've got a horse in this race, so interest is justified. Part two, and perhaps more compelling, if the Architect has a shooter or even shooters on the ground, it's not impossible that he's uncovered Blackfriars's part in Heatdish's capture. This could put Blackfriars at risk, and if there's one thing that Emmet Brock is certain of, it's that Abigail Heath will mama-bear to shreds anyone or anything that threatens one of her operators. Casting it as concern for Chief Petra Nessuno will not only make it palatable, it'll give it all urgency.

He reaches for the phone.

"Heath."

"Captain, Brock."

"Sir, what can I do for you?"

"I've got a whisper that Heatdish was taken out of play during transport this morning out of Leesburg."

There's just a fraction of a pause before Heath says, "Whisper?"

"I'm not going to call up Colonel Ruiz and ask him, for obvious reasons. But I've got a bigger concern here."

"I think I'm on the same page."

"Do you know where she is?"

"I can locate her."

"Maybe you want to bring her in and keep her close to you for the time being. Set up out at Belvoir, see if she can't help you confirm this, confirm what happened. If Echo has this reach and she's compromised, I do not want him looking to settle accounts with her, not after everything she's done for us."

"Understood."

"Let me know what you find," Brock says.

He goes about his business then, because frankly, there's a lot of business for him to attend to. A half dozen more meetings before two that afternoon, by which time he's back in his office and Heath is waiting for him on the line. She's confirmed the attack and is trying to get a positive identification on the body. By four, she's able to do that, too, and declares that Tohir is dead.

"Send me what you've got."

The files are on his computer within five minutes. He transfers them to a thumb drive, takes it with him when he leaves the Pentagon at half after six. He heads with the rush-hour traffic in the direction of home before pulling off in a supermarket parking lot and taking his burner phone from the glove compartment. His first call goes to voice mail.

"Twenty-one hundred," is all he says before he hangs up. He dials a second number.

"This is Jordan."

"Make time for me tonight," Brock says.

"I have plans."

"I'll be there at ten thirty."

Jordan laughs softly. "All right. Should I make you something? Will you have eaten?"

Brock finds himself wondering if she did it, if she could've murdered Tohir. He dismisses that thought as absurd, as paranoid. She belongs to the Architect, yes, but she's a different weapon entirely.

"I'll be there at ten thirty," he repeats.

"Very mysterious," Jordan says. "I'll be waiting. Will you be staying?"

Brock hangs up, enters the supermarket. He drops the phone in the trash can beside the shopping carts, buys a gallon of milk, a box of cereal, some veggies, just to make everything look good, just in case he's being watched. He gets back to his car and resumes the battle against the traffic, and when he gets home his wife isn't there, and he's relieved. He puts the groceries away, gets out of his uniform, and takes a shower. He shaves, even though he'd shaved that morning. He wonders if Jordan is going to shave, too, and when he thinks that, he has a moment of self-loathing unlike any he's ever felt, so strong he swears aloud.

"Fuck honor," Brock says.

He struggles. He calls himself a traitor and calls his own actions treasonous. He calls himself weak, and venal, and old because he cannot stop himself from wanting this woman as much as he does, knowing everything he knows. He calls himself stupid, and a coward.

None of this keeps him from getting dressed again, this time in civvies, or from writing a note to his wife saying that he'll be late, or from stopping to buy a new burner phone. He puts it in the glove compartment where the old one went. The thumb drive is in his pocket. He tells himself that life is about compromises, and that he is and always will be a patriot, that what he does he does for the safety and security of his country, a country that is naive and asleep and complacent.

He tells himself that he is using Jordan just as much as she is using him, and that in the end he will come out ahead.

Then he tells himself that Jordan probably thinks exactly the same thing.

Larkin is seated at the bar when Brock arrives. "Bar" is probably a misnomer, although there is a long counter with a bartender behind it. Calling the place a private club gives it too much credit. Rather, it's a place for people who can afford to meet discreetly and socially in the D.C. area to do just that; it's the kind of place where the clientele is almost invariably white, and if you see a woman who isn't serving drinks or isn't keeping someone company, you mark it in your calendar as a day to remember. Larkin calls it the Four-Four-Two, because that's the number on the brownstone, and Brock has never asked who owns the place or who runs the place or how many people know about the place. This is Larkin's world, and Brock always feels like he's invading whenever they meet here, and he resents it like hell. Brock is two years Larkin's junior, but put them side by side and Larkin looks ten years younger, because Larkin comes from a class and a level of wealth that can afford doctors to defend against his particular means of self-abuse. Like the clientele, Larkin is white, and like the rest of his associates in this matter, with the notable exception of Brock himself, Larkin is very, very rich.

"I bought you a drink," Larkin says, waits for Brock to take it. He raises his glass, waits for Brock to do the same. "To Jamieson."

Brock refuses to echo the sentiment, but he drinks just the same.

"Are we on again?" Larkin asks.

Brock runs his eyes around the room. There's piano music playing from somewhere invisible, and muted conversation, and nobody is giving them any attention. It doesn't make Brock feel better. The problem with D.C. is that the town is lousy with people listening, people who know people, and you never know where or when you'll be recognized, even in a place like this. They meet here because it limits exposure, but it doesn't eliminate it entirely. So Brock takes an extra minute to be sure, and Larkin waits because he doesn't want to draw attention.

"I'll know by this time tomorrow," Brock says.

"I'll tell the others. They'll be pleased," Larkin says. At least he isn't whispering. Brock had to explain to him that when people whisper in public, that's what draws attention.

"What changed?" Larkin asks.

"The problem went away."

"Most do if handled properly." Larkin finishes his drink. "Has he set a price?"

"I'll know that by this time tomorrow as well."

"It's getting expensive. For all of us."

"We can call it off," Brock says. "Just let things run their course."

Larkin shifts on the stool, looks at him, curious.

"You've seen the news, you know the climate. We don't need another one."

"You're losing your nerve, Emmet?"

Brock just stares at him, wondering what it must be like to never have doubts. He thinks that Larkin has never seen violent death outside of fiction. He thinks that Larkin and the rest of them must be very sure in their beliefs to raise the question of courage.

Larkin shakes his head, reaches for his wallet, puts a hundred dollars down on the bar.

"We want what we paid for," Larkin says. "We don't intend to pay again."

"We got what we paid for."

"Not the result. We're halfway there. Halfway isn't far enough."

Larkin gets up, motions to the bartender, points to Brock's still half-filled glass. He puts a hand on Brock's shoulder.

"You don't change the world by being timid, Emmet," Larkin says, and leaves.

Brock waits until she's let him in, until she's kissed him once, those lips smooth as satin. Then he takes hold of her by the shoulders and drives her into the wall.

"Did you kill him?" he asks.

She does what she always does when he puts hands on her. She yields. He can feel his fingers digging into her flesh. She looks up at him.

"Tell me," Brock says.

"Who are we talking about?"

"You know who."

"I may know who. I want to be sure."

"Where were you this morning?"

"More specific, baby."

"Early this morning. Before dawn. Where were you?"

"I was here."

"Prove it."

"And how do I prove it, Emmet? I was here alone. Do you want to ask the neighbors? I had thought our goal was discretion always." She cants her head to one side, looking up at him. "Why are you angry at me, baby? Did I do something wrong?"

"Tohir," Brock says.

"Tohir's dead?"

"Yes."

She relaxes further against the wall, smiles up at him. "Tell me everything."

Brock watches her copy the files from the thumb drive, go through them on her laptop.

"The photographs aren't pretty," he warns her.

"You're sweet."

"There wasn't much of him left. No dental, but we had prints."

"And the rest of these files, they're what he asked for?"

"They're exactly what he asked for — information on all the shooters involved in the capture operation and in the operation in California."

"The same men in both cases?"

"Mostly."

Jordan nods, shuts the laptop, returns the thumb drive.

"I don't need it anymore," Brock says.

"Then destroy it."

"Contact him." He nods toward the closed computer. "That's how you do it, isn't it? Online somehow, a chat room or e-mail. Tell him we want what we paid for."

"I'll tell him."

"Do it now."

"It doesn't work like that."

"Then how does it work?"

"Not like that, baby." She gets up, steps to him, places her palms against his breast. "Are you staying?"

"Are you asking me to?"

"I'd like it if you stayed."

"Why do you do this?" Brock asks abruptly.

She moves slightly, lets her hand roam. "This?"

"That's not what I mean."

"How about this?"

"Stop it." He takes hold of her wrist, moving her hand away. "You work for him, you've always worked for him."

"Perhaps."

"It's true."

"Perhaps."

"So work for me."

Jordan's hands climb his torso again, fingers drag slowly through his cropped hair.

"Baby," she says. "Are you in love with me?"

"I can take care of you. If you're afraid of him, I can protect you."

"I'm not afraid of him."

Brock stares at her, this woman he thinks is flawless and that he wants more than anything, anyone, and finally, he thinks he understands. She doesn't love him, and she never will.

He puts his hand between her legs, uses his other to gather her hair into a fist. He kisses her mouth, her throat, feels the pulse rise in him, anger and rejection and lust. She whimpers.

"So," she says. "This means you'll stay, then."

Chapter Thirteen

BELL RIDES WITH Steelriver and Cardboard in the back of the Humvee, all of them wearing cuffs, two MPs up in the front and the third with them. Nobody says a word. They pass through the checkpoint into Fort Detrick, come to a stop a few minutes later, are escorted from the vehicle into the building that houses the stockade, and no sooner are they behind closed doors than Ruiz is there.

"Cut them loose," Ruiz says.

The MPs exchange brief looks, then proceed to remove the cuffs. They don't need to be told a reason; it's a full bird colonel giving them the order. Bell makes loose fists of his hands, rolls his wrists about, stretching the muscles in his forearms.

"They weren't here," Ruiz tells the MPs.

"We haven't seen anything since we came on post, sir."

Ruiz turns, and Bell, Steelriver, and Cardboard fall in behind him. They head away from the door where they entered, make a left down a quiet corridor, then a right, then Ruiz pushes a door open and they're back in the midmorning sun, where a Chevy van is waiting. Jorge — Bonebreaker — is behind the wheel. Ruiz waits until they're loaded.

"One hour," he tells Bell, handing him a key card, an address.

Bell tucks the card in a pocket, climbs into the vehicle, slams the door shut. They start moving almost immediately, and he has to put a hand out to steady himself. Steelriver and Cardboard have already rearmed with their recovered gear, and Board hands Bell his .45 in its holster, then his phone. Bell checks the weapon out of habit, settles it back into its holster, and settles the holster back on his hip. There are a couple of bottles of water, and Steelriver hands him one, and Bell takes it with him as he wedges himself up to the front and into the empty passenger seat beside Jorge. They're already on the 550, heading south, light traffic, and it's a beautiful drive on a beautiful day.

"You thought I'd miss," Jorge says.

"Never crossed my mind."

"I thought you'd miss," Steelriver says, behind them.

"I'm just saying, broken ribs, three hundred meters, moving target," Jorge says. "Eight shots, all in group. You thought I'd miss."

"I am grateful to the United States Army and the taxpayers who trained you that you did not," Bell says.

Jorge keeps his eyes on the road, but his grin is broad.

"You're welcome," he says.

The key card opens room 121 at the Best Western Westminster, and Bell steps inside to find Ruiz already there. The colonel has changed out of his uniform and into business casual, which goes with the venue. Outside, there's the faint sound of a single-prop flying overhead; from its sound and its direction Bell figures it to be coming in for a landing at the Carroll County Regional Airport, less than a mile and a half away.

"Clear?" Ruiz asks. He's sitting at the round-top table, with its fake wood pattern, two paper cups of coffee in front of him. He pushes one of them in Bell's direction.

"If not, they're better than me."

Ruiz nods, waits for Bell to take a seat and the coffee.

"Status update," Ruiz says. "Isaiah has Heatdish en route to Hailey, should be there within the next hour. Rest of your team is heading out to join him, including O'Day. You'll need the extra manpower. You've got an objection."

"I've got an objection," Bell says.

"Speak it."

"You have cover on my family?"

"Counterintelligence is handling that, has been keeping watch on Amy and Athena since you got back from Burlington."

"And?"

"And nothing so far. They're fine, Jad."

Bell nods, takes the top off his coffee, tastes it. It's awful. He drinks some anyway.

"So here's where we are," Ruiz says. "Right now, it looks like Heatdish died outside of Leesburg, and there's not enough body left to disprove that quickly. Hopefully that'll put Echo in something of a fit."

"Echo."

"It was good enough for the Chief, Blackfriars, it's good enough for us. Tohir may be selling us bullshit at wholesale, but we know California was bought and paid for here, at home. There's a legitimate conspiracy here, a treasonous conspiracy, but we don't know who's involved. All leads off of Jamieson dead-end with Heatdish. We've got a triangle, Echo on one point, Heatdish on another, and a big fucking unknown on the third. That third—that who—that's who bought the California attack. Who that is, what they want, why they did it, those are all open questions."

Bell considers this, remembers the old man from Texas who bragged about what he'd done before he died. The attack at the theme park in California had led back to him, had been bought with his money, a hell of a lot of his money, at that. Jamieson had given up Tohir, and he'd additionally given up rhetoric of the kind that at the best of times annoyed Bell and at the worst of times made him truly angry. It was the talk of a man who combined a perverted faith in God with an inflexibility in politics, spoken with the righteous arrogance and condescension of someone who believed he could have things his way because he was never wrong. To Bell, there was no difference between that brand of zealotry and the kind that brought young men into the arms of al-Qaeda and its subsidiary holdings around the world.

"We know why," Bell says. "They want a war. Jamieson said so."

"Whoever 'they' are."

"You should probably find that out."

"I probably should. Maybe you can help." Ruiz tries his own coffee. "You're clear to run, but the fact is that until we get a nibble on the decoy operation — *if* we get a nibble on the decoy operation — our options are limited. You need to talk to Heatdish again."

"Wallford hasn't?"

"Wallford is cognizant of the fact that we are compromised and fears his direct presence might reveal Heatdish's location. He's backed off of his own volition."

"That's remarkably gracious of him."

"I was thinking the same thing."

"Who knows Heatdish is in Hailey?"

"At this moment, we and your team. Wallford knows he's still alive and was moved, but he doesn't know where to."

"As far as we know."

"Correct."

"Anything on the name Tohir gave us? Zein?"

"Added urgency. Jacob Zein arrived at JFK three weeks ago, traveling on a German passport, and dropped into the void promptly thereafter. He doesn't exist before he gets on his Prague–Munich connection, and he ceases to exist upon exiting the international terminal at JFK."

"Oh, that's lovely."

"We have differing standards of beauty."

"Where there's one…"

"…there's certainly more. Getting number and purpose from Heatdish is a priority."

"How much of a priority?"

"High enough that I want you to reach out to someone who knows him. She might be able to get him to talk. She was next to him for over eighteen months, after all."

Bell watches his thumbnail pick at the rolled edge on the top of his coffee cup. "He's not very fond of her."

"Better for us. You have a problem with this, Master Sergeant?"

"She hasn't had any time to reintegrate. She was under for two years, more, and she comes out and she thinks it's over, and it's not over."

"Which means she's not done. You think she's compromised?"

Bell shakes his head, maybe a little too quickly, maybe a little too vigorously. Yes, she is compromised, but not in the way Ruiz means; she is compromised in the way that Bell is compromised, he realizes; his failed marriage a symptom like her broken identity, the demands of two different worlds.

"So you trust her."

"I trust her loyalty."

"But."

"I don't trust her mind-set."

"Then it seems to me you're worrying about a null sum, Master Sergeant. She goes into that room as the chief, she goes into that room as her cover, both get us the same thing, just through different avenues."

"I think she's having trouble telling the difference between the two, that's what I'm saying."

"I ask again, do you trust her?"

"Yes, sir."

Ruiz looks at him hard. "There is a timer running, and we don't know how long until zero. The only people on this we can trust are the people we *know* weren't involved in California, which numbers your team and a Bravo-Interdict operator who warned us about it in the first place. I am willing to extend that to her handler, who could've killed that intel before dissemination but clearly did not, but it ends there. So you will bring the chief on board with you, and you will proceed to interrogate Heatdish together."

"And then?"

"And then you will deploy to terminate the sons of bitches who are threatening American lives on American soil."

Bell tries more of his coffee. It's sitting sour in his stomach. He makes a face.

"Where is she now?"

"I understand she's staying at the Hotel Palomar," Ruiz says. "But you already knew that."

Chapter Fourteen

THE PROBLEM NESSUNO has is that she knows she hates Vosil Tohir, but she also kind of loves him.

It takes her only eight minutes from Heath's wake-up call to the shower to her clothes to downstairs, through the lobby of the Hotel Palomar, which looks entirely different during the day, and then outside. She cannot get a fix on what she feels. She walks east two blocks to Dupont Circle, jaywalks across into the park, passes the Red Line entrance at the metro station. She's missed the morning rush hour, but the dregs remain, a few people scurrying, the rest of them tourists.

Unbidden, she's remembering riding the U-Bahn, the S-Bahn, with Tohir just before Christmas. The trip, he'd claimed, had been nothing more than a vacation, a spur-of-the-moment break for the two of them, though Nessuno knew better than to believe him. Whatever business had brought them to Germany, she never found out. He stayed with her almost constantly, doting, spending money in a frenzy, almost all of it on her.

"Vosil," she'd said over dinner at Fischers Fritz, after he'd ordered Champagne. "What is this about?"

He'd smiled, shook his head. Adjusted his glasses as the wine was poured, waited until they were alone again at the table. "Does it have to be about anything?"

"With you? Always."

"Maybe I want to be alone with you, maybe that. You think that might be possible, Elisabet?"

"You have me to yourself quite often. Is this business?"

"There's always business. Business can wait. This is for us, just us."

She'd left it at that. Pressing him was always risky, and she was always careful about her timing. Over dinner wasn't the moment, nor was there one for it the next day, when he took her shopping at The Corner. It was their last night in Berlin, lying in bed in the dark, waiting for him to fall asleep. He always fell asleep before she did, a calculation on Nessuno's part, a safety measure that was more illusory than practical. If he was asleep, he couldn't be watching.

The room had been terribly dark, no ambient light at all, and she had been listening for that last change, the rhythm of his breathing settling, fighting her own drowsiness. When he spoke, it took her by surprise.

"You know I am not faithful to you," Tohir said. "When we are away from one another, there are other women."

"I know," she said.

"You know and have never said anything about it?"

"No."

"Why?"

Her answer was flawless Elisabetta. "Would it change anything?"

"No. No, I do not think it would."

"You're mine," she said. "You always come back to me."

She had been lying on her stomach, and she felt his touch on her again, palms against her backside until his hands settled on her hips. He'd shifted, lying on her, slid one hand between her and the bed. His fingers began to play.

"No." His voice in her ear. "No, Elisabet. *You* are mine."

The sight of Heath appearing from the metro stop brings her back. From the edge of the fountain, Nessuno watches her approach, rises to join her. Heath veers south, and they begin walking together, crossing the street—again jaywalking—to follow Connecticut Avenue down toward the Mall.

"It's still coming in," Heath tells her. "I have only the rough. Word is they were moving him this morning and got hit during the transport."

Nessuno thinks about Bell, but doesn't want to ask. Turns out she doesn't have to.

"Far as I know, he was the only fatality," Heath says. "Local law enforcement crawled up everyone's ass *tout suite*. Rumor is that they've got the protective team in custody."

"This is confirmed?" Nessuno asks. "This is real?"

"This is what I know that I'm sharing with you."

"Where are we going?"

"Belvoir."

"We walking there?"

"We'll double back for my car, which I presume you still have, and besides, walking is good for you."

"How'd they fuck this up?"

"Somebody talked, that's how they fucked it up." Heath is staring straight ahead, walking with her hands thrust deep in the pockets of her windbreaker. There's no need for the jacket, not this morning, not with the heat and the humidity, and Nessuno guesses that means she's carrying. "Somebody talked, and it's got to be on their end."

"Because I'm still breathing."

"There's that, and frankly, I'd like to keep it that way. Also, first anyone on our end knew he was being moved was when I got the call it'd gone tits-up. Though." Heath shoots her a look. "I am forced to ask where you were last night, what you did following your departure from the house. Why you changed hotels."

These are reasonable questions, and Nessuno knows they're ones that must be asked, but it annoys her anyway.

"You think I did it?"

"No. I just know you wanted it done."

"After we'd wrung him dry," Nessuno says.

"So?"

"So the hotel was a piece of shit, and maybe I also did some damage to the room, and the management didn't appreciate that. I had to find another hotel."

"Hmm."

"You want an alibi for me, you can talk to Master Sergeant Bell. He spent the night."

Heath grins. "You got laid; good for you."

"You've got an unnatural fascination with my sex life."

"It comes from not having much myself."

Nessuno doesn't say anything.

"If he was on the detail, I don't know," Heath says. "If you're worried."

"Why would I be worried? I fucked him, I didn't marry him."

"Aw, look at you. You've got a crush on the shooter who saved you."

"How the fuck did this go wrong?"

"That," Heath says, "is a very good question."

They drive out to Fort Belvoir, and Heath is uncharacteristically quiet, which leaves Nessuno alone with her thoughts. Memories of Tohir keep pushing their way forward, carrying conflicting emotions, and Nessuno is no closer to discerning her feelings than she was in the minutes after waking.

It had never been a question of what Tohir would do to her. He would have killed her, plain and simple, and done it slowly. It would have been the farmhouse outside of Prague, except it would've been her in the stall, and it would have been unimaginably worse. The torture would have begun with a search for the truth — who she really was, whom she really worked for, what confidences she had betrayed — but that would, perhaps, have been only secondary. Tohir would've made her pay for her betrayal, for his broken heart, with a cruelty limited only by his imagination. The end wouldn't have been pretty, and Nessuno had known that as a certainty for years.

All this, and still some part of her had fallen in love with him in return — the Elisabetta part, the part that reveled in his attention and could be what he wanted, what he needed her to be. Abstractly, she knows this was a survival mechanism, that it was inherently false, but there's the problem. The heart can be deceived — she wonders if her heart isn't already deceiving her about Bell — but once it is set, its mind is not changed easily. She had pretended to be his lover, and to survive, had come to love him. She tells herself again that it was Elisabetta, not Petra Nessuno, feeling these things, but it makes no difference. They are the same.

Tohir had been funny — not a comedian, but a quiet and very sharp wit. He had been smart and, with few exceptions, always very gentle, if not always so in the bedroom. He had loved her, in fact, and Nessuno wonders if that isn't part of what she's mourning; never mind what she feels about him. A man who loved her is dead. It would be absurd of her to expect to feel nothing. He had given his heart — a part of it, at least — to her.

And she had betrayed him. She had delivered him into the hands of the men who had gotten him killed. She had, if she were to be particularly savage to herself, slept with the man who had gotten him killed. Incidentally, yes; accidentally, perhaps; but she feels there's something profound in that, though she cannot be certain what.

"I think I'm mourning him," she tells Heath. "Jesus Christ, I think I'm mourning him."

"Don't," Heath says.

The rest of the day they're at Belvoir, using an office that's supposed to be tasked for accounting. It's not strictly cover, but it's out of the way, and they're left alone to try to gather the information as it comes in, as they're able to find it. In the early afternoon, they determine that the body has been recovered from the Loudoun County sheriff's department, is on its way to Bethesda for autopsy and verification.

"Apparently," Heath says, "there's not a lot of him to work with."

Nessuno remembers, unbidden, Tohir's hand along her spine, the light touch of his fingertips stroking the small of her back. An instant of sense memory, the scent of him, cigarettes and cologne, his breath and then his lips at her shoulder and neck.

"We know the means?"

"Sniper," Heath says. "Multiple head shots."

"And the shooter?"

"Got away clean."

Heath sends Nessuno out of the room while she makes a call, and roughly two hours later they get a positive ID on the body, and Heath sends her out again. Nessuno figures she's talking to Brock or someone higher on the chain, that there's some additional level of security to all this. It makes sense, but it makes her self-conscious, makes her wonder, irrationally, if she's somehow under suspicion herself. When she comes back in, Heath is packing up her notes, tells Nessuno to do the same, then takes the whole collection and stows them in the burn bag they've acquired for the occasion. She scans the office from her seat, looking for signs of anything they might've left behind, tapping the pen in her hand against the edge of the desk in a rapid, staccato burst. She settles her gaze on Nessuno.

"You might want to be careful."

Nessuno shakes her head.

"If it was Echo who settled Tohir, he may be looking to settle with you."

"Echo doesn't know about me," Nessuno says.

"He didn't know where Tohir was or that he was being moved, either."

"If he knew about me, I'd be dead."

"Somebody talked," Heath says. "About what, we can't be sure."

*   *   *

Nessuno returns to the Palomar a little after seven that evening, making her way there alone after Heath drops her at the Blue Line. She gets off at Farragut West, but instead of making straight for the hotel, she lets herself wander, telling herself that this is due diligence, that she's being as careful as Heath has urged. Shoulder checks and changes of direction, but it's a lie, and she knows it. She finds herself on Pennsylvania Avenue, looking at the White House through black bars and wiping tears from her eyes. An irrational anger in her grief, anger at the men inside that building who don't even know her name, fury at herself for even shedding these tears.

She clears her eyes, reorients, heads for the hotel. She wonders where Bell is, what he's doing. There's no other way to view Tohir than as a high-level asset, an asset Bell had been charged with protecting, an asset he's gotten killed. At the minimum, there's a dereliction of duty question at work. If he's not cooling in a stockade somewhere, he damn well should be.

She realizes she's angry with him. Furious, really.

She finds him waiting in her room, her bag already packed.

"I need you to come with me," Bell says.

Chapter Fifteen

THE MAN BRIGADIER General Emmet Brock, the soldier, has named the Architect, the man CW2 Petra Graziella Nessuno, also known as Blackfriars, calls Echo, the man Zoya, who uses the name Jordan Webber-Hayden, calls her Lover, has rules:

Never meet face-to-face if at all possible. Use dead drops and cutouts, witting or unwitting, whenever available. Engage in direct communication only when absolutely, unavoidably necessary, and keep it brief. Avoid acting in haste, and always engage with caution. Honestly evaluate your successes and, more vitally, your failures. Rely on intelligence over force. Use force with precision. Where precision fails, overwhelm. Employ the best wherever possible, but admit that who you have is not always who you want and account for their failings. Remain anonymous, even among those you trust most.

Never remain in the same place for longer than twenty-four hours.

It is this last rule that has made the Architect a nomad. In a world of cell-phone triangulation, surveillance satellites, closed-circuit television, and rapid response teams, even twenty-four hours is a terrible risk. He is more comfortable on the move and grows easily restless now. He has been doing this for almost twenty years. It has become habit. He eschews the permanent address.

When he communicated last with Zoya, four days ago, the Architect was in a furnished rental apartment in Berlin — relatively close, at least on the global scale in which he works, to where the capture team touched down at Ramstein AFB in Kaiserslautern, in fact. Since then, he has made his way south, and three hotels later he is now in Zurich, staying at the Swissôtel under the name Kranzler. He had considered, briefly, taking a room at the Baur au Lac, but Herr Kranzler is a businessman, and such ostentatiousness would not fit him. Tomorrow he will continue south, but he will make an adjustment to the east and spend the night in Milan, in a room already waiting for him there under the name DeMartino. Eventually, he'll cross the Med down into Africa to deal with business that requires his attention in Bissau. That is his intent, at any rate, but plans change, and he endeavors to always be flexible.

At the Swissôtel he takes half an hour to shower, shave, and dress in fresh clothes. He sends out his dirty laundry to be cleaned. He travels with two bags only, one an appropriate and innocuous briefcase, the other a Tumi rolling bag. He has four sets of clothes, one of them for exercise, chargers for all his electronics, and appropriate toiletries. He does not carry a gun, and he does not carry a knife, though he is sure of himself with both. He carries a laptop, because that is the most devastating weapon he has ever wielded.

It is the summer season, and he walks in the late afternoon sunlight with his briefcase until he finds a busy café and a Wi-Fi connection. He orders in German, an affogato, takes small spoonfuls of his espresso-soaked vanilla ice cream while an automated program of his design dances from one e-mail account to another, downloading and, where appropriate, decoding messages. There are reports from operatives all around the world, but none is so pressing that he risks compromising security by reading them in public. He is pleased to see that Zoya has sent him multiple files, heavily encrypted and bounced through countless accounts before they could reach him. This is the information he has been waiting on from Brock, he's certain.

He finishes his treat, closes his laptop, and goes for a walk through the Altstadt, treading carefully on ancient cobblestones. He has been to Zurich more times than he can count in his travels, but the visit he always remembers is the one with Zoya. Despite knowing better, they had gone out together for an evening, a dinner and a long walk, before returning to his hotel to make love. He had held her hand while they walked, and then he lingered an extra day in the city after letting her believe he'd departed, just to check on her progress and her lessons, all the time fighting the desire to be with her again. Walking now, he misses her more acutely than ever. He knows what he feels is a weakness, the same weakness that she has learned to exploit in others.

Once, he fought against these feelings, tried to silence them, and, failing, came to a horrible conclusion. It wasn't that he was in love with her; it was that he was powerless to *not* love her. He could not help himself.

The realization had caused him one of the only moments of true panic in his adult life. Zoya could rule him. Understanding this, he understood also that he would always love her, that this would never change, and he had been young enough and brash enough and arrogant enough that he couldn't stand the thought of her jeopardizing him, compromising him. The only escape from the problem he could conceive was to kill her. This would remove her power, he thought, though not his love, and he had brought about the deaths of so many already that the death of another caused him no pause, at least in the abstract. He followed this thinking so far as to actually plan her death, the where, the when, the how, before he had stopped himself in a fit of self-loathing.

He was planning the death of the woman he loved.

How fucked up was that?

It was so desperately fucked up, he concluded, that he had to alter his thinking. Yes, Zoya could make him vulnerable; yes, Zoya could compel him to act solely for her happiness and not his purpose. But to become someone who would kill her because she had claimed his heart? He was capable of monstrous acts; he knew this because he had done monstrous things, all in service to a vision of the future and the world he sincerely believed was better than today's.

But to murder the woman he loved? That *would* make him a monster, and it was a distinction that mattered to him.

So he allowed himself to love her entirely in return, and he forgave himself at once for doing so. With her, he broke every one of his rules, and did so willingly. With her, he communicated directly, and far too often. With her, he lingered. With her, he made choices that put her safety before her usefulness. He broke all his rules for her except one.

He would not visit her. He would not compromise himself, or her, in that way. He would love her from afar and trust that she knew he was true.

It is growing dark when he returns to the hotel, and he idles in the lobby, then heads into Le Muh Bar for a San Pellegrino. He drinks while watching the pattern of guests, their movements, their stillness, and just as he was assured during his walk and at the café, he is again certain that no one is paying him any notice. He retreats to his room, orders a room-service dinner, then plugs in his laptop for recharging. He removes his shoes and socks, flexes his feet against the carpet, contemplates the faint tracks his toes leave in the nap. There is a long list of tasks at hand, and ordering them properly, considering their causes and effects, is an ongoing effort. He sits like this for twenty-seven minutes, rising only at the knock on the door to receive his meal.

He positions the room-service cart carefully in his room, both to avoid blocking the exit and for another reason, too. He opens the wings, rearranges the setting, making it as close to a proper table as he can. Advice from his father, many years ago, that when a man dines alone, that is all the more reason to remain civilized. His eyes stray to his laptop as he starts on the Caprese salad, and he considers reading while he dines.

He recognizes this as impatience on his part and resists. He moves on to his entrée of filleted char. He eats slowly, actively forcing himself to wait. When he finishes the meal, he resets the cart and shifts it out of the way, and only then does he take a seat at the desk and open the computer.

The machine is a heavily modified and custom-made laptop housed in the ubiquitous chassis of a relatively new MacBook Pro, similar to the machine that Zoya herself uses, though hers is less sophisticated. Booting the laptop reveals the start-up that anyone would and should expect, culminating at a desktop littered with folders and files named things like TRAVEL EXPENSES_YTD and ITINERARY and NOTES ON SOUTHEAST ASIAN DISTRIBUTION. It all looks very convincing. Beneath this, however, runs a shadow operating system, wrapped in layers of security to prevent unauthorized or accidental access, and it is in these depths that the Architect lives and breathes. These programs fly out into the world and do everything from monitoring his many channels of communication to plotting, booking, and purchasing his randomly generated travel arrangements.

It is in these depths that he decrypts and then assembles the information Brock has passed to him through Zoya. There are two discrete packages, everything that he has hoped for. The first contains a handful of images from a crime scene in Virginia, what remains of a man lying on the asphalt, his upper body savaged to the point of destruction by high-velocity rounds. A sparse scattering of reports, some conflicting, some local law enforcement, some military. Pieces are missing, much as they are with the body in the images — evidence, to the Architect's eyes, of an attempted cover-up. This makes sense to him, but it makes him suspicious; he would prefer a hard verification, some undeniably positive proof that the dead man is, in fact, Vosil Tohir. The best he can find is a terse after-action report that, even through its militarese, declares that an asset named Heatdish was assassinated during transport by his personal security detail.

It took four days, but Brock has done as asked.

The Architect thinks about Vosil Tohir. It is a pity, he acknowledges, that it came to this, but there was no choice. Loyalty buys only so much, and he knows that Tohir realized quickly there was no escape, nothing the Architect could have done to purchase or steal his freedom. Once Vosil Tohir understood that, he would have also known his life was forfeit. With that, he would have offered everything he knew, everything he had.

How much he gave up before he was silenced the Architect can only guess. He thinks Tohir would have held back, because one never gives away everything if it can possibly be helped. Information was the only currency Vosil Tohir had. He would have shared what he knew carefully, hoping to use his knowledge to buy as much as possible.

With any luck, Tohir died before he could reveal too much.

The Architect lingers over the photographs for a minute longer, then closes the files and turns his attention to the second packet. This is the information he demanded as partial payment for services yet to be rendered, information that, by the laws of the United States of America, is a state secret. Brock has committed treason in passing them to the Architect. This is the truth about the men who unraveled the operation in California, who captured Tohir in Uzbekistan.

The Architect finds the files on their team leader, an Indigo master sergeant named Jonathan "Jad" Bell, particularly interesting.

Master Sergeant Jonathan "Jad" Bell is thirty-nine years old. He was born 18 January, in Portland, Oregon, the only child of Alana and Simon Bell, deceased. He attended Grant High School, ran track, played football. His graduating GPA was 3.8. He left for basic three weeks after graduation, returned home long enough to marry Amy Kirsten Carver, then reported for AIT, followed by Army Airborne School, and subsequently the Ranger Indoctrination Program, all at Fort Benning. Assigned to the Second Ranger Battalion, he proceeded to the Jungle Operations Training Center in Panama. A citation in the file from his command sergeant major, Gerard Hennelly, cites distinguished action during Operation Safe Haven and a recommendation that Bell be admitted to Ranger School. Upon graduation, he was promoted to private first class.

A variety of duty assignments follows, with various notes, commendations, recommendations, and promotions. After four years, instead of leaving, Bell extends his service under the BEAR program, retraining as MOS 97B. He attends the Counterintelligence Special Agent's Course at Fort Huachuca, Arizona, and is then stationed at Fort Belvoir, Virginia. It is as his extension is coming to an end that he is sent to Afghanistan, and shortly thereafter he applies for Delta selection. Accepted, he spends the next several years as a high-level door kicker until he becomes attached to Indigo under his Delta colonel, Daniel Ruiz.

The Architect takes his time reviewing the rest of the service record, the long list of commendations and citations. There is only one reprimand, during his first tour, an Article 15 for "failing to prevent a cold-weather injury," which resulted in a confinement to barracks for forty-five days and another forty-five days of extra duty.

Curious, the Architect goes digging and learns more. He learns that Bell and Amy Kirsten Carver are recently divorced. He learns that Jonathan Bell had been offered a full scholarship to the University of Southern California in exchange for his football skills. He discovers that Bell had accepted the offer then subsequently turned it down. The Architect checks the dates and discovers that Bell's parents died on the same day, the first of January. It is an easy matter to find the story online, reported in the *Oregonian,* of the MVA that took their life early on New Year's morning.

The Architect thinks about a seventeen-year-old in his last year of high school, looking at the University of Southern California in the fall. He thinks about a New Year's phone call to a young man who undoubtedly spent the night celebrating with Amy Kirsten Carver and perhaps others, friends or teammates or both. The only mention of extended family in the file is an uncle, the brother of Bell's mother, who lives in Alaska.

The Architect thinks of Amy Kirsten Carver, truly in love for the first time in her life, filled with ardor and romance, and of what she must have seen when she looked at her football player, whose life had been turned upside down. That the marriage lasted as long as it did is not surprising; Bell would've clung to family like a climber clings to his lead. The birth of their daughter would only have made any thought of separation or divorce that much more difficult.

Considering this, the Architect is certain it was Amy Kirsten Carver-Bell and not Jad Bell who asked for the divorce.

Athena Andrea Bell, their daughter, is sixteen years old. The Architect wonders if the child was planned — if she was an attempt to bolster an already collapsing marriage. He wonders if the fact that the child is deaf has only prolonged the inevitable, if the birth and discovery of her handicap weren't behind Bell's change of military occupational specialty, his MOS. Athena Andrea Bell, the Architect quickly learns, attends the Hollyoakes School for the Deaf in Burlington, Vermont. He confirms this online in a four-day-old story from the *Burlington Free Press* entitled "School Trip Becomes Student Nightmare," in which Athena Bell is listed among seven students who were visiting WilsonVille when the attack on the park took place. Amy Kirsten Carver-Bell is listed as a volunteer at the school, also present on the trip. She is also, he learns, a licensed real estate agent.

So Bell, his ex-wife, and his daughter had all been in the park that day. He cannot imagine that Bell would have been so negligent as to have welcomed this, and he concludes that the relationship between the two is therefore likely strained, if not adversarial.

It takes only a minute of additional searching to find a residence address for Amy Kirsten Carver-Bell and her daughter in Burlington.

*   *   *

The Architect reads the personnel files twice, committing to memory as much as he can about Bell and his team as well as a Master Sergeant O'Day, who was apparently attached to Bell for the Tashkent capture. He rises from the desk, stretches, moves to the bathroom to wet a wash-cloth and wipe his face and neck, thinking. He stares past his reflection, allows his thoughts to unmoor and take their own pathways, examining everything he has learned, considering his options.

He has no verification, but he is now certain that Bell or one of his team is responsible for the death of Brock's associate Lee Jamieson. Jamieson had been the money, and it had been via Jamieson, through Tohir, that the Architect had been paid for the attack in California. It follows that it was Jamieson who led Bell to Tohir, but this is not a tight fit; Jamieson could have learned who Tohir was somehow; the Architect concedes this. But for Bell and his team to have captured Tohir so quickly, so efficiently, must mean there was supplemental intelligence.

The Architect sees his reflection again. Tohir had been compro-mised, he understands. Someone in the organization spoke out of turn, or someone in his organization is not who he or she pretends to be.

He returns to his laptop. If anyone in Tashkent had survived, he could send an inquiry, but Tashkent is burned, and no one remains. He must, instead, go over Tohir's reports, beginning with the most recent and then extending back over a year, then another. But knowing what he is looking for now, it doesn't take him very long at all.

Tohir had a translator brought into the organization almost eighteen months back. He had vetted her appropriately, used her for several jobs before finally bringing her all the way inside. Her background check had been exhaustive — verified and then checked again. He had been sleeping with her, had moved her into his home in Tashkent.

Elisabetta Villanova.

He checks the Tashkent reports again. There was no woman found dead at the house.

In the District of Columbia it is also night, and he imagines Zoya in her home, almost certainly with Brock. He knows that Brock is impatient, nervous, perhaps frightened. Brock, and the men he speaks for, are zealots, and the Architect knows zealotry and patience are uneasy partners at best. Any questions for Brock will have to wait until the Architect speaks with Zoya again, in another six hours or so. But the Architect is certain what the answer will be, just as he is certain that Brock will lie about it. He doesn't need to ask, because the Architect knows what Brock does at the Pentagon, where he sits in the Joint Special Operations Command.

The Architect doubts that Elisabetta Villanova's infiltration was done under direct order; the timing doesn't work, and it is more likely that her appearance beside Tohir was the result of a different operation entirely, begun before Zoya had directed Brock, before Brock had directed Jamieson, before Jamieson had made contact with Tohir. But at some point, Brock must have realized that he had a Bravo-Interdict operator in Vosil Tohir's bed, and he had kept that knowledge hidden from Zoya and thus from the Architect himself.

This doesn't, actually, make the Architect upset in the least. If the situation had been reversed, he certainly would've done the same thing.

In fact, Brock has done everything that has been asked of him. He has held up his part of the deal, Elisabetta Villanova notwithstanding. He has killed Tohir, he has provided the information the Architect demanded. Now the Architect must do what he has promised.

It takes less than a minute at his laptop to put things into motion.

The contingency that Brock has demanded, while planned to follow along the events in California, is riskier than he imagines. The Architect wonders if Brock understands the scope of what he is asking. But Brock and the men like him, men like the late and unmourned Lee Jamieson, have a specific myopia; they imagine themselves endowed with a global perspective, but they also see themselves as patriots and saviors, and thus they bias their view. They imagine the results of their actions, of the Architect's actions, in the context of what it will do for and to their country alone.

The Architect abandoned his national identity long ago and believes himself more objective. What happens in the United States affects the world. A second terrorist action on American soil so soon after the first cannot go unanswered. Echoes will wrap the globe, destabilize tenuous peace in the Middle East, require reactions from Moscow and Beijing, set North Korea and Tehran ever further on edge.

Which may be precisely what Brock and the cabal who ride with him desire.

The Architect shuts down his laptop and takes to his bed. He moves the pillows about, conjuring Zoya beside him, before lying down, closing his eyes, and calming his breathing. One pillow he rests in the crook of his right arm, the other between his knees.

It's a pity about Tohir, he thinks. He'll have to be replaced.

He kisses the pillow in his arm gently.

"Good night, my love," he whispers to the goose down.

He is on the train and heading south when he opens the laptop again. He waits as one of his programs maps relay after relay, laying true paths within false ones.

Dorogoy, will you speak to me?

Camera.

She appears in a small window and he smiles, knowing she cannot see it. Not for the first time, he wonders if she will recognize him when they meet again. He has watched her age so slowly these past few years, each time he sees her thinking she looks even more beautiful than before.

You received what I sent?

Yes.

He asks if this satisfies you. He insists you begin at once.

You may tell him it is begun.
It will be this weekend.

He will be pleased. He was agitated when I saw him.

The Architect pauses. He's positioned himself in his coach so that he has no fear of their words being seen from over his shoulder, but the surprise is such that he checks his position again, just to be certain.

Agitated how?
Compromised?

The wrong word. Alarmed, perhaps? He loves me.

Of course he does.

He thought I had done it.

The Architect stares at the words on the screen for only a second, then types.

What did he say, exactly?

On the screen, he sees the tip of her tongue peek between her lips, sees her close her eyes as she tries to remember. It takes only a moment, and then she is typing quickly.

He arrived and took hold of me. He held me against the wall. "Did you kill him?" he asked. I said I did not know who he meant. "Where were you this morning?" he asked. "Before dawn." He thought I had done it.

The Architect falls back against his seat, aware of Switzerland passing the window out of the corner of his eye. He sees movement on the monitor, words appearing, Zoya moving closer to the camera. Yet more words appear. He doesn't read them.

He marvels, for a moment, at how everything can change in an instant. Everything, including his plans. He takes a breath, calming himself, straightens again in his seat. He types, not bothering to read what Zoya has written to him first.

We have a problem.

Tell me and I will make it go away, *dorogoy*.

You must do something for me.

I will do anything for you.

The Architect exhales, resolving himself. He sees no choice, not with this realization, not knowing that Tohir still lives. Everything is wrong now. He is acting in haste. He is putting her in jeopardy.

He is breaking every one of his rules.

First you will need a gun.

Chapter Sixteen

―――――――

NESSUNO WAITS UNTIL they're in the air, the Learjet wheels up out of Carroll County Regional Airport, then says, "I can get how you spoof the DNA, the prints, all of that. The dental records, easy, especially since I understand there wasn't much in the way of teeth remaining. But the body, where'd you get the body?"

"Afghanistan," Bell says.

"You just grabbed someone off the rack?"

"There was a height and weight requirement," Bell says. "Once they had one, they put it on ice and flew it out through Bagram."

"And that was Tohir?"

"Close enough."

"We really are sick sons of bitches, aren't we?"

"Whatever it takes."

She shifts in the seat opposite him, glares at him with those dark eyes. It's not too far from the look she gave him at the Palomar, when she found him sitting in her room.

"Am I AWOL?" she asks.

"How it'll look," Bell says. "But if it makes you feel any better, I'm supposed to be in custody right now."

"Dereliction of duty."

"That's right."

"And other pending criminal charges in the investigation?"

"That's right."

"Why?"

"To put us outside the chain."

She doesn't say anything, continues to stare at him for a fistful of seconds longer, then twists in her seat to look out her window. There's nothing but black night outside.

"Can I trust you?" Nessuno asks.

"I'm solid," Bell says. "Whether you choose to, that's your call, Chief. Now here's my question: Can I trust *you*?"

He doesn't get an answer.

They're in Hailey before 2300 local, Bell's pickup again waiting in the lot. He drives them out to his house, and she pauses on the way to the front door to look up at the sky and search the surroundings. He can hear a distant dog barking, the rustle of the boughs, and she doesn't move, just standing there. He waits her out, and she heads inside through the door he holds for her.

"Bedrooms," Bell says, indicating their rough direction. "Take your pick."

"You don't want me in yours?" she asks.

He just looks at her.

"That was sharper than I intended," Nessuno says. "When you said you wanted to see me again, is this what you meant?"

"You mean did I know this was how it would come down?"

"Yes."

"I did not. There are three bedrooms. One of them is spoken for. That is all."

She nods, just barely. She makes two fists, brings them to her temples, closes her eyes. "I thought he was dead. And I was...fuck me, I was grieving, I was mourning him."

"And now?"

The hands come down, and the eyes open. "And now instead of being glad he's alive, instead of being happy, I'm scared again. I'm scared again, I'm fucking scared *still*. I love him, and I don't, and you…you, I don't even know what to think about you."

"Then at least it's mutual."

"So I can trust you, but I can't trust what you're thinking?"

"Call it the bends," Bell says.

"The bends," Nessuno says.

Jorge appears at midnight almost on the nose, coming up from the basement. Nessuno is taking a shower in one of the bathrooms, and Bell is making soup from the cans he's found in the kitchen cabinets.

"Isaiah and Freddie are on watch," he tells Bell. "O'Day is crashing at my place. Heatdish is sleeping the sleep of a man who's getting what he wants."

"His standards have fallen. He talking?"

"Nothing worth repeating. He's still in a lot of pain from the hip, too, and the transport took more out of him than he wanted to show." Jorge inclines his head toward the sound of falling water. "Since you're standing in front of me, I'm forced to ask who's in your shower. You pull the stewardess?"

"It's the Chief."

Jorge arches an eyebrow.

"Brickyard's idea, not mine," Bell says.

"We can't use her for guard," Jorge says. "He'll go after her."

"She's here to talk to him."

"I get that. What I'm saying is that we're light, boss. We want two on him at all times, and that gives us dick for perimeter, never mind sleep. We don't know how long this'll take."

"We'll start in the morning."

Jorge nods, turns his head in the direction of the distant shower as they hear the water stop. Looks back at Bell. "I heard a rumor."

"Certainly actionable intelligence."

Jorge just looks at him. Bell waits.

"Yeah," Jorge finally says. "What I thought."

She doesn't want any soup, moves past Bell in the kitchen, opens the refrigerator. Pulls out the carton of milk from the door, gives it a sniff.

"I heard voices," she says.

"Bonebreaker with the sitrep," Bell says. "Heatdish is sleeping; he's under watch."

"I heard voices," she says. "But I didn't hear the door."

"He came up through the basement." Bell indicates the backyard, through the kitchen window, the darkness outside, the stretch of lawn that runs to the trees, the fence. The light in the kitchen kicks off the glass, makes viewing anything in the darkness outside next to impossible. "His house is that way."

"Tunnels?"

"The houses were prepped for us, yeah. We've got a run between, some storage for weapons and gear, range space, and a hard room about midway along. That's where he's staying."

"You've got a shooting range?"

"Use it or lose it."

Nessuno opens a cupboard, then another. "Where are the drinking glasses?"

"Your guess is as good as mine. This'll be my second night spent here."

She drinks from the carton, replaces it in the door.

"Good night," she says.

"Sleep well."

She doesn't answer.

When he opens his eyes out of sleep, he has no idea what time it is, only that the world is still dark. He drags himself up from a disjointed dream, something about his daughter and a shotgun and Amy, and he fights the urge to go for his weapon when he sees the figure standing in the doorway.

"Friendly," Nessuno says.

"Problem?" His voice is hoarse with sleep. He clears his throat. "Problem?"

She moves to the edge of the bed, opposite him, hesitates, then sits. The mattress shifts barely with her weight on it. She's wearing the same shirt from the day and her underwear. Her hair is pulled back, tied in a ponytail. Ambient light barely gleams off the chain of that saint's medal she wears. Bell sits himself upright, aware that he's wearing shorts and nothing else.

"I'm really pissed off at you," she says.

"I know."

"You're asking me to do something tomorrow I don't want to do."

"I know."

"I'll fucking do my duty; I know my job. I'll play him, all of that. I'll do it. Don't you doubt that."

"I never once have."

"Don't lie to me."

Bell shakes his head. "Straight shit. Do I doubt your loyalty? If I did, you wouldn't be here."

"Orders."

"I know how to disobey. You're compromised, you're not here. But you're here, ergo not compromised."

"But I am compromised. My problem is, I don't know what I'm feeling anymore."

"I have the same problem," Bell says.

Her fingers find the back of his hand, begin to trace his fingers with sudden intimacy. Bell doesn't move.

"There's a part of me, the Elisabetta Villanova part of me, that's still with him," she says. "I'm trying so hard to untangle that, to get the threads sorted, like. But there's a piece of me, this Stockholm syndrome bullshit piece of me, I can feel it, and I know what it is, you understand? The part of me that likes him, that loves him, that had to and still does. The part of me that made it okay to do what he wanted me to do. The part of me that needed him to want me. The part of me that made it okay to be in his bed, to have him inside me. That part."

She trails off, staring at him in the darkness, in the palpable silence of Hailey, Idaho, at night. She hasn't moved once since sitting down except for her fingers, still tracing his.

"You asked if you could trust me," Bell says.

"You said I could."

"You never answered my question."

"I am answering it now." In the darkness, she looks down at their hands. Her fingers leave his. "You can't."

"You turn or you face," Bell says. "You either come up all the way or you stay under. You stay under, then you're right—you're compromised, and you'll be his to the end. That's your choice."

"It's not as simple as that."

"It begins with the action. You're trying to be either Petra or Elisabetta, thinking you can't be both."

"One of them has to lead. That's why I'm here, because you need me to be Elisabetta. I'm here now because she's who you want."

"You're here now because there's a man who has information that will save American lives and you can get it from him. Petra or Elisabetta, it doesn't matter. Your job is to get him to talk. Can you do that job, Chief?"

She doesn't answer.

Bell pulls the blankets back on the side of the bed, shoves one of the pillows over. She turns, slides her legs beneath the covers, lies down stiffly. Bell makes sure there's space between them, careful to avoid contact between their bodies. He is surprised when he feels her hand come to rest on his forearm, settle there.

"Get some sleep," he says.

Chapter Seventeen

ATHENA BELL THINKS she's being followed.

It's not like it's obvious, and it's not like it's any one thing in particular, because if it were, then she could be sure. Like, if she were seeing the same people in different places, faces she had never seen before but that kept reappearing. If she were positive it was the same car, the blue Toyota she saw parked down the street from the house and then, two hours later, at the curb outside Nunyuns on Champlain Street.

But she's not, and she thinks she's being totally paranoid, and it's not like that's an unreasonable thing to be, given everything that happened when she and her friends from the Hollyoakes School for the Deaf went to California.

It had been so good to see her dad that day he'd come and gone and brought her that stupid dragon — better than she wanted to admit. Just to have him for a few minutes so they could talk, so she could tell him how it felt. She was sixteen and she thought she should be too old for such things, but his hugs were still the best, and he almost always knew what to say to make her feel like she wasn't just making shit up. He always treated her problems as real. He pissed her off, sure, but he was a dad, that was kind of what they did, and she knew that, and even after everything she had seen him do, she still thought he was more awesome than not.

Athena also thought it was most decidedly a fucked-up thing that, since the divorce, she saw her father even less than before. If, as her mother said, one of the reasons for the split was because Dad was never around, this hadn't exactly fixed the problem, y'know? It made her resent her mother, and it made her want to blame her mother for the divorce, though she knew it wasn't rational or even fair.

After the walk, Dad had brought Athena back to the house and had spoken just a little bit more with Mom. Athena caught, maybe, pieces of every third or fourth or fifth word. She was one of the best lip-readers she'd ever met, and still, if Athena understood 30 percent of what was being said, that was doing well. She'd seen television and movies in which deaf people and even people who had their hearing could lip-read from, like, fifty feet away, and they'd get every word, and every time it made her laugh. As if it were that easy.

___*got to go,* Dad had said.

That one was clear enough.

___*v c___ you do,* Mom had said.

A little harder. That *v* sound, that might've been an *f,* in which case maybe that was *of. Of course you do* — that would make sense.

Mom and Dad had stared at each other for a moment, and then Dad sighed and his whole body had sort of shifted; his shoulders had dropped a little. He'd shaken his head.

___ ___ *c___d get ___way, I wo___,* he'd said. *___ ___ lot go___ ___ r___t now I c___ju___.*

Most of that was a miss, but context is everything, and Athena had a good idea what he was saying. It wasn't the first time he'd said it. He's got work, he can't get away, he would if he could, but he can't.

Th___ ___ways a lot go___ ___, Mom had said. *Go. This ___ the s___ co__vers___n w___ ___ ___ th__d times. Nev___ m___d me nev___ m__d ___ job ___ve g___ ___ fucking duty. ___ go.*

Almost a total miss, but *fucking* was clear. Athena had learned to identify most profanity early. So the argument, this was the same argument. He has to go and stop Bad Guys, something that, to Athena, has much greater immediacy following everything that happened at the theme park, where she'd actually *seen* him do it. Before the trip, his work, what he did for the army, for their country, that was abstract. Now, though, she knew. She'd seen the gun in his hand. She'd seen the people dead.

Amy ___ n. Be ___ ful o___? Please?

Chot___ ___ful? ___ that what you m___ Jad?

Athena can't think of a *ch* word, revises. *Shot. Shotgun?*

Dad shook his head again, tried not to sigh, Athena could see it. Then he turned to her.

You be good Gray Eyes, he'd signed. *You take care I'll be in touch when I can.*

Better.

That got him to smile, and he'd given her another one of those hugs and kissed her forehead, and then he'd left. Mom had gone back to fussing in the kitchen, and Athena had gone back to her room and opened her laptop and had found Lynne and Gail both online, so they chatted for a bit. They'd all been in the park together, though Gail and Lynne hadn't been there when the woman died, the woman who'd saved Athena's life.

Sup?

Just saw my dad. He brought me this.

Athena used the laptop camera to take a picture of herself with the purple dragon. She took a couple, one of them with her biting its felt wing.

awww

Athena thought it was kinda typical that her father had been worried she didn't have people to talk to. She didn't have *adults* she was talking to, but there hadn't been a day since they'd all come back from California when Athena hadn't talked with Gail or Lynne or Leon or Miguel or Joel.

Things had been a little crazy when they all first got home. Everyone's parents had been in total freak-out, not unreasonably. Any parent who *didn't* freak out wasn't much of a parent as far as Athena was concerned. Gail, Lynne, and Miguel all had visits scheduled with a counselor, now, too — the same counselor, in fact, because he was the only guy any of their parents could find who was able to work with adolescents and was also fluent in ASL. Mom had asked if Athena wanted to talk to him, too. Athena had said no.

It was better, talking to friends, even if at first they didn't talk about what had happened at all. It was on the news all around them, on the television's closed-captioning and in the newspapers. You could see it on the street, too, if you were paying attention; there were more police around, and even the people who weren't the police, they were tense, edgy. It was a small thing, but it was everywhere, and to Athena and her friends, it was hard to miss.

It was Joel who got them talking, actually, after he got out of the hospital. He'd popped onto chat while all the rest of them had been online, and it turned out he couldn't remember much of what had happened. One of the Bad Guys had kicked him really hard in the stomach, hard enough to cause bleeding inside, and from that point on, Joel said, he was hurting too much to pay close attention.

When they did talk about it, Athena thought it was funny how each of them recalled different things, or sometimes the same things, but in different ways. All of them were having bad dreams, even Miguel, who totally didn't like to admit things like that. That was also when Athena had told them all about what had happened in the tunnels underneath the park, and about the woman who had saved her life.

No one ever asked her about her dad. Everyone but Joel had seen him, and Athena was sure that Miguel or Leon had told Joel by now. Everyone knew.

But nobody asked.

Today — the day she thinks that maybe someone is following her — Athena gets up and checks her e-mail, is surfing the Web, when Mom comes in, already dressed for work. It's her first day going back to the real estate agency since they returned from California, and Athena can tell Mom is looking to sell some property today from the way she's dressed. The skirt is just above her knee, and she's put on makeup, and she's wearing her low heels.

Heading out be home by five, Mom signs. *Text if you need me you behave yourself.*

Athena sticks out her tongue and spells out *P-A-R-T-Y* with her hands.

Mom grins. *Going to see Joel?*

Athena's stomach does a little flip, and she can feel heat in her cheeks. She wonders how her mother can read her mind, wonders how she can read such truth into a joke.

Tell him I hope he feels better.

Athena nods.

Walk the dog and clean up after him.

Athena rolls her eyes. She loves Leaf, but she hates picking up his shit, finds the heat of it through the plastic bag disconcerting.

Mom leaves, and Athena goes back to her computer for another ten minutes or so, then takes a shower and gets dressed and makes herself a bowl of cereal for breakfast. Leaf follows her around the kitchen, sits by her feet as she eats, looking up at her occasionally, expectantly. He knows they're going for a walk.

So they go for the walk, and that's when Athena sees the car, a four-door blue Toyota, just parked down the block. She sees it but doesn't think anything of it, only that there's someone behind the wheel apparently talking on the telephone. Big deal. On the way back, after Leaf has done his business and she's got a bag of crap in her free hand, the car's gone.

Athena takes care of the trash, makes sure there's food and water in Leaf's bowls, and then gets her bike from the garage. It's an absolutely beautiful day, no clouds, and not too hot, either. She puts on her helmet and rides down the Island Line Trail, arriving at Nunyuns a little after ten in the morning. Locks up her bike and steps into a cloud of baked delights, the heavy scents of spice and yeast. She buys two cinnamon buns to go, and it's easy, because they know her there, so there's none of the difficulty Athena sometimes has when she's out alone. She's unlocking her bike when she thinks she sees the same Toyota parked across the street. She isn't sure, though, because she didn't look at the license plate this morning, and when she thinks of it now, the car is already pulling out and turning off Champlain Street and onto North.

Athena puts the Kryptonite lock back into its holder on her bike, fastens her helmet once more. She looks around. She thinks about Dad, what he said about knowing who is around and knowing where to go and knowing how to get out and knowing where to hide and where to get help.

Around her, there are people. This, she thinks, is not useful, but she has a good memory, and she tries to study their faces without being too obvious that that's what she's doing. Some of the faces she's seen before, around town, and she figures they're safe enough.

Where to go? Well, this is Burlington. She's maybe six blocks north of downtown right now; it's not as if she couldn't find help in any direction she chose.

How to get out? See above, Athena thinks.

Where to hide? Too many places to count, beginning with inside Nunyuns. So that's definitely covered.

Where to get help? That makes her grin. There's a Burlington PD black-and-white coming down Champlain even as she looks.

Athena tells herself she's being paranoid, and then throws her leg over the bike and takes hold of the paper bag and the handlebars together, starts pedaling along North until she gets to Union, where she turns south. She's careful at the turn, looking all around, but then she's always careful on her bike, always snatching glances over her shoulder for traffic that might be coming up from behind.

She doesn't see the Toyota anywhere. Or, more precisely, she doesn't think she sees *that* Toyota anywhere.

She loops around on Hickok Place, then turns north again onto Converse Court, and near the end of the street she hops off her bike and walks it up the driveway, leans it against the side of the house beneath a massive maple, the shade so sharp there's a moment of blindness before her eyes adjust. She goes to the front door, hits the doorbell, imagines the light flashing inside, and then it opens and Joel is standing there, grinning. The surgery had been minor and the doctors hadn't had to open him up to do it. Athena thinks he looks good, but she's thought he looks good ever since they met, back when she first started at Hollyoakes.

Cinnamon buns, she tells him.

Awesome.

They eat their cinnamon buns and hang out in the family room for a while, playing video games and then just talking before doing anything else. Both of Joel's parents are at work, and his brother is away at summer camp, so they've got the house to themselves, and eventually they do what teenagers do when they're alone, unsupervised, and in love. They've talked about having sex, but neither of them is ready for it, they've agreed. Athena's thought about going to the Planned Parenthood on Saint Paul Street, just in case, but she hasn't gotten up the nerve to actually do it yet.

She's rethinking that choice when she leaves Joel just before three that afternoon, her lips swollen and chapped from making out for almost two hours straight. She climbs back onto her bike feeling almost sick but not quite, an aching longing that isn't necessarily between her legs but isn't entirely in her breast and stomach, either. Maybe it's because Joel's still recovering from his hospital stay, but everything they did they did slowly, and when she took off her shirt for him and he took off his for her, she can still feel the extraordinary pleasure of warm skin touching warm skin. He held her breasts as though they were made from crystal, and she had to put her hands on his to assure him he wasn't hurting her, the sharp contrast between her pale and his dark skin beautiful to her. She felt him through his jeans, had wanted to actually touch him there, for real, and she thinks he wanted her to do it, too.

Athena gets her bike onto Pearl Street, heading toward the lake, thrilling at the thought of being in love. She wonders if Mom thinks they've already done it, because she so clearly knows they're together, and she finds herself thinking about her parents, if they could've ever felt the way she's feeling right now. She can't imagine it.

She's forgotten entirely about the blue Toyota by the time she comes off the Island Line Trail and eventually finds her way back to Edinborough Drive and home. She hops off the bike and wheels it around to the back of the garage, heads inside, and is almost immediately tackled by Leaf, who's heard her coming and greets her, snuffling and licking her hands. She gives him a good scritch, and her phone vibrates, and there's a text from Joel.

I love you

She replies:

Ur just horny

that 2

I love you 2

She knows she's smiling and can't stop. She takes Leaf outside, grabbing the ratty tennis ball they use for playing fetch. It's been gnawed and slobbered almost smooth. She tosses, and he retrieves, and they do this around the front yard for almost twenty minutes before Athena sees the black Mazda, just sitting there, up the block. Not a blue Toyota, not in the same place, and even from here she can see it has Vermont plates. But she can't remember seeing a black Mazda on this street before.

This time, when she throws the ball, she throws it in that direction, harder than before. The ball bounces, rolls, and Leaf tears after it, and Athena trots after them both.

There's someone in the black Mazda. Someone who looks like he's talking on the telephone.

Leaf has the ball, is running back to her, and she takes it from his mouth, soggy and slimy, pivots, and chucks it hard back toward the yard. Leaf tears off in pursuit, and she follows him, forces herself to do it slowly. She finds the urge to look over her shoulder, back toward the black Mazda, almost impossible to resist, somehow fights it until she's on the porch, has opened the door. She turns to summon the dog, and that gives her a good excuse to look back to the street, and the black Mazda is exactly where it was, and then it's moving, and she and Leaf both watch as the car rolls past.

Athena could swear it's the same person behind the wheel, the same person she saw that morning.

The car disappears.

Athena stands in the open doorway, thinking. She tells herself she's overreacting. She tells herself that she knows where to go and what to do and where to hide and who to call for help. She tells herself she has no reason to be afraid. She knows there's a shotgun in the closet with the towels, and that it's loaded, and that Uncle Jorge and her dad both made sure she knows how to use it.

She texts her mother.

> where r u

The response vibrates in her hand perhaps a dozen seconds later. That's fast for Mom, and Athena thinks she must've had the phone in her hand.

> Office. Home at 5.

> comin to meet u

> Everything ok?

> kk

> I don't know what that means.

> ok

She glances up at the street again, seeing no strange cars, no strange people, seeing nothing much at all, in fact. Most of the time, Athena doesn't mind that she's deaf, doesn't really even think about it. It's what she is, it's her, it's all she's known as far back as she can remember. But times like this?

Times like this, she really wishes she could hear the sound of a car coming down the street.

She finds Leaf's leash, the dog going bonkers the moment he realizes what she's doing, and she motions him to stay. Clips him on, and they step out, and she locks up behind her. She checks the street again, then cuts across the backyard, then into trees so thick it's like a compacted forest. When she emerges, she's on Sunset Cliff, and she looks both ways, scanning for the black Mazda and the blue Toyota, and she doesn't see either.

She thinks that means she's safe.

Chapter Eighteen

JORDAN WEBBER-HAYDEN holds the gun in her hand and waits for the woman and her child to return home.

The gun is a Walther PPQ M2 and holds eleven rounds, one of them chambered and ready. She bought it within an hour of her conversation with her Lover from a gun store in Alexandria, along with a box of .40 S&W ammunition, using her ID. As Virginia requires neither a waiting period nor a permit for the purchase of a handgun, the longest part of the transaction was when the gentleman selling her the weapon had to call ATF to run her Form 4473. The check came back clean, the way she knew it would, because Jordan Webber-Hayden has never been convicted of a felony, has never done anything that would prevent her from lawfully possessing a firearm. She was back on the Capital Beltway within thirty minutes of entering the store, heading west toward I-95.

Jordan flexes her fingers around the grip, reawakening the memory of weapons training almost a decade old. It's coming back faster than she'd have thought, the weapon already familiar in her hand.

She checks the clock on the microwave against the one on her wrist. It's seven minutes to three in the afternoon, and from what her Lover has said, she can expect the woman and the girl to return shortly after five. She has just over two hours.

Two hours to consider what it is he wants her to do.

Two hours in which she could just walk away, leave everything behind, and not ruin the three lives she knows she is about to destroy.

It had been easier than she'd expected, getting into the house.

She'd found the place without difficulty. Her Lover had given her the address, and upon arriving Jordan had parked down the block, on the opposite side of the street. She'd killed the engine and pulled out her smartphone and spent the next twenty minutes pretending to look at that and not the street, the whole time watching the house and the traffic. There was almost no traffic at all, and nothing in the way of movement from the house.

Satisfied, she'd started the engine once more, driven away, turned, turned again, and ultimately parked four blocks away. She'd unpacked the Walther, loaded it, tucked it into her waistband at the small of her back, where her shirt would cover it, then gotten out of the car and taken her time with the walk.

When she reached the house, she'd headed straight to the front door and knocked as if she were expected. There'd been no answer, also as expected. She'd already noted the alarm-company decal on the window, peered through the glass to see the panel on the wall in the front hall, a single green light shining. She'd taken that to mean the system was working but not armed.

The garage was to her left, so she went around the side without pause, then through an unlatched gate and into the backyard, where she'd found the back door to the garage unlocked. Inside was everything one would expect, up to and including a workbench and a dust-covered Bowflex machine. The adjoining door into the house had been locked.

She had no lock picks, but she did have the tools from the bench, and for the next seven minutes she worked carefully and slowly, consciously trying to avoid marring the plate or the knob with any telltale scratches. Then the lock had surrendered, and she opened the door with her heart climbing, waiting for the trill of the alarm that never came.

There'd been a roll of old duct tape on the workbench, and she'd taken that, then locked the door behind her.

Jordan checks her watch again.

It's now three minutes to four, and there has been no sound from the garage. She moves the Walther from her right hand to her left, picks up the mask she's made from the watch cap she found in the front closet. It's not a ski mask, but there were scissors in one of the kitchen drawers, and it was easy enough to cut the eyeholes. With its edges pulled down, it's big enough to cover her chin. She fingers the mask, pokes her fingers through the holes she's made for her eyes. She wonders if she should've cut one for her mouth.

She considers wiping down the scissors, going back through the house, and clearing her prints from every surface she's touched, but it's not a pressing concern; Jordan Webber-Hayden has never been arrested, never once had her fingerprints on file.

It's a nice house, Jordan thinks. She wanders out of the kitchen, gun still in one hand, the mask now in the other, and into a comfortable family room with a big-screen television and a stereo stack. In another ground-floor room is a home office, bills and paperwork of everyday life. She thinks it's peaceful here. She could live in a house like this. She heads upstairs, steps into the master bedroom. It's very Laura Ashley, but a little off, and Jordan imagines money is tight in this home, but they're making do with what they can. She takes a moment to look at the photographs in their frames on the dresser, at this family of three. There's an adjoining master bathroom, and she notes the abundance of feminine products, the lack of masculine ones. She checks out the other bedroom on the floor, this belonging to the child. It's a bedroom on the cusp, transitioning from childhood to adolescence.

She wonders if she and her Lover will ever make children. Until this moment, she has never considered it, and she is self-aware enough to know that she is thinking this now because of what she is here to do. She wants children, she realizes, and though they have never spoken of it, she feels, absolutely, that her Lover does not. He is her Lover; he is not a husband.

She heads back down the stairs, wondering about what might have been. She does not have to do this, she tells herself.

Then she hears the garage door opening, the grinding of the motor, the sound of the car. She puts the mask on and steps around the corner to the hall, out of sight. Jordan hears their voices before the door is open. They're talking about dinner. The door falls closed, heavy, pushed, and the woman passes the open archway to the hall, not six feet from where Jordan is standing, a bag of groceries in her arm, sliding her purse down her other arm, sets both on the counter together. Her keys clatter on the tile. She's shorter than Jordan, and older, in her late thirties or even early forties, black hair in a bob, a little on the heavy side. Jordan thinks her clothes are like the decor in the master bedroom—trying too hard.

"Go get cleaned up," the woman says. "I'll have dinner ready in fifteen minutes."

The girl rounds the corner into the hall and sees Jordan and for a moment she has no idea what she's looking at. From what her Lover said, Jordan knows the girl is twelve, but like her mother, she's dressing to be something she isn't.

The moment of shock breaks, the girl starts to take a step back, starts to open her mouth. Jordan moves forward before she can, takes hold of her by the throat, points the gun in her face. Pushes the girl back into the kitchen.

There's the sound of glass shattering, and a strangled cry, and Jordan sees the woman turning away, lunging for the far counter.

"Don't," Jordan says.

The woman doesn't listen, spins back around, the biggest knife from the rack in her hand. She's holding it wrong, Jordan can see that, but even wrong, it can still kill her. The woman holds the blade out, the cooking island now between her and Jordan and the girl.

"Let her go!" the woman says. "You fucking let her go or I will kill you."

Jordan considers this. She needs them alive to do what her Lover requires, at least for now. In her hand, she can feel the girl shaking.

"Drop the knife," Jordan says.

"Fuck you! I will end you! Let my daughter go!"

Jordan releases the girl, and the girl recoils, both her hands going to her throat. The moment she's clear, her mother is moving, the knife high, and Jordan pivots inside the strike, slams her left forearm across the woman's jaw, snapping her head back. The woman staggers, tries to right herself, and Jordan hits her in the face again, this time with her elbow. The woman hits the counter, collapses to the floor, landing hard on her behind, the knife clattering away. Blood is flowing from her nose and mouth.

In her periphery, Jordan sees the girl start to move, and she turns, bringing the Walther up again. The girl freezes, one arm already extended. Jordan points to the roll of duct tape on the counter.

"Take that, start tearing strips," Jordan says.

She's about to add that she doesn't want to hurt them, either of them, when pain blasts along her right leg, out from the side of her knee, and she's falling, has to put her free hand out to catch herself. She twists just as the woman kicks at her again, and the blow misses the joint and lands on the inside of Jordan's thigh.

Jordan jerks back, trying to keep her feet, sees the woman is now pulling herself up, the blood still running from her nose. The girl is moving, too, again going for the knife on the floor, and in the way that adrenaline makes such realizations clear, Jordan thinks the girl is being stupid, that it would be much quicker to just grab another knife from the rack.

Jordan also thinks that this was not at all what she had planned.

The woman is charging at her, heedless of the gun, or perhaps realizing that Jordan doesn't want to shoot them, or perhaps not caring for anything but the safety of her daughter. There's no time to get out of the way, and Jordan tries to twist with the impact. The woman is heavy and has velocity, and together she and Jordan smash into the kitchen table. Both the woman's hands are on Jordan's wrist, fighting for control of the gun.

"Callie!" the woman says. "Run!"

Jordan punches with her left, the way she was taught by the man in Singapore, her fourth teacher. She hits the woman in the side, hears her grunt, hits her again twice more in the same place, and the woman's weight changes as her legs go weak. Jordan uses her knee, slams it into the woman's crotch, and the grip around her wrist slips, and she shoves, hard, and the woman again hits the floor.

The girl, Callie, is halfway down the front hall.

Jordan points the Walther at the woman on the floor.

"You open that door and I will kill your mother," Jordan says.

The girl skids to a halt, one arm extended, already reaching for the door.

"You open that door, I will kill your mother," Jordan says. "I will do it."

The girl doesn't move.

On the floor, the woman, Callie's mother, says, "Run, baby." The words come out on a wet wheeze.

"I will do it," Jordan says. She says this quite calmly, despite her racing heart and the ache in her right knee and the swirl of thoughts all saying that she should not be here, that she should have walked away, that she cannot fail at this, she cannot fail her Lover. "I don't want to do it, but I will."

The girl's hand is on the doorknob now.

"I don't want to hurt either of you. I don't want to kill either of you. But if you open that door, I'll do it. You'll make me do it."

"Lying," Callie's mother says.

"No," Jordan says. "Trust me."

Callie's hand drops. Her body sags. She turns around, looks at Jordan with an expression of hopeless confusion.

On the floor, Jordan hears her mother release a single, agonized sob.

"Come over here," Jordan says.

Callie comes over.

"Why are you doing this?" the girl asks. It's plaintive, almost bewildered. "What do you want?"

"I want you to call your dad," Jordan says.

Chapter Nineteen

SHE AWAKENS AND is once again unsure of where she is, sunlight cutting across a strange room, a ceiling unfamiliar. She smells coffee and eggs and bacon, the muted sound of a single voice in a one-sided conversation. The sheets are cotton. This is not a hotel room, and it is not Tashkent. She strains for the voice, recognizes it as Bell's and that he must be speaking on the phone. The memory of the previous night comes back. She feels a muted shame at herself, not for sharing her weakness but for admitting to it. Elisabetta shows no weakness; it's Petra Nessuno who doesn't know if she's coming or going.

Nessuno rises, drags fingers through her hair. It's still too long, outside of regulation. Elisabetta's hair. She knows she should have cut it by now.

She leaves his bedroom and returns to hers, the bed as pristine as the night before. She couldn't even bring herself to lie down on it. She grabs her jeans from where they're heaped in the corner, pulls them on, not bothering with shoes or socks, then heads in the direction of the scents and the sounds.

"No, I already confirmed," Bell is saying, his phone wedged between shoulder and ear. He's at the stove and cooking a genuine heart attack, eggs and bacon together. He catches her eye and motions to the coffee pot with the spatula in his hand. "It's a two-man team, they're supposed to be there, just let them do their job."

Nessuno fills a mug from the pot.

"Have her text me," he's saying. "I don't know. I haven't been here long enough to check."

Nessuno sips her coffee. She doesn't bother to pretend she's not listening, and Bell certainly doesn't seem to care, so she suspects whatever the conversation is, it's not operational.

"I don't know." This time, there's the edge of exasperation in his voice. "She'll have to text me until I know. As soon as I can get online, I'll let her know. But it's a standard detail, Amy. They're doing their job."

Whatever is said in response takes a while, and Nessuno watches as Bell tenses. He gives the pan a sharp jerk, makes the bacon and eggs jump, spattering grease.

"I will not ask them to be removed. No." A pause, and he catches her eye again, indicates one of the cabinets with the spatula. Nessuno opens it, finds glassware, opens the one beside it, finds plates. She takes down two, balances one in each hand. Bell serves up equal portions from the pan. He grins slightly, says, "I'm going to talk to someone about it, don't worry. At the least, she shouldn't have been able to spot them, let alone slip them...Amy...Amy...Amy, I am taking this seriously. That's a serious concern."

Nessuno takes the plates to the table, looks to Bell again, mimes for silverware. He shrugs. She begins going through kitchen drawers, all of them with generic contents, as if whoever stocked the house had done the shopping in one go at the nearest Walmart.

"Have her text me," Bell says, now putting pan and spatula in the sink. He frees the phone, brings it with him to the table, sets it beside his plate when he takes the seat opposite Nessuno.

"You cook," Nessuno says.

"And clean and sew. I'm a complete soldier." He gets up again, realizing that he has no coffee. "Juice in the fridge."

"I'm fine."

He returns with the pot and his cup, tops off her mug.

"What was that?"

"My daughter made the security watching her and my wife," Bell says, cracking bacon with his fork. "But she didn't know it was security, and it scared the hell out of her."

"Counterintelligence?"

"Yeah. They're keeping an eye on them."

"How old's your daughter?"

"Sixteen."

"And she spotted them? Were they being sloppy?"

Bell mixes broken bacon with his scrambled eggs. "She's deaf, so she's a watcher by nature. She doesn't miss much."

"I'd never thought of that."

"Most people don't."

"That's why she has to text."

"We do video when we can so we can sign, but I haven't had a minute to find out if they set up wireless with the house. Jorge's place has all the bells and whistles. I'll try to reach her from there later."

Nessuno tries the eggs. They're moist and taste good, and she can practically feel her arteries seizing from the bacon fat. It's an American breakfast, the first one she's had in as long as she can remember, too heavy for her. In Tashkent, it was always tea and bread and milk. Bell is watching her as she sets her fork aside, the meal unfinished. She wishes she could read him, wishes she knew what he was thinking, and it frustrates her that she can't. He cleans his plate, then takes both to the sink and begins washing up. When he finishes, he dries his hands on a dish towel.

"Chaindragger stuck his head in before you got up," Bell says. "We'll start when you're ready, you want to shower or anything first."

She wants to say yes, anything to forestall the inevitable. Instead she says, "I'll save it for after. That's when I'll need it."

It's a semifinished basement with a washer and dryer stuck in one corner, an old couch in another, some cardboard boxes labeled in black marker with different words: CLOTHES, PERSONAL, BABY STUFF. The walls are open post with wooden boards, and on the north side, five feet from the corner, there's a metal light switch box. Bell pops it open, and there's a separate switch inside. He throws it, and Nessuno doesn't hear anything, doesn't see anything change.

"Letting them know we're coming," Bell says.

He reaches up behind one of the crossbeams, fiddles with something, then pushes on a section of the wall and the wall swings open, becoming a door. The tunnel she sees is wider than she'd expected, finished concrete, with fluorescent fixtures running in a straight line along the center of the ceiling. Bell lets her in first, then closes up behind them. They walk abreast, and she can smell moisture and the faint traces of gunpowder.

"Very high speed," she says.

"Isn't it just."

"They do this for every team?"

"I wouldn't know," he says. She can't tell if he's lying or not. She can't tell if the distance she's suddenly feeling from him is the shift to operational stance or if it's a distrust of her. The vague, indefinable sense that something ominous is approaching. The instinct that tried to warn her that night in Prague, is whispering to her.

About twenty-five feet along, they pass an open room on her right, small, storage. The brief glimpse she gets tells her enough; it's a loadout room, weapons and gear. Another twenty feet past, this time on the left, is the range, lights on inside, and she sees the man called Steelriver at the bench. He's got range glasses over his eyes, his ear protection around his neck, and two pistols in front of him, one of them in pieces. He looks up when Bell stops.

"Master Sergeant," he says.

"Master Sergeant," Bell says.

Steelriver grins at Nessuno. "Blackfriars. Gonna give that son of a bitch one hell of a jolt when he sees you, huh?"

"Yeah, that's the plan." It comes out flat. Nessuno's words, not Elisabetta's.

She sees Steelriver's grin falter, then fade, a new gravity apparent. Nessuno thinks it may be sympathy, or at least empathy, but maybe it's something else.

"No easy days," Steelriver says.

"Only if you're a marine," Nessuno says.

Bell's laugh surprises her. Steelriver goes back to rebuilding his pistol. "Holler if you need me," he says.

The hard room is just beyond the midway point of the tunnel, its door to Nessuno's right. There's a keypad beside it, but Bell ignores that, just taps the door three times, and the one called Cardboard opens it immediately.

It's a larger room than Nessuno expects, almost twenty by twenty, with an industrial carpet that she's sure is called seafoam or ocean mist or like that, which she can feel through her boots has been laid over the same cold concrete that lines the hall. Walls and ceiling covered with waffle pattern acoustic tile, and an open archway off to the far left. She can hear the sound of running water, the distinct slap of it hitting plastic, and Nessuno concludes that it's a basic bathroom, a shower and shitter and not much else. The one called Chaindragger is leaning against the wall by the opening, but he straightens up when they enter. Nessuno sees a cot against the far wall, blanket folded, pillow atop, a set of clothes beside them. A sink and mini fridge are to the right, along with a couple of folding chairs. In the center of the room is a six-foot-long table that folds width-wise in the center, and it matches the chairs, all from the same set. In two of the corners, where the ceiling meets the walls, she sees cameras, small and black and glassy-eyed.

"We're recording?" Nessuno asks.

"Yeah," Cardboard says. He's got a southern drawl she hadn't noted before. "So watch your language, missy."

"Bone still asleep?" Bell asks.

"Presumably."

"How about you?"

"We're both awake, even if we don't look it."

Bell takes his .45 from his hip, makes it safe, then hands it to Cardboard. "You two watch the feed."

"He's not going to try anything. He's on easy street."

"Take a hike."

Cardboard tucks the .45 away, and Bell and Nessuno part to let him and Chaindragger pass. They step out, and the door falls closed, latches with authority.

The water in the shower stops. Bell moves to the table, pulls one of the chairs out for Nessuno. She considers not taking it, wonders at the message she will send if she remains standing, decides it will make her look defensive. She sits, and Bell shifts to her right, to get a better view of the bathroom as Tohir emerges. He steps into the room slowly, favoring his good leg, a surprisingly lush-looking blue towel wrapped around his waist, hair heavy and wet. He's carrying his glasses in one hand, puts them on as he speaks.

"Your shower is shit," Tohir says.

Then he sees her.

"Elisabet."

"Vosil."

He speaks softly, and deliberately, and in Uzbek. "I am going to kill you for what you did."

For an instant it's everything out of her nightmares. It's the road to the farmhouse and the tangled sheets and the difference between standing before him naked rather than nude, and she knows that's absurd, with him wearing a towel and her fully clothed. Not a threat or even a promise, just a recitation of fact. He will kill her.

Then the fear snaps into fury, and she's out of the chair and lunging at him before Bell can move, driving him back into the wall, fists working into soft tissue and bone. The glasses drop, Tohir trying to both cover and defend himself, and she's snarling, spitting rage, cursing him in Italian and Uzbek both. He screams in pain, the sound deliciously gratifying, and she punches at him again, now shouting, barely able to make out her own words.

"Don't you threaten me," she's saying. "Never again, never again, you bastard, you piece of shit, you bastard piece of shit. Never threaten me, never again, I am not yours, I was never yours."

Bell has an arm around her waist, one hand at her right wrist, she feels the floor leave her feet. The room turns, she's standing again, and Bell is pushing her back, toward the door.

"I was never yours." She starts forward again, blocked by Bell, who sends her back again, until she can feel the acoustic tile digging into her skin.

"We're all right," Bell's saying. "We're all right, we're all right."

She realizes he's talking to the others, Cardboard and Chaindragger, the men watching them on video. She can feel the heat high in her face.

Opposite her, Tohir is down on the floor, wedged against the wall, one hand straining for his glasses. The towel has slipped, bunched around one ankle, and his other hand covers the wound at his hip. He is naked, and raw, and when he brings his glasses to his face and raises his head, hissing in pain, his lips are bright with blood. It's only then that Nessuno feels the ripped flesh on her knuckles, the soreness where her fist met his mouth.

"She does that to me again," Tohir says, "you get nothing. Nothing."

"It's not going to happen again," Bell says. He's still fixed on her, not him. "Is it?"

"He threatens my life, he tries to —"

"Is it?"

Nessuno shakes her head.

Bell takes a step away from her, moves to Tohir to offer a hand that Tohir petulantly shoves away.

"I can get to my own feet."

"Then do it, and put on some clothes."

Tohir works himself upright, using the wall and the cot, dripping beads of water from his hair, the room cool enough to bring goose bumps to his flesh. His mouth has tightened, and his nostrils flare as he inhales. Nessuno sees his nakedness in a new way, sees the vulnerability of his body, the still-puckered and inflamed flesh around the stitches at his hip, a narrow thread of blood running from the sewn skin. She hit him in the wound, she knows, just as she knows it was no accident but pure malice.

She should feel remorse, or guilt, or shame, she thinks. Watching him struggling into his underwear, his pants, she should at least take pleasure in his suffering.

As it is, she's feeling nothing at all.

"I haven't eaten," Tohir says. "You have to feed me something."

"In a bit," Bell says.

"Now."

"Vosil," Nessuno says. "You're acting like a child."

He blinks at her behind his wire-rimmed glasses. In his eyes, she sees his desire to hurt her, so palpable it's a presence of its own in the room. He moves with effort to the table, seats himself with a grunt.

"So you starve me, you beat me, that's how this is going to go?"

She stares back at him, finds that he cannot hold her gaze. It's almost satisfying.

"Tell us about Zein," she says.

Tohir smirks. "You can't find him, can you?"

"We will," Bell says.

"And if I told you there were five other men just like him, all of them here, now, in your country?" He shifts his gaze from Nessuno to Bell. "What would you say to that?"

"I'd say you're trying to buy yourself more with what little you've got left." Bell takes one of the folding chairs from the wall, snaps it open, and turns it in his hand, sitting on it backwards. "At a certain point,

Vosil, the shop closes, you understand? At a certain point, we're not buying what you're selling. You're at that point."

Tohir matches gazes with Bell, and for a moment, Nessuno is certain this is about to devolve into a cock contest. Then Tohir looks at her.

"You remember in March?" he asks her. "When I sent you to Moscow?"

"I remember."

"Did you fuck him, too? That's what you do, right? Fuck for your country?"

Nessuno almost dignifies that with a response. He'd sent her to talk to a man who was laundering money for them, the proceeds from the heroin that Tohir was bringing up from Afghanistan. It had been a lunch meeting at Bar Strelka, she bringing the routing numbers Tohir had made her memorize and the banker swearing up and down that he was taking no more than was his agreed-upon cut. He'd tried feeling her beneath the table, fat fingers on her thigh, and she'd taken his thumb and twisted and told him that if he tried it a second time, she'd be sure to tell Tohir that he was skimming the take. He'd lost his color but found his manners.

"I went to Africa to make arrangements for travel. Mostly, we sourced out of Guinea-Bissau."

"Sourced what?" Bell asks.

"Everything," Tohir says. "Drugs, weapons, people. Lots of people. Route from Europe or the rest of Africa or the Middle East, arrive as one man, leave as another."

"Zein started in Guinea-Bissau."

Tohir smirks. "Zein was created in Guinea-Bissau. So were Hawford, Dante, Verim, Ledor, and Alexander. All of them are now in this country, all of them are now on their way to their target."

"They're all here now?"

"Yes."

"When did they arrive?" Bell asks. "How long ago?"

"Some of them? A couple of months. Zein was one of the last."

"This was planned before the California attack?"

"That is correct."

"Why?"

Tohir shrugs. "I don't ask. He tells me what to do, I do it."

"What's the target?"

Tohir shakes his head. "Not yet." He adjusts his glasses, spits again on the carpet, more blood. He leans forward on the table, bringing his face just that much closer to Nessuno's. He's feeling better about himself, feeling much more in control. "You know I loved you, Elisabet?"

"You thought you loved me," she says. "What's the target, Vosil?"

"Don't you miss me?" He gestures at her, indicating her clothes. "You look like a matron dressed like that. You're beautiful; why do you hide it? With me you never had to hide it. You took pride in it, the way I looked at you. The way you made other men look at you with desire, the women with envy. Everything you've given up. Don't you miss it at all? Miss me, just the tiniest bit?"

"Answer me first."

He inclines his head, and Nessuno is surprised to see what looks like the glimpse of a human being behind his eyes. The anger and hatred have gone.

"It wasn't all an act, was it? It wasn't all a lie?"

"No, Vosil. It wasn't all a lie."

"Tell me you love me."

"She loves you," Nessuno says. "I don't."

Tohir sits back, jaw clenching, and Nessuno hears the lock behind her snap open, then the door. She doesn't look away, leaving that to Bell. Tohir's eyes flick away from hers, but his expression doesn't change, and again he's staring at her.

Steelriver moves into view on her right, approaching Bell. He leans down, whispers in Bell's ear. Nessuno thinks she hears the words *brick yard*.

Bell pushes up from the chair. "The shop's closing, Vosil. You don't want to talk to me, fine, talk to her. We want the target and the timetable."

He leaves, the door latching after him once more. Steelriver moves to the vacated seat, but he doesn't take it, remains standing.

Tohir sets his palms on the table, looks at them, then at Nessuno. "I don't know when. Soon, perhaps the next week or so, I should imagine on a weekend."

Weekend venue, Nessuno thinks. *Tourist destination? Sporting event?*

"Where?" she asks.

Tohir wipes his mouth with the back of his hand, looks at the blood staining his skin. He exhales, straightens, and then the bullet rips through his head, the gunshot and the impact so near to instantaneous that it's beyond Nessuno's ability to perceive. Tohir's eyes open and look into hers, the right side of his head breaking open. He holds for a fraction of a second that seems much longer before gravity remembers him, then pitches face-first to the table, a thin blob of blood spilling from his skull. Nessuno chokes on a cry, pushing back, sends her chair tumbling as she finds her feet, and Steelriver is holding his .45 in both hands, and now he's pointing it at her.

He's a shooter and she isn't; he has a gun and she doesn't; there's twelve feet between them. There's nothing she can do. As she watches, his expression changes, moves from pained to placid.

Outside, Nessuno can hear Bell shouting through the door. He's working the keypad as fast as he can, and it isn't fast enough.

Steelriver puts the barrel of his gun beneath his jaw.

"They've got my wife and my daughter," he tells her.

The door opens, and she hears Bell shout Steelriver's name, hears him say, "Tom! Jesus Christ, don't —"

And the gun goes off.

And Steelriver falls.

And Nessuno feels like she's falling, too.

Chapter Twenty

IT IS THE first time in years that the Architect has had to travel like this, and it makes him nervous. He relies on his programs to define and direct his movements, the programs that he created, programs that generate true randomness, stochastic systems entirely of his own design. He has kept faith with them for several years now. He knows they work, not because of their speed-of-light computation but because of the time and deliberation he put into their creation.

He cannot use them now.

His original destination had been Milan, and he disembarked there as planned, but only because he was required to change trains in order to continue to Rome. He purchased a new ticket for the high-speed express from one of the automated machines, boarded, and once under way returned to his laptop to begin the painfully slow process of planning his new route and matching that route to each ID he planned to use and then destroy upon completing each leg. This last part pained him, because despite his resources and his reach, these identities were precious and would be both time-consuming and aggravating to replace. This occupied him for most of the four-hour trip.

At Roma Termini he disembarked and made his way through the station, again pausing at one of the automated machines before threading his way through the ticketing hall, beneath the glittering tesserae that decorated the ceiling. He did not look up. He had been through this station seventeen times in the last five years alone, and always he had made a point to appreciate the beauty of the mosaic ceiling. This time, his preoccupation and paranoia were such that overhead was the only direction in which he did not cast his eye. At track 25, he boarded the Leonardo Express with two minutes to spare, and thirty-three minutes later he was exiting his third train of the day at Fiumicino-Leonardo da Vinci International Airport.

He checked in for his flight to Amsterdam, still using the DeMartino identity. He remained DeMartino all the way to Schiphol airport, flying coach, at which point he became Ronald Spencer, passenger 12B on KLM, now traveling business class to Montreal. He slept during much of the journey, spent the time he was awake staring out the window. The nervousness had decayed into boredom, then returned in a different form.

It had been so long since he'd seen her. He doubted she could recognize him, hoped she would all the same.

Five hours after clearing Canadian customs—the purpose of his visit: business; his profession: software design—the Architect is walking around the building in D.C.'s West End for a second time. He has his briefcase, but the rolling bag he left behind at his room at the Watergate, a room taken in the name of Willem Smart. It's two in the afternoon here, and he's aching for sleep, and despite the effects of the sunlight on his body clock, he doesn't trust his judgment. He wants to circle the block a third time, but twice was one too many already. He sees nothing to give him alarm, but that doesn't make him feel any more secure.

He looks at the building, its facade, and it is everything he remembers. He can pick out the windows that belong to her, and if his Zoyenka has done everything he required, and if those she compelled did what was required of them, she should be back home by now. But the Architect sees only closed blinds and no sign that she is home.

If it has gone wrong, he has lost her. The thought makes his stomach ache. Only the first of many things that will go wrong if he has miscalculated, he knows.

Heading for the front door of her building, the Architect finds himself wondering if he should have brought flowers for her.

He enters the lobby, glass and hardwoods, and a smartly dressed young man at the concierge's desk watches his approach, asks, "May I help you?" before the Architect has come to a stop.

"Jordan Hayden," the Architect says.

"Miss Webber-Hayden, yes. She's expecting you?"

"She is not." The Architect thinks his English sounds stiff, wishes he'd taken more time using it.

The concierge reaches for the handset of the house phone. "And your name?"

"Dorogoy."

"Russian?"

"It's a Russian name, yes."

The concierge nods, smiling slightly, puts the handset to his ear, but not before the Architect can hear it ring. He turns away to look out the wide windows at the street, at the traffic, but it's an idle scan. He doesn't want the concierge to see his smile as he hears her voice, unmistakable if faint, the glee.

"You can head on up," the concierge tells him. "You know the number?"

"I do," the Architect says.

He knocks once, and before he can knock again, the door is open.

"Jordan," he says.

She doesn't move, so still for an instant. She looks tired, wearing just jeans and a sweatshirt, and her hair, he sees, is wet. He smells the last traces of soap or shampoo on her, lemon and ginger. She doesn't smile.

"Perhaps you'd like to come in?" she asks.

"Very much."

She steps back, closes the door behind him, throws the locks, and when she turns back to him she says, "What is my name?"

"Zoyenka," the Architect says. "My little Zoya."

She plunges into him, throws her arms about him and her weight along with it, so forcefully he loses his briefcase and nearly his footing, stepping back, just managing to stay standing. She mashes her face against his breast, nose and mouth followed by her cheek, and he puts his arms around her, feels her shudder as she sobs.

"It's all right." He speaks softly, resists the urge to switch to Russian. "It's all right, I'm here now."

She shakes, sobs again, loudly, trying to muffle it against him. He can feel her tears leaking through his shirt. He runs his fingers through her still-wet hair, tightens his other arm around her.

"I would do anything for you," she says to him, and her voice is hoarse. "I would do anything for you, you know that, but please, *dorogoy*…please…"

He strokes her back, her hair. "I know."

"Never ask that of me again." She lifts her head, swipes at her nose. "Never ask me to do that again."

He brushes a tear along her cheek, erasing it with his thumb. He kisses her brow, then her nose, then her lips.

"I won't promise you that," he says. "I won't lie to you."

She blinks at her tears, and he feels her hands on him, fingers curling, nails biting at his skin. But her expression doesn't change, pained, staring up at him, and he doesn't look away, despite the urge to do just that, despite the urge to lie to her, to tell her anything that will make her anguish in this instant vanish.

"No," Zoya, who is Jordan Webber-Hayden, says. "No, you won't lie to me. So when I ask why you came, why you are here right now, you will not tell me what I want to hear."

"You wish me to say that I wanted to see you."

"Yes."

"I always want to see you," he says. "But that is not why I'm here."

"Tell me you missed me."

"In every moment."

"Tell me you want me."

"More than anyone I have ever imagined."

"Tell me you have been faithful, even if I have not."

"But you have been faithful. You give them your body, not your heart."

"And have you been faithful?"

"Yes."

She brushes at her cheek with the back of her hand, snuffles a last time. The hint of a smile appears.

"I like that," she says. "I like that you have been faithful."

He kisses her brow again. "I will prove it to you later, I promise. But I need something first."

"Tell me."

"I want to meet the soldier," the Architect says.

Zoya, who is called Jordan Webber-Hayden, makes a call and leaves a message, and they wait together to hear back, curled on the couch. Even when she is on the phone, she refuses to not be touching him somehow, a hand on his arm or her foot against his calf, and the Architect reciprocates, so eager to learn her again.

"How long does it normally take him?" he asks.

"He calls within twenty minutes," Zoya says. She puts her palms on his cheeks, fingertips tracing his cheekbones. "You changed your face."

"Do you like it?"

"I am getting used to it." She grins. "Did you change anything else?"

"No."

"Good." She kisses him, and he feels her smiling, feels her teeth pull at his bottom lip. Her hands unfasten his belt, unfasten his pants. "Undress me."

The Architect pulls the Georgetown sweatshirt up and over her head, reveals her bare chest. He kisses each breast, greeting them, and she sighs as his fingertips stroke their swell, slide along her ribs. He thinks the years have made her even more beautiful, and he tells her as much, and she kisses him again, sliding down his body, sliding his clothes down with her. She works her way slowly up again, and he finds his fingers have become clumsy, and she helps him tug her jeans and panties off her hips and down her thighs until she can shake them free, kick them away. There's a fresh bruise on her thigh, above the knee, and when she moves to mount him he sees a line of scratches at her shoulder, but if she feels the pain, he can't see it through their shared desire. She rides him on the couch, staring at him with terrible intensity, and he clutches her closer and closer, aching to be surrounded by her, and that is when the phone rings, and she doesn't stop moving, just picks up the handset to answer.

"When can you come?" she asks, and the Architect has to stifle his laugh between her breasts. "As soon as you can. I need to see you. No, I understand. I need to see you. Please."

She thumbs the phone off, drops it, and the Architect thrusts, relishes the quick intake of her breath in response. Her hands find his shoulders, grip tightening.

"He says an hour," she tells him. "Say you love me."

"I love you."

"Say it again."

"I love you."

"Say it again."

He says it again, and again, feeling her tremble around him, says it again as she voices her climax. He shouts it against her neck in his own orgasm, murmurs it in her ear following, whispers it as a mantra as she lies against him, breathless, light-headed.

"I believe you," Zoya says.

*   *   *

They are dressed when Brock arrives, and the Architect waits in the kitchen as Zoya goes to answer the door. The Architect wonders if he should have brought a gun for this part, but the plan, as of now, does not call for one. When he asked Zoya what she had done with hers, she told him it was in the Potomac.

He hears her greet him, hears the man's voice in response, hears the door close. Hears the moment of silence and stillness that tells him Brock has his hands on her, his mouth on her, and for the first time since sending Zoya away from him, sending her here, he feels a twinge of jealousy.

He hears them moving, watches as Zoya leads Brock into the room. The soldier's eyes are on her, and she's pulling his vision away from the kitchen, and he turns to follow her as she moves toward the bedroom.

"You needed to see me," Brock says. "Why?"

"I'll be right back," Zoya says. "Just a moment."

She disappears into the bedroom. The Architect watches as Brock stands there, back to him, looking after her. He's changed out of uniform, he's in a blue cloth windbreaker and khakis, and he looks uncomfortable in them. The Architect wonders if he showered before coming over.

"You're going to do something for me," the Architect says.

To his credit, Brock doesn't react as if surprised. He turns slowly, looks the Architect over. His hands go into the pockets of his jacket, and his chin drops a fraction, and the Architect imagines this demeanor must be very effective on those of inferior rank.

"You're him," Brock says. "Holy fuck and angel choirs, you're the Architect."

"Is that what you call me? I'm vaguely flattered."

"In lieu of some other things."

"That's very generous, considering everything I've done on behalf of you and your partners. Considering everything you've failed to do."

"I gave you everything you asked for."

"No, you didn't. As of twenty-four hours ago, Tohir was still alive, General Emmet Brock."

Brock's brow creases. "You did him."

"No; you assumed I had. Our agreement was that *you* would take care of that, if you recall. Someone played us. Which brings me to what I need you to do."

The Architect can see Brock processing what he's said, the ramifications. He starts to speak, but the Architect cuts him off.

"I had to do what you failed to do, General. But I need it confirmed, and that is what I need you to do now. It shouldn't take more than a phone call or two."

"Bullshit," Brock says. "You're playing games with me, you're trying to get something more."

"You think this is about your contingency?" The Architect shakes his head. "It's all set. It's ready to go. Just a little over forty-eight hours away now. If I give the word."

"So you are playing a game."

"I suppose I am. Two phone calls. Make them, get me the answers I need. Do that, and we can discuss what happens next."

"I should take you down."

"You shouldn't make idle threats."

"It's not an idle threat."

"Then you're not thinking things through," the Architect says. "Never mind my guilt — let's talk about yours. You want to end me, you're welcome to do it. You might succeed. But you and your partners will tumble down with me. And we're not even talking about Jordan, what will happen to her."

"You're a piece of shit."

"I'm not the one committing treason. Two calls at the most, General. Make them now."

Brock's hands come out of his pockets in fists. The Architect watches as he unrolls his fingers, stretches them to reveal empty palms, then reaches again into his jacket for his phone.

"And who am I calling?"

"Whoever you need to," the Architect says. "Just confirm that Tom O'Day has killed Vosil Tohir."

It takes Brock only one call.

"He's dead," Brock says. "They're all dead."

"You're certain?"

"I'm as certain as I can be without drawing a line directly from him to me to you," Brock says. "You realize what you've done?"

"Yes."

Brock continues as if he hasn't heard him. "You leaned on him. Leaned on his family. You used information I gave you."

"Yes."

The Architect watches as Brock makes his hands into fists again. They are big hands, and clearly strong, and what Brock wants to do with them now isn't in doubt, but he keeps himself in check.

"They're going to know," Brock says. "There's only so many places that information could've come from. You've driven them right to my doorstep. You've exposed all of us."

"Including myself, yes."

"The contingency—"

"Is secondary. Our survival is primary."

"We agree on that."

"Then you'll also agree with this." The Architect smiles. "It's time you introduced me to your partners."

Chapter Twenty-One

THE DEATH TOLL, Bell thinks, now stands at three, and he wonders if it's about to climb higher.

He resets the pistol in his hands, resets his grip, thumbs lying together. He pushes thoughts about Tom O'Day and what's being done with his body back in Hailey out of his mind, does the same with the memory of Tom O'Day's family, imaginings of his wife and daughter, found dead in their home. Callie O'Day, who will not see thirteen years, who is not anything like Athena except that she's another soldier's daughter. Stephanie O'Day, who clearly went down fighting, and, yes, that is just like Amy.

The voice comes in his ear. *"Stand by."*

He checks Nessuno, on the opposite side of the door, Provo, Utah, SWAT team surrounding them as they wait, poised to move, outside this second-floor walk-up, this apartment. She's miked and harnessed just as he is, a pistol in her hands. He remembers what she said on the ride in, remembers another woman saying the same thing not so very long ago, the woman who saved his daughter's life and lost hers in trade.

I'm not a shooter.

Nessuno moves her head, just enough to dip her chin. Nodding. Yes, I am ready.

There's the creak and rattle of men wearing body armor and holding weapons, all of them waiting on the razor's edge. The door man on the SWAT team shifts, brings the mallet up, ready to strike.

In Bell's ear, *"Go go go."*

The hammer falls.

He goes to work on Tom O'Day at once, trying to bring him back to life, but even as he starts he knows it's futile, and even though she knows it, too, Nessuno tries to help. Then Freddie and Isaiah pour through the door, and Bell abandons the room and sprints the length of the tunnel to Jorge's. Brickyard is already on the line, Jorge hurriedly uploading everything that has happened in the interview room. Bell takes the phone.

"Steelriver?" Ruiz asks.

"He's gone. We need a response to his residence, now."

"Already en route."

"I want a response to mine, I want a status."

"Danso reported on the hour, all clear."

"Have him check again. Have him do it now."

"We will call back," Ruiz says.

Fourteen minutes later, Ruiz does, and that's when Bell learns what has happened to Tom O'Day's wife and daughter. That is when Bell learns that Callie and Stephanie O'Day have been murdered in a home that only a handful of people in the world knew truly belonged to Tom O'Day and his family. A home that even fewer than that number should ever have been able to identify as the residence of the Indigo Second Team lead.

"We're backing up Danso and Harrington in Burlington," Ruiz says. "I'm dispatching an additional CI unit to Hailey; they should be there in three hours."

"Not fast enough," Bell says. "Freddie's got two kids. I want to move them. We're bleeding here."

"I am well aware."

"Nobody should've been able to find him. Nobody should be able to find us, and right now they can."

"Second Team is not First Team, it's not your team. We've no reason to believe you're compromised."

"And no way to assure me we're not. I am moving Freddie's family, with or without your permission, I don't care, sir."

It's remarkable insubordination for Bell, and he knows it, and at any other moment, any other place, he would care. Right now he doesn't, and right now, it seems, neither does Ruiz.

"Jet should be wheels down for your team in twenty minutes," Ruiz says. "Westminster. We have receipt of the interview, will run the names. I'll have a team handle the scene there. You lock it down."

"We've sealed the room," Bell says. "I'm moving Freddie's family."

Ruiz pauses. "Negative. I want you and Blackfriars in Westminster, I want to circle this thing, and I don't want all of you on the detail. Chaindragger, Bonebreaker, and Cardboard, but you and Blackfriars, you come in."

Bell rubs a thumb against his temple, feels the adrenaline beginning to leave. "How the fuck did this happen?"

"You said it. We're bleeding from inside."

"My family," Bell says. "They have to be safe."

"They're out of our orbit, they're not in Hailey. That might make them the most secure of all of us for the moment."

"'Might' isn't enough."

"Which I recognize, Master Sergeant. It will be handled. Take Black-friars. Westminster."

Bell kills the connection.

"What's the word?" Jorge asks.

"Break it down, you're rolling out with Chain, you're going to make sure Board's family stays safe."

"It cuts that deep?"

"Someone reached out to Tom and threatened his family, Jorge," Bell says. "They held his wife and his child, and instead of turning to the men who've had his back since day one, instead of turning to us and trusting us to do what we've trained every fucking day of our lives to do, Tom shot Tohir in the head and then ate his gun."

"He should have told us. We could've gotten them back."

"That's what I'm saying. But he didn't."

"Why?"

"Because someone had to have talked. Because, despite everything, he *didn't* trust us."

Jorge is heading for the basement stairs. "We're fucked."

Bell says, "We've got an active cell planning an action for this weekend, maybe. Tom O'Day was compromised, his family has been murdered. Brickyard wants me and Blackfriars to come in for reasons I don't begin to understand. We are thoroughly fucked, Jorge."

"Tell Freddie I'll meet him at his house."

"Will do."

Bell leaves the room, makes his way back down the tunnel, slower this time. Isaiah is standing post at the interrogation room door.

"Freddie?" Bell asks.

"He went home, and I don't fucking blame him," Isaiah says. "We were watching on the monitors, we heard what Tom said."

"Jorge's packing up and heading there now. You're going to join him, and then you're taking Freddie's family to ground until you hear otherwise."

"Roger that."

"Where's the chief?"

"Getting cleaned up. You should, too."

Bell looks down at himself, sees that he's covered in Tom O'Day's blood.

"Come with me," Bell says.

They stop at the gear room before reaching Bell's basement. Isaiah grabs three of the ready bags, Bell takes another two. Once in the house, Isaiah heads for the front door and out, and Bell finds Nessuno coming out of her bedroom. He pulls off his shirt without breaking stride, heads into the bathroom, and runs water, finds it already hot.

"We move in five," he tells her.

"Tohir's dead, I'm not going anywhere. I'm done."

"You need to sit with the body?" He rounds, angry at everything, at Tom O'Day's death, at the murder of O'Day's wife and daughter, and — not in small measure — at this woman he cannot track, who keeps slipping between the lines and making him question what he feels. "You need to make your good-byes, is that it? You work it out yet?"

"I told you not to put me in that room, I told you —"

"Did you know?"

She stares at him, loses her color. "How can you fucking ask that?"

"Did you know?" He steps forward, and Nessuno's arms snap up, ready defense.

"You touch me you're striking an officer, Master Sergeant. How dare you fucking even ask me that question."

"So you're an officer now? Is that who you are? Were you an officer when I had to keep you from putting your fist into his wound?"

"He said he was going to kill me, he said it like I was on a fucking to-do list." Her arms come down, but instead of keeping her distance she steps up, lifts her chin, close enough for him to feel her breath. He can see that amber in her eyes, and it seems to flare. "Ratfuck sitting in that room, shooters on all sides, he threatens me? Like I'm his fucking *toy?* Like I'm his motherfucking *plaything?*"

"I have to know who you are. Right now. I have to know if I can rely on you."

"Who am I? Who do you want me to be? You want the woman you fucked in D.C., is that what you want? Or the broken goods who came to your bed last night? You want me to show you my moves? You've fucking seen them. You know who I am. I'm all of it, Jad. You don't live a lie without some part of it becoming true. Who am I? I'm all of it."

Bell doesn't speak, turns back to the sink, the condensation rising to cloud the mirror. He can see her through its mist. He can see himself.

"Your friend is dead, I understand that," Nessuno says. "The situation is what has changed, Jad, not me."

"You're supposed to transit with me. Brickyard's order. Grab your bag."

Bell scrubs at his hands, at scrapes and cuts that still haven't fully healed. The bandage around his palm came off at a time he can't even recall, and the sting of the healing wound is galvanizing. He splashes water on his face, uses the damp hand towel to dry off, and Nessuno sidesteps out of his way as he heads for his duffel at the foot of the bed to search for a clean shirt.

"I've got to reach out," Nessuno says. "I've got to report to Heath."

"I would not do that."

"I look AWOL."

"You're covered."

"You think she's wrong?"

"The only people I trust right now are headed out of town."

She goes to grab her duffel, returns in seconds as Bell is shouldering his. He tosses her a gear bag, leads the way out of the house, locks up quickly. They make the drive to the airport in eight minutes, find the Learjet waiting for them when they arrive.

They're in combat climb before Nessuno speaks again.

"They had his family."

"They're dead," Bell says.

She doesn't say anything.

"Brickyard says there were signs of a struggle," Bell adds.

"How old was his girl?"

"Twelve, I think. Maybe thirteen."

"Maybe forensics will pull something."

"Yeah, that'd be nice, wouldn't it?"

"You've got to hope."

"Oh, I hope," Bell says, and once he starts speaking this time, he can't stop himself. The anger that flared when talking to Ruiz, the fury he directed at her, it surges, rises like a boil, inflamed, infected, aching. "I hope a lot of things, Chief. I hope there are forensics, absolutely. I hope we get a lead. I hope that lead gives us a name and an address, and I hope that gives us a positive identification. I hope we undeniably identify the piece of shit who pulled the trigger on Stephanie and Callie and, yes, Tom. I hope we put the fucking gun in their hand at the exact moment, without any doubt. Because once we have that, I am going to kill that motherfucker."

The plane banks sharply, abruptly.

"I am going to pay this one in full," Bell says.

Nessuno nods once, then points past his shoulder, and Bell looks to see the call light blinking beside the headset mount. He pulls the phones over his ears, jabs the button.

"Warlock, we have Brickyard."

"Go for Warlock."

Ruiz's voice. "Jackpot. Ledor, first name Michael. You are being diverted to Provo, Utah. Your mission is to capture this asset for interrogation, to capture this asset for interrogation. Stand by for briefing."

Bell listens, confirms, and from the corner of his eye, he can see that Nessuno has shifted in her seat, pivoting to face him, leaning forward. She catches his eye, but Bell just shakes his head slightly.

"What's the support?" Bell asks.

"Local only, SWAT," Ruiz says.

"They know we're coming."

"They will be aware. I need answers, Master Sergeant. This man can give them. Bring him to me."

Bell replaces the headset on its hook, reaches for one of the gear bags he pulled from the tunnel storage. He indicates the second one, the one Nessuno had brought aboard.

"They've located one of the names, Ledor. We're going to bring him in," Bell says.

"I'm not a shooter," Nessuno says.

"Local will effect the breach. You'll stay on me," Bell says.

"You'll trust me that far? Put a loaded gun in my hand at your back?"

"You want to go through first, be my guest."

"We square?"

"For the moment. They'll take the door, deliver the first bangers, we'll buttonhook the entry. You know what I'm talking about?"

"I know what you're talking about, but you're not hearing me. I'm not a shooter. I can't cover you right."

"You hit what you aim at?"

"Most of the time, yeah. I'm out of practice. I'll get us killed." She pauses, shakes her head. "I'll get us both killed."

Bell has his bag open in front of him, looking at the equipment neatly strapped down and arrayed, the magazines and the extra rounds and the weapon, the grenades. All the tools, all of them treacherous if not granted respect, and even then all of them willing to betray their masters at the slightest hint of negligence. Doubt kills. Doubt in ability, doubt in your fellows. To do this, he has to believe in her absolutely. To do this, she must have the same belief in him.

He turns in his seat, reaches out, and takes her hands in his. The tiny medallion she wears has come free from where it was tucked inside her shirt, swaying gently on its chain.

"No, you won't," Bell says. "I'm going to walk you through this."

"Jad."

"It's just playing another role, Chief."

"No, it's not."

"Right now it is. You're going to do this. Today you're a shooter."

She closes her eyes, exhales, opens them on the inhale.

"Talk me through it," she says.

The doctrine is simple. Speed, surprise, and violence of action.

Speed. Hit fast, as fast as possible, so fast there's no time to think.

Surprise. Don't let them know you're coming, don't strike where expected, when expected. Violence of action. Hit hard, hit so fucking hard they can't think even if they weren't surprised, so hard that they can't fight back even if they want to.

The mallet hits the door, and the door hits the floor. Bell turns his head as the banger sails past, hears its muted blast behind his ear protection, and the SWAT team is through the door in a fluid rush. Another banger detonates, then a third. He hears the first "Clear!" and goes into motion, enters fast and going right, gun high and ready, and Nessuno, bless her, is stacked tight behind, covering left.

The first room is a rectangle, and they've entered at one narrow end. Thin curls of smoke from the banger hang in the sunlight coming through the now-broken windows. Bell sees a couch, a low table, a television, screen also cracked. He sees newspapers and a box from Domino's and a half-empty bottle of Sprite Zero. He does not see a man who might be named Michael Ledor.

There are three doors, two left, one right, and an open square of kitchen. SWAT has moved left to clear, Nessuno's side, giving good cover, and they bust the near door open, give it a banger, and one pokes his muzzle in and there's another "Clear!" It's outside of Bell's sector, his slice of the room, and he doesn't dare look away to confirm what he's heard. He hears another door burst, another bang, and "Clear!" and the team is sweeping into his field, and only then does he change his aim, and they take the door and he turns his head to dodge the blast of light, and, doing that, he sees the first door, left, hanging broken and open, sees it's a bathroom.

Two things happen at once then.

Behind him, the door right, the door the team has cleared. An explosion from within, a scream that makes it through the protection at Bell's ears. He knows it's a grenade without thinking, knows the sound intuitively, knows it's a booby trap, maybe a trip wire; knows at the same time that someone wasn't discreet, that they never had surprise.

Michael Ledor knew they were coming. Somehow, some way, he saw something or heard something or someone just wasn't as careful as he needed to be, but Michael Ledor knew they were coming.

He knows all this, understands all this, as he looks past Nessuno into the bathroom and sees the man lurching up and out of the tub, the long gun in his hands. It's an instant impression, flash-burned, the assault rifle and the man. Blue jeans and a checked blue-and-white overshirt, unbuttoned to reveal a white T, untucked and splotched with water from the tub. Black hair, slight curl, almost to his shoulders, stubble over his mouth and on his chin, as though he's trying to grow in a beard. The glimpse of neon orange, earplugs to protect from the blast.

Then the third thing, the thing he couldn't teach Nessuno, because there wasn't the time. He could teach her to cover her sector, he could teach her to buttonhook the entry, he could get her to trust him, he could make himself trust her. But to teach her not to react to the unexpected explosion, to the grenade and the scream, that takes more than he could give. That takes years, working day in and day out, live fire in the shoot house and on the field and in battle, and her reaction is human, instinctive.

She turns away and gives the man that Bell believes must be Michael Ledor her back.

Bell has no shot.

He lunges, hand out, grabs hold of Nessuno by the front of her harness, yanks her down with him. The gunshots wrack the small apartment, rip the air overhead, and Ledor is firing like a pro, controlled bursts, over and over again, and Bell is on the ground, tumbling on top of Nessuno to cover her, and he sees SWAT falling. They're wearing all their protection, but Ledor is firing 7.62, Bell knows, and there's only so many of those that threat level III body armor can take before the protection gives up and allows the rounds to do their business. Everything goes clumsy, he's atop her, tries to roll free, but Nessuno's arms are around him, holding him against her, trapping him there, as if in some mockery of that night they shared, and he senses the movement above and behind him more than sees it, more than hears it, and he goes limp. Something hits the floor, a follow-through vibration of footsteps beating retreat, and she slackens her grip. Bell rolls off her, tries to get his weapon up, but Ledor is out of the room, an empty magazine on the ground not a foot from where they lie, and he understands. Ledor should've stopped, he should've delivered rounds to them, but he must've believed they were down, too, or else he'd certainly have paused to finish the job.

Then Bell is up, keying his mike, officers down, he's rabbiting, he's rabbiting, he's armed. Nessuno shouts something after him, but he doesn't understand it, and he doesn't stop, rushing out of the apartment and into the railing in time to see the man and his rifle break out of the doors to the street in a flood of too-bright daylight.

Bell vaults the railing, lands badly, tumbles down the stairs, back to his feet. His ankle tells him that was a stupid fucking thing to do, but he's ignoring everything now, running with gun in hand and crashing through the doors and into the sunshine. He's thinking of Tom O'Day turning to deadweight on his feet and Stephanie and Callie and Amy and Athena and they're bleeding, and Ruiz wants this one alive, and, goddamn it, so does Jad Bell. He can hear Nessuno in his ear, calling it out, they've got a runner, rabbit, rabbit, one in pursuit. Officers are down, repeat, officers are down.

The apartment complex is off South Meadow Drive, two identical structures built facing one another, separated by their carports. One police car is here, pulling to a stop, and Bell strips the phones from his ears, lets them fall, immediately hears the chatter of that assault rifle once more, another terse, controlled barrage. Someone, somewhere, screams, but it sounds like terror and not pain. Bell sprints in that direction, cutting between parked cars, between pockets of shadow and washes of sunlight, comes around the south side of the building to see the man who is—and please God let him be—Ledor perhaps sixty feet ahead, crossing a new stretch of parking lot.

Bell skids into the side of a parked car, braces himself on the hood, dimly aware that there's someone behind the wheel. He tries to control his breath, sights, and fires twice. It's a hell of a distance for a pistol shot, would be the first break they've caught if he manages to land a round, and he's both a little surprised and, more, grimly satisfied when the man stumbles, tumbles, skids along the pavement. He loses the rifle. The driver hits her horn, screaming at him behind the windshield, but Bell doesn't care, he's already running again.

And the son of a bitch is up again, too, now forcing himself forward. He's got a hand at his left side, and there are trees at the end of the property line, and that's where he's heading. If he's slowed down at all, Bell isn't seeing it, and his own lungs are beginning to burn and the sweat is beginning to race down his back as he sprints after him. There's more chatter through his earpiece, police response, calls for backup, for ambo, for evac, for information. Four officers are down, the suspect is armed and dangerous.

Through the trees now, and green grass that ends in yet another parking lot, another set of paired apartment buildings, and Bell can see that the man is slowing, because Bell himself sure as hell isn't getting faster. His ankle renews its protest as he comes off the grass, chasing between the buildings, onto the asphalt at the end of a cul-de-sac. He sees the safety orange of the earplugs on the ground, wonders idly if they've fallen or if he somehow missed Ledor, if it is Ledor — it must be Ledor, please let it be Ledor — removing them. Forty feet between them now, and Bell is definitely gaining. He can hear someone running behind him, one of the cops, perhaps.

The cul-de-sac dumps onto South Stubbs Avenue, and the man continues across, and Bell has closed to thirty feet but loses at least ten when he has to dodge traffic, a little black Fiat that swerves the wrong way. He spins about, sees it's Nessuno behind him, sprinting for all she's worth, arms pumping and knees high. He finishes his turn, and Ledor hasn't changed direction, straight for the retaining wall against a berm dead ahead, a hard earth slope, and atop it the interstate, where midday traffic is roaring at them from above. Ledor goes over the wall, and seconds later so does Bell, and his ankle makes it a point to tell him what it *really* thinks of that the moment he comes down. The man is scrabbling his way up toward the road, and Bell shouts at him to stop, to stop or he'll shoot. More blood has fallen, turned black on the dry earth. He sees Nessuno drop down beside him, her weapon up and ready and in both hands.

"Stop!" Bell shouts. "Michael Ledor, stop!"

He's at the top of the slope, and Bell and Nessuno are at the bottom, but somehow, Ledor hears him over the traffic. He rises unsteadily, turns to look down at them, and Bell sees he's got a second weapon, a pistol, in his blood-soaked left hand, held limply at the ground. Bell has a good shot, can take it, but he wants him alive, and he holds his fire, and Nessuno does, too.

"Michael," Bell shouts at him. "Drop it, come down here, we'll take care of you. You're out of run, you understand? You've got none left."

Michael Ledor looks at the guns pointing at him, then the one in his hand. There's a wide stain of blood along his left side, and Bell thinks the man must be close to decompensating, that the shock from the blood loss will take him down in just a few more seconds. In his ear, Bell hears officers saying they're en route, they see the suspect, they're close.

"Just drop it," Bell says again.

Michael Ledor drops the gun.

Then he turns and throws himself into sixty-five-mile-an-hour traffic.

Chapter Twenty-Two

LARKIN IS WAITING at Four-Four-Two when Brock arrives, but this time he's not at the bar. Instead he's in a private room on the second floor, what was maybe a bedroom once but has been since converted into a study slash card room. The floors are hardwood hidden beneath Oriental rugs, and the furniture is all wood and leather, and the books on the shelves are bought by the yard and bound in leather, too, or at least imitation leather. There's a Waterford crystal clock on one of the shelves, and it's creeping up on one in the morning.

"What?" Larkin demands. His mood shows his age, brings out the lines around his mouth and eyes. He's wearing a tuxedo, the bow tie loosed and his collar unfastened. Brock wonders whether the meal was political or business or whether Larkin even differentiates between the two.

Brock moves to the sideboard. He's never liked being anyone's whipping boy, didn't like it when his father did it, didn't like it when he was at West Point, didn't like it as he worked his way through the ranks, and one of the perks of being a fucking *general,* goddamn it, is that he doesn't have to take it now. He picks up a glass and ignores the ice in the bucket, pours what he thinks is bourbon from an unlabeled decanter, drinks most of it before refilling. It is bourbon, and, unsurprisingly, a good one.

"Emmet," Larkin says. He says it, Brock thinks, as though he's issuing a warning to one of his snot-nosed grandchildren.

"Where are the others?" Brock asks.

"I saw no reason to bring them in."

"Despite what I said."

"Precisely because of what you didn't say. You want all of us in one place, you need one hell of a good reason for it, and it's not something that can be done quickly, anyway. Anderson is in Vienna right now, and Lenhart is fishing in Alaska."

"You're going to have to reach them," Brock says. "You're going to have to have them come here."

Larkin takes a moment to study him, then sits in one of the overstuffed armchairs. The room, Brock realizes, is decorated in an American version of some British manor-house fantasy. There's even a bellpull by the curtained windows.

"This isn't like you, Emmet," Larkin says. "You're acting alarmingly close to petulant. You know how this works, the way this has worked from the start. We don't work for you."

"And I don't work for you," Brock says.

"We're all in this together, always have been."

"It's good to hear you say that, Bobby," Brock says. "I'm glad to hear you say that. Because that means you're fine with us all going down together, too."

Larkin doesn't like Brock using his first name, likes him using the familiar diminutive even less. He likes his final implication least of all.

"Perhaps you better tell me what's happened."

"Our partner paid me a visit today."

Larkin's reaction isn't anywhere near as gratifying as Brock had hoped. "He met with you in person? I assume with discretion?"

"Oh, he was discreet," says Brock. "What he's done, not so much. All you need to understand is that I'm two days, at the outside, from having army counterintelligence so far up my ass they'll be able to count my fillings. From me, it's not a long walk to you, and Anderson, and Lenhart, and Frohm, and our dear, departed Jamieson."

Brock finishes his drink, pours another. Larkin sits back in his chair, starts to open his mouth to speak.

"I'm not done," Brock says. "There are two positives in this. The first is that, according to our friend, everything is moving forward. The contingency is in motion, and he's promising we'll see it this weekend. So that'll coincide nicely with my arrest."

The humor is either too bitter for Larkin's taste or missed entirely. "And the second?"

"The second is what's going to save us. Our exposure will expose him, and he sure as hell doesn't want that to happen."

"If he didn't want it, he should've been more careful in the first place."

"It doesn't matter what he should've been, Bobby. What matters is how it is right fucking now, and right fucking now I'm in the crosshairs, which means we're all in the crosshairs. He used intelligence I gave him to kill four people. Like I said, we've got two days at best before that leak gets traced back to me."

"You're certain of this?"

"Process of elimination." Brock gets halfway through his third drink, finally, gratefully, beginning to feel the edges of the alcohol. He exhales, looks at the glass in his hand. "They get me, they're getting everything."

That, finally, seems to get a reaction from Larkin. The man straightens, his jaw tightens, and the look he gives Brock is savage.

"I thought you were a patriot, Emmet."

"You don't get to question that," Brock says. "You never get to question that, you arrogant fuck."

"You'd betray us, that's what you're saying."

"Once they put me under the glass, they're going to trace it all, don't you get it? It's all going to come out. All of it, including him, including you, and I don't have to open my mouth. There's a fucking trail here, and once they find me, they're going to find *it*. He understands that, at least. You need to understand that, too."

"Two days?"

"Outside."

Larkin thinks, his gaze going to the books on their shelves. The Waterford timepiece is silent, and Brock thinks that's wrong, that what this room needs is a ticking grandfather clock with its pendulum swaying. There's no other noise, not traffic at this hour, not music piped from some unseen source, not even the sound of movement from the hall.

"In two days, I would think they'll be too busy to care," Larkin says. "If he's done what he's promised."

"And that's why we need to meet, all of us. Because that's what he's holding. He gets a meeting with all of us, he'll give the go-ahead."

Larkin shakes his head. "No; impossible."

"Then we need to start looking at real estate in countries that don't extradite."

"He's already made contact with you, he can meet with you."

Brock feels the glass in his hand, the etched crystal heft of the tumbler, and he wants to throw it in Larkin's face. He wants to overhand it, pure fastball, see the glass hit and shatter and punish Larkin and his arrogance.

"You're questioning my patriotism," Brock says. "You're all fucking talk. Talk about saving our country, talk about needing to put the fight where it belongs, talk about God and socialism and government repression and correcting our national course and right down to the fucking Resurrection. Nothing but talk, but now your ass is on the line, and you need to step up."

"Emmet." It's a warning. It doesn't take.

"No, shut up, listen. You and the rest, you were happy to pay the money so this fucking Architect would attack us in our *home*. So he would kill people in California, so he will kill more people God knows where. You're happy to have me run between you and him, all to make the war you believe in, but you won't go further. You won't go all the way."

"You believe in it, too," Larkin says. "Your words, if I recall, were 'We're not making war, we're just trying to win it.' Don't divorce yourself from what we've done. You've as much to gain as any of us."

"Don't bullshit this back on me. I know your interest as much as I knew Jamieson's. At least Jamieson was a true believer, at least he thought he was doing Christ's work. How's business, Bobby? You short-selling those stocks tomorrow? You got some other way to make another cool billion off of what might — and I stress *might* — happen this weekend? Don't bullshit me."

"It doesn't matter why we believe it needs doing, just that we agree it needs to be done."

"Sure, so long as you never have to get shit on your white shirts." Brock finishes the last of his drink, sets the glass back upon the tray. "You're getting to clean the shitter now, Bobby, and it's backed up and full to the brim. One way or another."

Larkin goes back to looking at the shelves, but Brock can tell he's not seeing the books or their titles. The hour and the moment have further conspired to reveal Larkin's age, the slight sag of the flesh at his cheeks, the lines defining his mouth. He frowns, purses his lips for a moment.

"I'd like a drink, if you would," Larkin says finally.

There's enough in his tone to let Brock know he's won. He knows Larkin now sees what Brock has been staring at from all angles since he left Jordan's apartment, left without even seeing her to say goodbye. Left with the Architect saying that Jordan would see him the next morning to give him the details of the meeting.

"What's your poison?" Brock asks.

"Genuinely?" Larkin shakes his head. "I don't care."

Brock leaves Larkin and drives home, and although he's had enough to drink to know he shouldn't be behind the wheel, he hasn't had enough to make him wrap himself around a tree. He wonders if that wouldn't be a better resolution, to take himself out of the equation entirely. He's never had a suicidal thought before in his life, not even at his worst, but alone in his car he's dwelling on death, not least of all his own. He's lived far more of his life under pressure than not at this point, but this is different. This is inevitability. He's half expecting to find the FBI or CI or both waiting for him in the den when he gets to his house.

So wrapping the car around a tree at seventy miles an hour, that's not out of the question.

He remembers wondering what the Architect was like, the imagined man, Eurofag and effete. He hadn't been prepared for the real thing, the confidence and the arrogance. He'd been plain, average — even the clothes were average, midrange and off the rack, not the tailor-made bespoke suits that Larkin and his ilk favor, that Brock will never be able to afford. It was an alpha-male reaction, Brock measuring himself against this man, the one who had Jordan. They'd fucked, he could tell. He was probably fucking her right now, and that thought keeps him on the road, keeps him driving toward home, keeps his mind focused.

The end may be inevitable, but it will not, Brock resolves, be his end alone.

Larkin calls the next morning, while Brock is having his breakfast. His wife had been asleep when he'd returned, had already left by the time he rose. That was their life, had been for years. Brock made coffee for himself while wondering what she was doing, where she was going, whom she was seeing. He couldn't remember the last time they'd exchanged more than a dozen words all together. He thinks the only reason they've not divorced is because they're too old and it would be too much bother. He used to wonder if she had a lover or a string of them. He had ways of finding out, but after he'd met Jordan, he couldn't stomach that hypocrisy. She did her duty by him, stood at his side at the White House, at other events. Beyond that, she'd made her own life, and he wasn't in it. It was one of the things that had made Jordan so appealing when they'd met. The choice between her and the work required to repair his marriage had been an easy one.

"Lenhart can't make it before noon," Larkin says. "But he'll come straight. We're set for two."

"He can't get there any sooner?"

"You're lucky he's coming at all. You're lucky any of them are coming. They don't understand why this is needed. I don't understand why this is needed."

"Mutual survival," Brock tells Larkin. "Or mutual destruction."

"We've no reason to trust him."

Brock doesn't bother responding to that.

"Two," Brock says, and hangs up. He drinks his coffee, finishes going through the correspondence and reports that have backlogged over the last eighteen or so hours on his computer. Everything looks normal, no signs of him being cut out of the loop. There is nothing about an Indigo operation gone wrong or an Indigo operator's murder, but it doesn't matter. Brock thinks, at the most, he's got a day before the trail leads to him.

He takes his coffee with him into the small home office where he and his wife have their desks, positioned back-to-back rather than facing each other. He picks up a piece of his monogrammed stationery and a pen, spends the better part of a minute staring at the blank page before he begins writing, and is finished in less than another. He folds the paper, closes it within an envelope, then takes it with him upstairs.

He bathes, goes to dress, stares at his uniform on its hanger on the hook on the closet door, feels a surge of disgust. He cannot go into work today. He cannot wear it.

He replaces the uniform in the closet, puts on civvies instead, then kneels and opens the trapdoor to the small compartment hidden in the floor. He puts his fingers into the slots of the safe, taps in the code with his other hand, and the lock snaps back. He takes one of the bundles of cash, another burner phone, the gun, the ammunition, and the magazine. Some of the ammunition goes into the magazine, and the magazine goes into the gun, and for the first time in years, the gun goes onto his hip. He closes everything up, heads downstairs, grabs his jacket, and stows the envelope in an inside pocket. He pauses at the window, looks out at the street. It's another in this string of endlessly sunny summer days. A kid with his pants too low skims past on a skateboard. Brock sees no signs that he's being watched, but he knows that means nothing.

He leaves the house without his laptop or his secure phone, and as he pulls out of the driveway, he thinks this is the last time he will see his home.

It's less than ten minutes to the nearby Starbucks on Connecticut Avenue, where Jordan is already, standing in line and waiting to order. She shoots him a smile when she sees him, one unlike any that he's seen from her before, genuinely happy. He wants it to be because of him. She moves to pick up her drink, and Brock doesn't bother with the pretense of ordering one of his own, just waits until she's done and holds the door open for her, following her back outside.

"He let you out alone?" Brock asks.

She moves to her Jetta without pause, but smiles at him again. "You make it sound like I wear a collar and chain."

"Don't you?"

"Jealousy unmans you, Emmet."

"Where is he?"

"Are you asking if he's watching us?"

"Is he?"

"Did you talk to your people?" She's reached the car, unlocks it with the fob, opens the door. He watches her bend and put her drink in the cup holder between the front seats. She's wearing a summer dress, and her legs are bare, and the length and tone of muscle is magnetic. Then she straightens, turns so she's wedged between door and seat. "Do we have a place and a time?"

"I talked to them. They're not happy."

"Well, we knew they wouldn't be, didn't we? Where and when?"

Brock tells her. He can feel the gun at his hip, acutely aware of its weight, the way it presses against the bone. He puts a hand lightly on hers where it rests on the frame of the door, his skin ruddier, so much older and more used than hers. She's watching him, curious.

"I want you to come with me," he says.

"Where?"

"Anywhere."

She laughs softly.

"Come with me," Brock says. "We can go right now."

She stops laughing. "You're serious?"

"You and me. We can go, right now, we can go, Jordan."

She looks past him, turns her head slightly, as if checking their surroundings. Her expression doesn't change, but her manner, he thinks, does, a new weight settling upon her.

"You think we'd be able to hide?" she asks. "Honestly? You think we could get away from everyone? Your people? Him?"

It's a question that gives him hope, and he seizes it. "I told you before, I can protect you."

The smile remains, but now he can read the change, the edges of a sadness he's never seen from her before, even a fatigue. "I think you really are in love with me."

"It was what you wanted me to be."

"Yes."

"Then you shouldn't be surprised."

She takes the corner of her bottom lip between her teeth for a moment, again switches her focus past him, over his shoulder. Her hand on the door frame, beneath his, turns, and he feels her fingers entwining his. She kisses his lips lightly.

"He has a plan," she says. "It will work."

"His plan," Brock says. "For him."

"For all of us."

Brock squeezes her fingers in his. "Do you really think he cares more for you than I do? Do you really think that when it comes down to survival, his or yours, he'll put you first?"

"But you will?"

"I love you. Of course I will." He says it knowing the hoped-for response won't come. Her answer delivers on that anticipated disappointment, yet brings with it an exquisite elation.

"I love him. But I think I might love you, too. I don't know what to do."

"Will you be there this afternoon?" Brock asks.

"If he wants me there."

"You can't trust him."

"He has a plan, Emmet."

"So do I," Brock says.

A flicker of something in her expression, the corner of her mouth turning down slightly, and Brock thinks, for the very first time, he's seeing confusion, even doubt, from her, and it renews his hope.

"There's a Hilton near BWI," Brock says. "The one on West Nursery Road. Meet me there. I'll leave a note at the desk for you. Just meet me there, we can go, he'll never find us."

"You don't know what he can do, Emmet. You don't know how far he can reach."

"I know what I can do. Noon. Can you meet me there at noon?"

She slips her fingers free from his.

"Will you be there?"

She kisses his mouth softly a second time, then climbs behind the wheel. He holds the door open as she puts her hand out to close it, and there's a moment where he feels her pulling, and he can't bring himself to let go. She looks up at him, that sad smile, and he releases his grip.

"Maybe," she says, and the door closes, and the engine starts, and he watches her drive away.

Chapter Twenty-Three

"It's Brock," Heath says. "If I wasn't sure before yesterday, I'm solid fucking gold on it now."

"That doesn't make sense," Nessuno says. She looks to Ruiz for support, but he's already up and getting on his sat phone. She looks to Bell, who's seated on the floor just inside the door of the hotel room, his back to the wall, looking as wrung out as she feels.

Nessuno turns her gaze back to Heath. "You're saying our oversight, Interdict's oversight, is rotten."

"I know damn well what I'm saying, Chief. You think I'd throw that down without paper to back it up?" Heath gestures at the folder spilling its guts on the little round table in the corner, where Ruiz was seated until a moment before. Now the colonel has retreated to the far corner of the room, by the curtained windows, and he's got someone on the other end of the line, and he might as well be alone for all the attention he's giving them.

"It doesn't track," Nessuno says.

"Not that you're seeing."

"And you are? The only reason to kill Tohir is to keep him from talking, to keep him from fingering Echo, right? You don't have that if we don't have Tohir to begin with, and we don't get Tohir without BI putting me next to him! It's not like Brock didn't know what I was doing!"

Heath gets angry. "I'm not explaining it, I'm telling you what it *is*, goddamn it. This is the fucking evidence, Chief, this is the paper trail, this is the call logs, this is the goddamn time stamps, you clear? This is Brock accessing Indigo personnel files. It's not a motive, no, it's not, but you know what? Fuck the motive. I don't know the motive, and none of us will until we've got that ratfuck son of a bitch in irons and talking, which, by the way" — Heath pivots, points at Ruiz — "better fucking well be what you're working to achieve right now."

Ruiz hears that, raises an eyebrow, continues speaking on the phone. By the door, Bell clears his throat.

"Sir," Heath adds.

"There's another reason," Bell says.

Nessuno shakes her head. "I know what you're thinking. You're thinking that Tohir was about to give up the action."

"That's what I'm thinking."

"That assumes Echo cares about the action."

"You think he doesn't?"

"I told you — the only thing Echo ever seemed to care about was money." She takes the vacated seat at the table, finds herself sitting more heavily than she'd intended, bone-tired and aching. It's well after midnight here in Westminster. The last thing she ate was the breakfast Bell made that she barely touched, and that seems eighteen days, not eighteen hours, ago.

She thinks of what happened in that apartment in Provo, and the shame scores her so suddenly and sharply she has to fight the physical response, the urge to vocalize. The last they'd heard, two of the SWAT team were dead from their wounds, one was still in surgery and it didn't look good, and one was post-op and in recovery.

She wants this day to end.

She's covering her sector, her slice of the room, and the blast comes, and before she can stop herself, even as she's thinking she shouldn't, her head turns to the noise. The SWAT team is stacked at the door the way they've taken each door, one after the other — breach, banger, clear — except at this one there's chaos, and Nessuno can see blood spatter on the door and the wall, pieces of drywall and wallpaper all flying.

Bell grabs her then, and she barely keeps from shooting him by accident, gets her trigger cleared, her finger safe, and she hits the floor on her side. Her breath goes, her own elbow in her stomach, and she can't get it back because he's on top of her. Then the shots, burst after burst after burst, and she sees this guy come out of the bathroom that was supposed to be cleared but wasn't, and instinctively she wraps her arms around Bell, holds him to her as tight as she can. The guy is dropping the mag on a motherfucking assault rifle and swapping it and she holds on to Bell, clamps his arms against hers, and thank Saint Nicholas or thank God or thank the fucking Higgs boson but the shooter doesn't look down at them, he's in too much of a hurry to get to the door and out of there.

Then Bell is up and going after him, and Nessuno is trying to follow suit, fumbling, clumsy, and she sees these men, their broken movement, and through the dulled world behind her ear protection, she hears their pain. The amount of blood spilled on the walls, on the floor, is shocking. She keys her radio, calls it all in. The urge to stop and render aid, to begin triage, is at immediate war with the need to follow Bell, to give him cover, to be his backup.

He is relying on her. She has no choice.

She goes out the door in pursuit, exits the building with no idea which direction to go. She pulls the phones down around her neck in time to hear shots, a pistol double tap, makes the corner in time to see Bell sprinting away from her, in time to see a woman in a parked car screaming. She gives chase, following Bell following the shooter, and by the time she's caught up it's all but over. Ledor turns at the edge of the interstate, and she can see what he's going to do before he does it.

At the bottom of the slope, her angle on the action narrow, she watches him disappear, then reappear suddenly, thrown high into the air. He comes down, vanishing again, and she's racing up the slope, this time ahead of Bell, and Ledor reappears for an instant, tossed once more, body twisting, the angle unnatural. It's not a fall, it's a throw, she thinks.

She reaches the shoulder of the road first, asphalt under her boots, and Ledor is easily eighty feet away, where he's finally come to rest. Traffic is jerking to a desperate halt, cars sliding at angles. She hears metal meeting metal, plastic and glass shattering. She races along the side of the highway, but part of her wonders, what's the point? Why waste the energy? Michael Ledor has become meat in torn clothes, avulsed, all abraded flesh and cracked bone. She takes a knee beside the body, sees the eyes, one wide open, pupil exploded, the other half lidded and leaking fluid. She checks for a pulse anyway. He has none.

Bell stands beside her, chest heaving, sweat running down his face. She's feeling defeat when she looks up at him, but that's not what she sees. She sees cold anger.

Then Bell squats on his haunches, sets his pistol aside, and begins going over the body, emptying pockets, checking his hands, his wrists, his neck, his legs. He finds a wallet and a cell phone, and he tosses the cell to her, opens the wallet, pulls out a driver's license issued by the state of Utah. He shows it to her. Michael Ledor.

"The apartment," he says.

It's a long walk back, and she sees that Bell is limping slightly.

"Ankle?" she asks.

He grunts.

"This is my fault," Nessuno says. "I thought the bathroom was cleared."

Bell says nothing.

*   *   *

There's chaos at the complex when they return, police and ambulance and crime-scene people, and Bell leads, pushes his way past officers and technicians to get them back inside. Someone from the bomb squad tells them that they found another trip wire, another grenade trap, that it's been disarmed. They should wait outside until they're finished.

"Sure," Bell says and doesn't leave, and so neither does she.

They stay until after dark. They go through everything, every drawer, every cabinet, every closet, every bag. Bell finds three grand in mixed bills wrapped in a plastic bag that's been taped to the back of the medicine cabinet in the bathroom. Nessuno finds a passport hidden in one of the DVD cases stacked beside the television, the photo and name both Michael Ledor, the issuing country Belgium.

The alarming shit, she thinks, is what they don't have to search for, what the police have already found and begun to catalog. There's more than twenty thousand rounds of ammunition, half of it for that assault rifle they've recovered, the rest in 9mm and .40. It's stacked in boxes in the cupboards, stored beneath the kitchen sink. There's multiple magazines for all the weapons and four more grenades. Most of the heavy gear is recovered from a bag in the bedroom closet, not hidden so much as it was placed out of sight, with boxes and boxes of ammunition neatly stacked beside. Bonus items in the bag included a gas mask and a vest that Nessuno thinks is rated at level II, maybe IIA.

She does the math, quietly asks Bell, "If they're all geared like this?"

"Nothing good," Bell says.

Nessuno understands. Six of them working together, armed like this, it's been seen before. The Mumbai attacks come immediately to mind, small terrorist fire teams looking to spill as much blood as possible. This guy, Ledor, he knew what he was doing with his weapon; his fire had been disciplined. If they're all trained like that, the body count will easily reach triple digits.

There's another option that is potentially more frightening. If Ledor was in Provo to stage before moving on to target, before meeting up with the rest of the cell for their action, that's one thing. But if the plan is not for a group action but rather for individual attacks, the result could be truly horrifying. To Nessuno, that would be true terror. Not one target but five, hit all in concert, different places at the same time or in quick succession, one here, one there, sowing widespread panic and, subsequently, terrible paranoia.

Those five could be anything, she thinks. Movie theater on a Saturday night, shopping mall in the middle of the day, church on Sunday morning.

She thinks about Ledor, his willingness to fight and his desire to survive right up to and until the moment he knew it was over.

She thinks about five more men, similarly motivated, similarly trained.

Everything in this apartment hints at what they're planning, but nothing tells them when. Nothing tells them where.

Everything tells them they're running out of time.

Ruiz isn't having any of it. He's off the phone now.

"Walk us through it," he says to Heath.

"That's the problem, there isn't an 'it.' There're two things here." Heath holds out her hands in fists, straight ahead of her, looks at Ruiz, at Nessuno, at Bell. She opens her left, palm up. "Here's the attack in California, bought and paid for, and another one coming up. According to Heatdish, it's one that's been built by Echo for the same buyer. That's what you found in Provo, right? One of those elements. That's Ledor, that's Zein, Alexander, Hawford, Dante, and Verim. We have anything more on those guys, by the way?"

"Working on it."

"That CIA guy, he's leading?"

"Wallford, yes."

"We know he's solid?"

Ruiz nods.

"Fine." Heath opens her right fist, turns it palm up.

"Thing two, 'it' two, is Brock. The guy who's having the chief and me confirm Heatdish's death and who CI confirms accessed Indigo personnel files and who has been sharing God knows what with God knows who — Echo, certainly, maybe others."

Heath lowers her hands, sets them on her thighs, rubs her legs as though she's trying to make fire with the friction.

"Brock didn't lean on Steelriver," Bell says.

"Doesn't look that way, no, at least not directly. His movements put him out of the running for the death of O'Day's family."

"Which means it was Echo."

"Jesus fuck," Nessuno says. "Brock isn't working for Echo, he's working *with* him."

"You said Echo was about money," Bell says. "General may be well above our pay grade, but he's not into that kind of money."

"But Jamieson was," Ruiz says. "And men like Jamieson have friends."

Bell makes a noise, almost a growl. "We get anything off Ledor's cell phone?"

"It's a burner, and clean. We've got it on, if a call comes in."

"Assuming they think Ledor's still alive."

"I'm not holding my breath."

Ruiz's phone bleats. He turns away to answer it.

"This is follow-the-chain," Bell says. "There's a cutout in here somewhere, has to be, someone between Brock and Echo."

"At least one, maybe more," says Heath.

"We squeeze Brock for the cutout, that should lead to Echo."

"We jump on Brock —" Nessuno says.

"Assuming we get clearance to go after a fucking *general,*" Heath says.

" — and Echo will know," Nessuno continues. "Just speaking from experience with Tohir, now, but if that cutout gets a whiff that Brock's compromised, he's going to vanish. We'll get nothing."

"We can't sit here and wait," Bell says.

Ruiz is getting off the phone again. There's something in the way he says "Yes, sir" before hanging up that catches their attention.

"Here's what's going to happen," Ruiz says.

Bell drives, Nessuno beside him. She slides the seat back, draws her knees up to her chest, stares at the road appearing ahead of them in the predawn hours. The traffic is light, and the drive from Westminster to Chevy Chase should take only an hour, but Bell is lead-footing it, and she knows it'll take less. There's at least one counterintelligence team moving in on Brock at the moment, their orders to maintain surveillance until Bell and Nessuno can get on-site and to break off entirely if there's fear of exposure. Bell has a reason to speed.

"How you holding up?" Bell asks. The tone of the question surprises her more than the content. He asks it like a human who cares, not like a soldier who's worried.

"I'm still in Provo."

"With the bends."

"With the bends, yeah."

"You need to set Provo down," Bell says. "You can't carry that, not right now."

"You're not the one who blinked."

"You'll have plenty of time to pick it apart later, trust me."

"The voice of experience?"

"I've made more mistakes than you can count, Chief. Find me someone who hasn't."

"How many have gotten men killed?"

He shakes his head slightly, then reaches out and sets his hand on her arm. She takes it in her right, laces her fingers with his. His hand is large, and strong, and everything she likes.

"I can't read you," Nessuno says.

He laughs.

"What?"

"It's mutual, Chief." He glances to the mirrors, then to her, and she's surprised again, because he's grinning. He goes back to looking at the road. "We didn't fuck."

"What?"

"In Hailey, when I asked who you were. You said we fucked. It's schoolboy, I know it. I'm soft on this, I know that, too. But if that's what you think, you need to know you're thinking it alone. That's not what that was."

Nessuno stares at him, trying to understand what she's feeling. When she does, she looks out her window, sees her own smile in the reflection.

She doesn't let go of his hand.

Chapter Twenty-Four

CI HAS A command post established and operational before Bell arrives at Find Your Space Storage in Chevy Chase, pulls up to the gate as dawn is creeping into the sky. Nessuno has been asleep, or nearly so, for the last twenty minutes of the drive, head against the window, but she opens her eyes as Bell comes to a stop, and she releases his hand at long last. The plainclothes on the gate ID's them and lets them through, pointing the way to the row of units that's been commandeered for the operation. One is being used for command, another for commo, and there are soldiers sorting wardrobe choices for quick change and checking gear as Bell and Nessuno approach.

In the command post they find a sergeant who identifies himself as Lopez.

"Warlock?"

"Warlock," Bell says. "Blackfriars. What's the word?"

"We've got a watch on the subject at his residence." Sergeant Lopez checks a sheet on his clipboard, looks at the digital clock that's been hung on one of the unit's walls. "His wife left four minutes ago, alone. We've got a team following her now."

Bell looks at the maps that have been taped to the wall, the photographs of the house and of the man. "What's on the residence?"

"Three teams, one static."

"Stand off?"

"We're under orders not to spook him."

"Positive he's still there?"

"As positive as we can be without getting into bed with him."

"Radio? Phone?"

Sergeant Lopez grins. "We're assured a warrant is on its way."

Nessuno has moved to one of the two long tables pressed against the side of the unit. She pulls two radios from their chargers.

"We need another vehicle," she says.

Sergeant Lopez looks to one of the soldiers, who immediately nods and heads out of the unit.

"My understanding is that we're to render all aid to you for this operation," Lopez says.

"That is correct."

Nessuno whistles, and Bell turns to her, catches the radio she's tossing his way just in time in one hand.

"I want everything light on the house until we're in position," Bell says. "He moves at all, you let us know."

"Understood."

Bell checks the radio, takes the earpiece that Nessuno is offering him, fits it into place. It's uncomfortable; unlike the ones he uses in the field with his team, this one is generic and hasn't been fitted for his ear. The soldier who was sent for the car returns, holds out a clipboard in one hand and a set of keys in the other. Nessuno takes the keys and ignores the clipboard, and Bell follows her out of the unit. A navy blue Prius, almost black in the shadows cast by the units, is parked five meters away.

"I'll follow you," Nessuno says.

There's been no change by the time they reach the residence. Bell parks around the corner, with an eye on the house; Nessuno continues another two blocks along before pulling over.

"Kill the engine," she says. "Don't show him exhaust."

"Already done."

She laughs, the sound soft in his ear. He hasn't heard her do that enough. "Of course."

Bell checks in with Lopez and orders the surveillance withdrawn even farther. He wants them as backup if things go south. The beauty of having resources is that they're fully staffed. The downside is the co-ordination, and the dangers of miscommunication, and Bell tells Lopez he wants confirmations across the board. Within three minutes, he has them, and settles in to wait.

The sun comes up, and the neighborhood stirs, and with it the exhaustion Bell's been fighting finds his seams, begins to sink toward bone. His ankle throbs, and the stitches, cuts, and scrapes on his hand and arm itch. He's tired, and feeling it, tries to remember how long it's been since he's had a full night's rest, how long it's been since he's had a chance to heal. Too long, he thinks, and it makes him feel old, and he acknowledges that he's been feeling that way a lot lately.

Sleep tries to catch him, and Bell pushes it away again. He shifts in the seat, tries to make himself uncomfortable. It helps, but not enough.

He thinks of Petra, of Elisabetta, of Blackfriars, two blocks away, waiting in her Prius, that she's at least ten years younger than he is. He hopes he's wrong about that, that their ages aren't so disparate. He's only ever been in love the once, with Amy, and he's suspicious of what he feels for CW2 Petra Nessuno, wary of making it more than it is, wondering if that isn't just what he's doing because that's what he wants. What the fuck is he doing, thinking like that? he wonders. He doesn't know her. There are times she has seemed to not even know herself.

Yet thinking that, he knows he's trying to retreat, and he thinks that cowardice. He's been afraid too many times in his life to count, but he's refused to ever let it rule him. He refuses to let it happen here. Turn and face it. She's tearing herself up over Provo, but the fact is she was there, she took his back. The fact is he liked her hand in his. The fact is that whatever began with mutual attraction and a mutual need, with them trying to unpack their varied baggage, it's become something else.

It's getting harder and harder to stay focused, to stay awake. The sunlight brings pleasant warmth, and it's seductive. He blinks, blinks, blinks, and then he's seeing Emmet Brock's car backing out of the driveway, and he swears.

"He's moving," Bell says to his radio. He clears his throat. "Heading east."

"I'll pick him up," Nessuno says. "Hang back."

"Confirmed."

Bell watches the car finish its reverse, the white lights flashing off, then it's pulling away from him. It makes the turn north at the opposite end of the block just as the Prius passes him, and Bell waits a fifteen count before starting his own engine and following. Nessuno is giving updates, calling out the turns as she follows onto Woodbine Street, now west onto Leland; he's at the speed limit.

Bell follows the turns, can see the Prius ahead of him.

"Break," he tells her.

Brock's car continues through an intersection, and the Prius makes a left and Bell maintains the distance, and now it's his turn to give the play-by-play. He varies his speed, risks putting more cars between his and Brock's, until he sees him make the right onto Blackthorn, then into the heavier four-lane traffic, heading north. He closes the distance, has a moment of alarm when Brock hits his brakes, wondering if it's not an attempt to flush the tail. Then Brock turns across traffic, pulls up at a Starbucks, and Bell continues north another two blocks before taking the turn to bring himself back.

"I have eyes on," Nessuno says. "He's parked, heading inside."

Bell pulls into the lot north of the shop, facing south. He checks left, sees that the Prius is similarly parked across the street, opposite the store, positioned to head north.

"I have eyes," Bell says.

"He's inside," Nessuno says over the radio. "No, coming out."

"Guess he didn't want coffee."

"You see her?" Nessuno says.

"Oh, yes," Bell says.

"We have a vehicle, Volkswagen Jetta, black. D.C. plates, can't make them out."

"I've got them," Bell says, and he gives the string over the radio. For the first time since the tail began, Lopez's voice comes on, repeating the sequence.

"Running it," Lopez says. "Registered to Webber-Hayden, Jordan; we've got a D.C. address."

"Subject two is female, Caucasian," Nessuno says. "Five eight, maybe five nine, brown hair, shoulder. Wearing a summer dress, white, with black and gold print."

"We have a D.C. driver's license for Jordan Webber-Hayden," Lopez says. "Address matching vehicle registration. Fits your description, brown hair, eyes hazel, five foot nine, weight one thirty-two."

"My ass," Nessuno says.

Bell grins.

"Warlock." Nessuno's tone has changed. "She's the cutout."

"Maybe his mistress?"

"Maybe both. Look at the body language."

"What am I seeing?"

"You're seeing him being played."

Bell watches the woman and Brock.

"Designating subject two as Hardball," Lopez says.

"I'll take her," Nessuno says. "Warlock, you keep the primary."

"Got it. Command, you still have teams in the area?"

"I have teams at standoff," Lopez says.

"One for Blackfriars, one for me," Bell says.

Lopez confirms, and there's a crackle, then the odd, dead sound of a muted line in Bell's ear. The woman is getting into the car, but Brock won't let her close the door. From where Bell's looking, he can't make out expressions, can't tell if it's a fight or something else. Then Brock steps back and the door closes and the Jetta pulls out, turns, and Nessuno is rolling after her.

Brock just stands in the lot, his hands at his sides, his head down, his chin to his chest. Then he squares his shoulders and returns to his car, starting it immediately and quickly pulling out, heading north.

Bell spins his wheel and moves to follow.

It's forty-five minutes of tag, with Bell swapping positions with the CI team that's come in to back him up. Most of it is on I-95, and after half an hour, Bell is certain Brock is heading for the airport, that he's going to rabbit. He's fallen back, letting the other team hold position, and is reaching for his phone to call Brickyard and seek permission to detain Brock.

"He's exiting onto Aviation," the CI team says. "We stay on him, he'll make us."

"Roll," Bell says. "I'll take him."

He makes the off-ramp just in time to see Brock heading east on Aviation Boulevard, makes the turn to follow. Another turn, this one a sharp left, and there's no traffic to speak of. Bell feels horribly exposed as he follows suit. Hotels are springing up like weeds, suddenly, and Brock makes a right onto West Nursery Road and now they're passing the National Electronics Museum, aerials and radar dish installations out front, crimson awning over its entrance. Bell finds himself marveling at the fact that such a place even exists.

There's more traffic now, and Bell watches as Brock turns a last right into the Hilton parking lot. Bell goes left, into the lot of the Marriott opposite, parks, and leaves his car. A jet thunders overhead, taking off from the airport, and Bell jogs across the street in time to see Brock heading into the hotel ahead of him, his hands free.

"I'm at the Hilton on Nursery," Bell says. "He's gone inside, hands are free. No bags, no plan to stay, might be a meet. Question is with who."

"I've got a good idea," Nessuno says.

The second team comes in five minutes after Bell, and then a third, which gives Bell four soldiers to play with, all of them in plainclothes and most of them wearing it well. The ones who haven't quite shed their soldier bearing he posts outside the Hilton, covering the exits, leaving him with two, one male and one female, that he sends into the lobby.

Bell returns to his car, gets on the phone with Brickyard.

"I need a go order," Bell says. "I need to know if I can take him."

"Blackfriars is still on Hardball?" Ruiz asks.

"She is. Hardball has moves."

"So I heard. It confirms she's the cutout."

"Blackfriars believes Hardball is en route. We can get them together."

"We need her alive," Ruiz says.

"That's understood."

"You think it's a quickie?"

"I think there are easier places they could've gone to get laid."

"So what is it?"

"I eyeballed his vehicle," Bell says. "No bags visible, but I didn't pop the trunk."

"So possible rabbit."

"Possible, but if Hardball is coming here, does that mean he's saying good-bye or he's taking her with him?"

There's a brief pause, then Ruiz says, "You are authorized to arrest as acting CI. Get them together and take them down."

"Roger that."

Bell kills the connection, stows his phone, thinking about just who has the power to grant the authorization required to take down a brigadier general.

*   *   *

Bell waits until Jordan Webber-Hayden is in the lobby before moving to join Nessuno. She's switched cars, coming out from behind the wheel of a white Subaru.

"She's at the desk," Bell says.

Nessuno slips her arm around his waist. They start for the doors.

"Talk dirty to me," she says.

"Seriously?"

"Honest autonomic reaction." She nudges him with her hip, and her smile is dazzling. He flashes back to the woman he met in Tashkent, the dark eyes and pride, and thinking then that she must've been very good at her job. He's seeing that now. She is relaxed and self-assured, but more, she is happy. Flushed with the chase and confident in her skill and as sure as any door kicker he has ever known.

"I want you," Bell says.

"I want you, too. But you have to do better than that."

"No." He brings his mouth to her ear. Everything they're saying, it's on the net, he knows, it's being recorded for posterity. "I want to be inside you again, I want to hear your joy again. I want to feel your hands and your breath and your body, and I want to make you shake and make you know how stunning you are, how rare, how precious. I want to make love to you and make you forget everyone and everything until it's just us, to do it for hours, and days, and weeks, and as long as you'll have me."

Her hand tightens at his hip.

"Okay," she says. "That was pretty good."

"She's heading for the elevator."

"We have a room?"

"CI badged the manager after Brock checked in. Four forty." With his free hand, he takes the key card from his pocket, shows it to her. She plucks it. "Passkey."

"Guess we know where we're going."

"Guess we do."

She keeps her arm around him until they're in the elevator, his arm around her shoulders. Once the doors are closed, she turns and kisses him, keeps kissing him even as Lopez comes on the radio in their ears.

"In position."

Nessuno breaks off long enough to say, "Confirmed," then brings her mouth back to his until the elevator chimes and comes to a halt.

That's when they hear the shots.

That's when Nessuno opens the door and Bell goes through it. Jordan Webber-Hayden is on the floor, and there's a smear of blood on the bed, and Bell has his weapon up and ready and in both hands, and there's Brigadier General Emmet Brock with his. Bell gives the warning, knowing it won't be taken, and he shoots, understanding that is exactly what Brock wants, and hating Brock's guts for making Bell give it to him.

Chapter Twenty-Five

JORDAN LEAVES BROCK, drives a dozen blocks, doglegs another four, and then reverses direction and returns to the Starbucks where she started. She parks in a different spot, even though the one she's left only minutes earlier is still vacant, and she takes a moment to pretend to check her hair and makeup in the mirror, but in truth she is trying to confirm that Brock has departed and that she is, in fact, being followed.

About Brock, she's certain he's on his way to the Hilton at BWI. He'll get there early, she knows, because he'll want to make certain he's gotten there clean. The clock on the dashboard is reading eleven past ten in the morning. She has plenty of time.

Whether she has picked up surveillance is uncertain. There had been a navy blue Prius with Virginia plates behind her when she left, and through the start of the first dogleg as well, but it had turned off before she'd completed the maneuver and begun the second. When she'd reversed direction, she thought she'd seen it again, but that could have been paranoia; the model and color are common enough, and she hadn't been able to see its plates.

She finishes up in the Jetta, climbs out, taking her messenger bag. Inside she orders a green tea latte, finds an empty table, and opens her laptop. She doesn't bother with the camera this time, or even with a direct link to her Lover. Just sends a simple e-mail, the address and the time for the meeting, adding that she had to do nothing, that Brock did it all himself. She contents herself surfing from one news site to another while awaiting a response, but she's not really reading, and when she sips her drink, it tastes off. She knows why; she can feel the adrenaline and her excitement and her anxiety. She is on the cusp, she can feel it; she can jump either way.

She genuinely doesn't know if she can do what her Lover has asked. The sincerity, the desire of Brock's offer was unexpected, even though she suspected the depth of his feeling for her. All the doubts she had put aside when her Lover returned — Brock brought them forth again. She wants to be pure and certain, not so suddenly conflicted, and she thinks that if Brock had made the offer only a day earlier, before her Lover had reappeared, she would have taken it gratefully. She would have walked away with him, leaving everything behind.

Now her Lover has returned, and that changes everything, the way what he asked her to do to that mother and her daughter changed everything. She has his promise. She has him again.

From her seat, she can see where she's parked, and she keeps glancing up, and there are no navy blue Priuses in sight.

Then the e-mail she is waiting for comes, and she opens it and reads what her Lover has written.

> There is a house in France I bought for us years ago. Tell me you like France.

She can't keep herself from smiling, can't keep the small squeak of joy from escaping.

They had fought the night before, the first time they had ever fought.

She'd asked him to stay with her, to spend the night in Jordan Webber-Hayden's home, and he had refused. It was too dangerous, he said; it would put them both at risk. There was the chance that Brock would return, and his passion for her made him unpredictable. If he came back to find them together, it could jeopardize everything. She knew he was right, she didn't need to remember any of her tutors or any of her lessons, but she had argued with him anyway.

"I don't care," she said. "Please, *dorogoy*, just this night. I don't want to be alone. I don't want to be without you."

"Zoya." He cupped her face in his hands, kissed her lips. "You think I do not wish to remain? You think there is anywhere I would rather be than with you?"

She pulled away. She struck at his arm, not to hurt him but to tell him that his touch was unwelcome, and took some satisfaction that the gesture seemed to both surprise and wound him.

"Zoyenka," he said.

Her leg ached, and her arm. She squeezed her eyes shut, and it was a mistake, because the memory of the woman and her child came back, sharp with detail. She could again smell the rank fear in that house, see and hear the sobbing girl, the anguish of her mother. She had killed the girl first, and her mother's scream had been primal, had continued in anguish until Jordan had silenced her with a shot.

"I can't do this anymore." She opened her eyes, saw that he hadn't moved, that there was sadness on his new face. "I do not want to do this anymore."

"You don't have to."

She didn't understand.

Her Lover said, "Pack a bag. Clothes, things you would take on a short trip, and Jordan Webber-Hayden's passport. One bag only, you understand? Nothing more. Everything else here you leave behind."

"I'm leaving?"

"You are compromised, and I will not allow it. After I meet with the soldier's friends tomorrow, I will return to you here, and together we will leave."

"I'll come with you?"

"Yes. We are both in danger now, and I will not allow it. I cannot allow it."

Her hands were shaking, she realized. She clenched them together, and he came and put his arms around her.

"You have been everything I needed, done everything I hoped," her Lover said. "Now I need you to do one more thing. Just one more thing, Zoyenka, and I will give you everything I promised you all those years ago."

The pressure in her breast was becoming unbearable. She buried her face against his shoulder.

"The only thing I have ever wanted is you," she said.

It is ten thirty exactly when she leaves the Starbucks in Chevy Chase, and she takes the next ninety minutes for a drive that in the best of circumstances lasts only thirty. She doglegs, doubles back, takes the highway and varies her speed, and all the while she is watching the vehicles as much as the traffic, trying to spot patterns, trying to flush any possible surveillance. There are navy blue Priuses on the road, but the one she sees with Virginia plates doesn't match the one in her memory, and the driver is a black male, not a white female with dark hair.

At the Hilton, she parks the Jetta in the lot, then makes her way to the lobby. It's only two minutes before noon, and there is a cluster of pilots and flight attendants waiting for the shuttle, and some business types, nothing that raises an alarm. She goes to the desk and gives her name, and the young woman there brightens and gives her an envelope. Inside Jordan finds a slip of hotel notepaper, a room number written on it.

She goes to the house phone, asks the operator to connect her with the number she's just read, and the phone rings twice before Brock answers it.

"I'm in the lobby," Jordan says.

"Come up."

She hangs up, moves to the elevators. The airline personnel are filing out the front doors, and a couple is entering after them, arms around each other, shoulder and waist. She thinks of her Lover and Brock at once, because everything about their manner tells Jordan that they're in love. He's whispering in her ear, and the woman's expression tells Jordan that the proposal is indecent and welcome.

She rides the elevator up alone, reaches Brock's room and knocks, and the door opens at once. She steps into his arms before he can speak, kisses him, and his surprise gives way to his passion, the way it always has. He turns her, knocking the door closed, and his hands are eager, fingers dragging along her thighs, slipping beneath the hem of her dress. She wraps her arms around his neck, makes a sound into his mouth before pulling her lips away.

"How much time do we have?" she asks.

"All of it," Brock says.

She brings her mouth in close to his again, runs her hands from his shoulders down to his chest, but instead of keeping her close and taking the kiss, he steps back. His hands slide along her bare arms, down to her wrists, holding them gently. He smiles at her, and Jordan thinks this is the first time in a very long time that she has seen that smile.

"I'm so sorry, Jordan," Brock says.

"What?"

"This is how it has to be." He lets go of one hand, takes the gun off his hip. The sound of the weapon going off safe is damning.

"Emmet," she says.

"You would never leave him," Brock says. "But you came here anyway. There's only one reason you would come here anyway, Jordan."

It's not entirely true, but she knows there's no point in denial, in trying to explain to him her conflict, how close he came to having her. No purpose to showing her desperation or making a plea. She is here to kill him, and he knows it; whether he intends to kill himself along with her doesn't matter.

She doesn't think about what to do or why to do it. She thinks that her Lover will be waiting for her at her West End condo, and she thinks that there is a house in France waiting for them tomorrow, and she knows that she will not allow everything she has done, everything she has sacrificed, to go to waste.

She thinks all this instantly, intuitively.

Brock brings the pistol up, his other hand still on her wrist, and she twists her arm away from him, slams the palm of her free hand into his face. The weapon discharges, and she feels a sear along her chest, and she cries out as she grabs for the barrel. All the tutors, all the lessons vanish, and she screams at him that she will not let him do this, will not let him take this future from her, wrenching the gun. Brock shouts in pain, and suddenly the weapon isn't in her hand, but it's not in his, either. He yanks on her wrist, spears heat into her shoulder, and she punches at his throat and gets his chin instead. He hits her, and she finds herself on the bed, bouncing off of it, and he's reaching for the gun on the floor.

She kicks, digs a heel into his side, and Brock falls to a knee. She kicks again, skims his back, and he's coming up with the weapon. She tumbles to one side, off the bed and onto the floor, and he is rising, steadying himself.

The door flies open, and she sees the man from the lobby, the one who made her think of her Lover in attitude, if not in body, and he has his own gun in his hand, advancing. The woman hugs the wall of the hallway outside, just visible.

"Brock!" the man shouts. "Drop it!"

Brock does not drop it, pivots, and the two shots come rapid, and the man advances and the woman takes the corner into the room behind him. Jordan launches herself forward, throws her shoulder into the woman, slams her against the door frame, hears her grunt with the collision.

Then Jordan is out of the room and not looking back, and running with everything she has, trying to get away.

"Jordan Webber-Hayden," the woman shouts, and somehow a neuron connects for Jordan, and she realizes that this woman shouting and the woman in the blue Prius this morning, they are the same. "Stop!"

Jordan Webber-Hayden does not stop.

Chapter Twenty-Six

THE GENERAL HITS the floor, and Hardball hits Nessuno, and for the second time in twenty-four hours, the chief thinks that there's a reason why specialists train day after day after day to clear rooms. She's not a specialist, not at this, but this time, she's not having any of it.

"Rabbit," Nessuno shouts, sending it out on the net, sending it wide, and she shoves off the door frame and pivots into the hall. She shouts after the woman, "Jordan Webber-Hayden! Stop!" and gets exactly the result she'd expected. The door to one of the neighboring rooms flies open, one of the CI agents posted there swinging out, SIG in his hands. Hardball is at the end of the hall and crashing through the fire exit.

"No shot." Nessuno barks it, makes it an order, already chasing. "We need her alive."

Responses crash in her ear, radio traffic suddenly nuts. Bell's voice, and it's the second time she's heard him speak amid chaos and adrenaline, and, as before, he's almost unnaturally calm. Brock is down, need medic, need evac, Blackfriars is in pursuit of Hardball.

She catches the door just before it swings shut, slams it open but pauses, checks low first, and sees a pair of black heels discarded on the landing, spatters of blood. Checks high, and there's a flutter of white summer dress with black-and-gold pattern rounding a corner.

"She's in the stairs," Nessuno says, repeats it, adds, "She's heading up."

Taking the stairs now, as fast as she can, racing past droplets of blood on the cold concrete. She's tired, she's smelly, she's hungry, but all that vanishes, adrenaline and fury propelling her to take the stairs two at a time. She rounds one corner, another, and Jordan Webber-Hayden is fast or inspired, but Nessuno thinks if she can keep up the pressure, they'll have her. They can cut her off at the roof. They can cut off her route.

Except Nessuno is rounding the landing at seven, and she hears the door being knocked open above, and she looks up just in time to see Hardball wrenching the fire extinguisher from its holder. The canister comes crashing straight for her head, and Nessuno jumps back, feels the air shift her hair, brush her face. She leaps over it as it begins to spit on the stairs, nearly loses her footing, rights herself, and is onto eight as the door is again closing. This time, she goes through without pause, and Jordan Webber-Hayden is running barefoot away from her down the carpeted hall.

Full sprint after her, gun in one hand, and Nessuno won't even consider trying the shot, doesn't dare risk it. She's shouting that they're on eight, and wondering where Bell is, where anyone is. Jordan Webber-Hayden cuts right around a corner and out of sight, and a second later Nessuno rounds after her, into the short hallway of the eighth floor's elevator bank, trying to stay on her feet.

Something bashes her shoulder, catches her across the jaw, and Nessuno tastes blood and realizes she's on the ground, rolls in time to avoid the foot trying to find her neck. Jordan Webber-Hayden stands, holding the house phone from the table, handset gripped in her right, base unit in her left. She's spitting fury, swearing at her, fabric ripped in a line across the left side of her torso, dark blood shining. She kicks, barefoot, and Nessuno gets her hands up and catches her foot, twists, brings her down, and that's when she realizes she's lost her weapon.

Jordan Webber-Hayden lands facedown, lashes back with the handset of the telephone. It cracks audibly against Nessuno's forehead, makes her see dancing light, rocks her back, and Jordan Webber-Hayden lunges forward again, phone jangling miserably as it's discarded. She reaches for the gun with both hands, still cursing, and Nessuno hears seven-tiered Russian insults blending with English calling her a cock-sucking cunt.

Nessuno throws herself forward, lands on the other woman's back. An elbow comes around, hits her hard in the side, but Nessuno gets her left arm beneath, up, drives her right thigh between Jordan Webber-Hayden's, locks her ankles around the woman's left leg. She grabs her wrist, yanks, closing the chokehold at the woman's throat, pulling with all her might, and Jordan Webber-Hayden won't stop fighting, even as the blue streak turns hoarse. They rock together, and Nessuno flips onto her back, now with the other woman on top of her, pulling and pulling, and she can hear the radio in her ear spewing nonsense. Jordan Webber-Hayden drives her elbow back into Nessuno's side again, but this time it's weaker, and her other hand is clawing at Nessuno's wrists, nails tearing skin and drawing blood, trying to break the hold. There's a distant chime, the sound of Bell's voice, and then there are hands on her, pulling at her, and she realizes that they've been separated, that CI has the other woman facedown on the carpet once more, cuffs snapping around her wrists.

Bell helps her to her feet, and she spits out a mixture of saliva and blood, wipes at her mouth with her sleeve. She's drenched with sweat, and when she touches her forehead with her fingertips, she can feel the goose egg coming up.

Jordan Webber-Hayden has stopped struggling, and she's stopped swearing.

Nessuno realizes that the woman is sobbing, choking out one word over and over again.

"What's she saying?" Bell asks. "Anybody know what she's saying?"

"Dorogoy," Nessuno says. "It means 'my love.'"

Chapter Twenty-Seven

SO MUCH FOR rules, the Architect thinks. Rules are made to be broken. Some things, he acknowledges, have to be done himself.

The first communiqué from Zoya comes, and with it the address and the time, and it gives him roughly three hours to do what must be done. He's anticipated the day's work and has done his shopping already, fortunate to find an electronics store open at nine that morning. The camera is a new Canon EOS, and he charges the battery while working at his laptop at the hotel. He sends her a response, imagining her smile when she reads about their plans.

Then he sets to work. There's a backlog of reports and messages from other operatives around the globe, and he barely gives them the time they deserve. Right now, his primary concern is twofold. The day's business and the exfiltration. The exfiltration is easier, and he spins out his programs in search of flights. When Zoya was placed all those years ago, he set two caches for her should everything go wrong, one at a CubeSmart on Upshur Street in D.C., the other out in District Heights, in Maryland. Each exists only for emergencies, and, since stocking them, the Architect has made certain that their contents are maintained and all their paperwork remains current. Zoya, who has been Jordan Webber-Hayden, can become Evelyn Bridger or Claudia Voss, depending on the route they decide to take.

The day's business is an entirely different challenge, and while he has operatives he could reach out to for assistance, he is resolved to do this alone. Already he and Zoya are horribly naked; he has no wish to compromise any other operations.

He goes back into his own archives, in particular the reports from Tohir about his contacts and meetings with Lee Jamieson. Jamieson had communicated via Tohir, the relationship put in motion by Zoya through Brock. Once the request had come, the Architect had vetted Jamieson himself, acting with what he viewed as expected caution; after all, Jamieson wanted a very dangerous, very expensive service provided. The Architect needed to be certain he would be both safe and paid upon its execution at the very least.

Now the Architect views the Jamieson bio again, not to learn more about the man himself but rather to learn about his associates. Tohir had concluded early on that Jamieson was acting with others beyond Brock, and the Architect had agreed. Thus the question had become, who are Lee Jamieson's friends? More precisely, who among those friends are both wealthy enough to afford the Architect's services and sufficiently ideologically aligned with Jamieson to contribute to his cause? Who is in it with him?

The initial list was longer than the Architect liked, though he'd finally been able to winnow it down to eleven names. One has since died from apparent natural causes, and upon reflection the Architect determines that another would never associate himself with Brock and Jamieson in such an endeavor.

The remaining nine get his full attention now. He reacquaints himself with their biographies and photographs, committing everything to memory. He doubts all nine are involved; the difficulty in maintaining any conspiracy increases exponentially with the number of the participants. Nine, he thinks, is untenable, but with no further data he has no means of revising his estimate.

The Architect thinks that it would be so much simpler to just kill them, but of course that points back to the problem of who "them" is. That is the real reason he needed Brock to set this meeting, a meeting that the Architect has no plans to actually attend.

He wants to identify the cabal.

Once he's done that, he'll have the luxury of controlling or destroying them as he sees fit.

Just after noon, the Architect leaves the hotel in his rental car. He spends the next twenty-seven minutes driving a random route, crossing the Potomac twice, turning at random intervals, cutting back on his trail. He is as certain as he can be that he's clean, and this makes sense to him. The only person who could have put surveillance on him is Brock, and Brock, he knows, is too obsessed with the idea of losing Jordan Webber-Hayden to risk compromising them all in such a fashion.

It's eleven minutes to one before he finds a place to park in front of a brownstone in Capitol Hill numbered 432. His view of number 442, a block away, is unobstructed and, as seen through the Canon's telephoto lens, clear. He positions the camera on the dashboard carefully, checks the view again. He takes out his smartphone and opens the EOS remote application, sees the view through the lens duplicated in real time on the screen in his palm. He takes a half dozen test shots like this, reviews them, and, satisfied, leaves the car, locking it after him.

He takes a walk, testing the range of the application, and is pleased to discover that he maintains control of the EOS from almost two blocks away. He posts at a bus stop, focused on his phone, and every person he sees entering 442 he photographs, some of them arriving on foot, others pulling up in luxury cars that are almost instantly met by fleet-footed valets rushing from the building. The Architect stands for fifteen minutes or so and takes four pictures, and a bus comes and he waves it off. Ten minutes or so later he's taken another two pictures, and a new bus pulls up, and he waves that one off, too, then heads back up the street, walking along the redbrick sidewalk. He passes his car, passes 442, and in the process snaps three more people entering the building. The clock at the top of the smartphone's screen tells him it's nine minutes to two. He crosses the street, doubling back, takes one more photograph, and returns to his car, where he sits, still focused more on his phone than on his surroundings. One more photograph, this at three minutes past the hour.

He shuts down the application, takes his laptop out, and opens it on the seat beside him, connects it to the camera. He's working quickly now. Of the eleven pictures he's taken, his hope is that at least one will match to the men associated with Jamieson. But he needs to make the match quickly. He didn't see Brock entering the building, and that means that Zoya has done what was necessary. Brock will not be coming.

But that will make the cabal anxious, turn their suspicion into fear, and it won't be long before they leave, before they separate.

The photographs transfer, and the Architect quickly begins flicking through them, comparing them to the ones in his files. If his angle had been better for the photographs, he'd leave the search to one of the facial recognition programs he possesses, but even the best software currently fails when presented with only profiles, and most of it only works if the subject is facing the camera directly. This requires an eyeball search.

It takes him less than five minutes to match four faces to the photographs in Jamieson's file. Two of them he is willing to rate 100 percent positive. The remaining two he is less certain of, but it doesn't matter. He has four names now, and two choices.

He stows the laptop, the camera, returns to his watch on the brownstone. At seventeen minutes past two, the first one leaves, the man the Architect has positively identified as Donald Lenhart. A black Mercedes-Benz pulls up for him as he exits the building, and he's in the back almost without pause. The Architect watches him go.

Three minutes later two cars pull up, the first a blue BMW delivered by a valet, the second a yellow-and-black D.C. taxi. The two men the Architect could not be certain of emerge from the brownstone. One of them, he believes, is Emanuel Frohm, which would make the other Victor Anderson. Frohm takes the BMW; Anderson leaves in the taxi.

This leaves Robert Larkin, president and CEO of Larkin Industries. Fifty-seven years old, son of Frederick J. Larkin, company founder. Educated Princeton, MBA Harvard, married to Marguerite Pierson, since divorced, father of three, Robert junior, Frederick, and Lenore. Larkin Industries began as a machine manufacturing company but in its fifty years has diversified, becoming what is referred to in government circles as a general service provider. Larkin Industries now supplies vehicles and civilian services to government agencies, everything from the National Science Foundation operations in Antarctica to military bases around the world.

The Architect starts the car, checks his watch, feels a surge of confidence that makes him realize just how much worry he'd been carrying. It's gone now. Brock is dead, and Larkin is coming out and taking the keys for his Porsche from the valet, and Zoya is on her way back to her condo in the West End, and tonight they will fly to either Rio or Berlin, whichever she prefers.

Everything, the Architect feels, is going exactly as planned.

For a moment, crossing the Potomac, the Architect wonders if Larkin is heading for the Pentagon in search of Brock, an act of almost impossible folly. Certainly the cabal is now spooked, but the Architect worries if Brock's absence was too much, if he should have waited before Zoya took him out of play.

It's an ill-founded fear; Larkin turns off almost immediately upon crossing the river. He pulls up at Le Méridien, is out of his car and into the lobby with barely a pause for the valet, and his haste forces the Architect to abandon his own vehicle illegally across the street, and he has to run through the doors, hating the attention it draws. Larkin is already at the elevators. The Architect takes out his phone once more and busies himself with its screen, glances up to see that Larkin and two others are entering a waiting car. He hurries, extends an arm, catching the doors before they close.

"Sorry," he says. "Sorry."

Larkin glares at him, and one of the others hits the DOOR OPEN button, and the Architect steps inside, turns.

"Floor?"

Three lights are already lit.

"Ah, you've already got it," the Architect says, and then goes back to checking his phone. The elevator stops twice on the ride, until it's only Larkin and the Architect, and when it comes to a stop the third time, the Architect cuts in front of him to step out first, then pauses again with his phone. Larkin steps around him, heading down the hall, and he's taking out his own phone in one hand, digging for his key card with the other. There's no one else in the hall, a housekeeping cart at the far end, but that's all. The Architect hangs back, waits until the key fits the slot, until Larkin is pushing the door open.

"Sorry," the Architect says. "Robert Larkin?"

Larkin turns, suspicion, and it's flaring into alarm, but by then it's too late. The Architect hits him in the face with the base of his palm, connecting with the man's chin, forcing his teeth together with a definitive clack. Larkin's arms go out and he steps back, into the room, and the Architect punches him once in the stomach, closed fist and knuckles this time, kicks him in the knee. Larkin drops, and the Architect pivots, shoves the already closing door shut, throws the lock. When he turns back, Larkin is trying to get up on one leg, and the Architect slaps him across the jaw with full force, knocks the older man into the bureau against the wall.

"Brock is dead," the Architect says.

The Architect steps forward, Larkin straightening up, dazed. He's leaking blood from the corner of his mouth. The Architect grabs him by his necktie, slaps him twice more, releases him. Larkin blinks, unsteady, tries to raise his hands again. His phone and the key card are now both on the floor.

"Jesus Christ," Larkin says. "Stop it."

"Brock is dead," the Architect says again. "Do you know who I am?"

Larkin shakes his head, but the Architect reads it as an attempt to clear it, not as a confession of ignorance. He takes a step forward, and Larkin immediately takes another step back, waving him off.

"Stop hitting me."

"You know who I am," the Architect says. "And I know who you are. I know who Emanuel Frohm is, and Donald Lenhart, and Victor Anderson, and I can tie each of you to Emmet Brock and the late Lee Jamieson. I can tie you to California. Do you understand?"

Larkin wipes two fingers at the corner of his mouth. He looks at the blood he's removed. "What do you want?"

"I want you to understand." The Architect takes another step forward, and, despite himself, Larkin takes another step back.

"Stop hitting me."

"Do I have your attention?"

"Jesus Christ, we were willing to meet with you. Why do it like this?"

"I can find you," the Architect says. "I can find your children. I can find your friends, and your partners, and their children. You have wealth. I have wealth and power. Do you understand?"

"Yes, I understand. Jesus Christ, I understand."

"Then tell me why I'm here."

Larkin clears his throat, a wet sound.

"You're warning us. You'll take us down if we betray you. If we ever talk about you. You don't have to worry about that. No one is going to talk. No one is going to touch us."

"Brock is dead."

"Brock lived in a different world. His world made him touchable. We're not touchable."

"Look in a mirror."

Larkin loses some of the color he's regained. "That's not what I meant. We have friends. Anything Brock could've said, he'd have fallen, not us."

"For your sake, I hope you're right."

The Architect turns to go.

Larkin says, "The contingency. It's still on?"

The Architect stops with his hand on the lock.

"You're going to go through with it, yes?" Larkin asks. "We'll get what we paid for?"

"Mr. Larkin," the Architect says. "I couldn't stop it now even if I wanted to."

The rental is where he abandoned it, and the Architect is pulling away as the tow truck is arriving. He grins at the vehicle receding in the rearview mirror, feeling pleased with himself. It has been a long time since he's gotten his own hands dirty, since he has inflicted violence instead of inciting it, and the adrenaline is still singing to him. He feels good.

Larkin understood, he knows. His arrogance had been broken enough by the beating to listen, and the Architect thinks that the warning will take, that it will be shared among the entire cabal. Once Larkin knows for certain that Brock is dead, he will have no choice but to tell the others about what's just happened, and not one of them will believe the Architect's threat is an empty one.

He drives, early rush-hour traffic now beginning on this Friday afternoon, and it's almost five o'clock before he's back in the West End. He leaves his car around the corner from the condo, starts along the sidewalk up to the home of Jordan Webber-Hayden. There's light foot traffic, heavier on the street, and something in the movement of people, in the pattern, catches his mind, sends him a warning. It registers as instinct first, and he heeds it, continues past the front doors without breaking stride, trying to find what it was he saw without seeing. Is it the man down the block and across the street, leaning against a parked car? The woman he passed who wasn't actually going anywhere but was arguing on her phone?

He stops, looks up, looks around. From this angle he can just see the facade of the condo, can count the floors to what should be Jordan Webber-Hayden's home. The curtains are open.

She does not leave her curtains open.

He keeps going, and the victory he's been feeling is gone, replaced by a whole new dread. This is a town filled to cracking with security and spies and surveillance; it is a dangerous town to operate in, and he knows this. If he's walking through an operation, it needn't be one targeting Zoya, targeting him.

Wishful thinking.

A man dressed as a jogger is at the end of the block, stretching his calves against the side of the building. Everything about him looks right, the shoes, the shorts, the shirt, but he's got a fanny pack resting at his stomach. There's a discoloration at his ear, so faint the Architect could believe it's nothing but a shadow rather than an earpiece.

There is no doubt.

He rounds the corner and continues walking, rounds the next, and makes the full circuit until he's back to his car. His hands are shaking as he drives back to his hotel.

They have her residence. If they have the residence, they have her. If she is alive.

The thought that she might not be is too much to bear. It nearly brings him to panic, and the Architect has to pull over and catch his breath. His grip on the wheel tightens, tightens, until he forces his fingers to unclench. He has to think. He has to plan. It's what he does.

They found her through Brock, he concludes. That's the only way they could have, which means they found her after Brock died, or Brock is still alive, or he doesn't know, but Brock didn't go to the meeting. If they found her through Brock, then they found Brock, and they found Brock through the death of Tohir.

He thinks about Zoya, and he again asks himself whether he is a monster, or someone forced to do monstrous things, but he already knows the answer. He's answered it years ago, and seeing her again only proved he was correct.

The Architect fumbles for his laptop, snaps it open, hurriedly passes through each plane of his security. He brings up the files Brock passed to him via Zoya, the files that had given him the home of Master Sergeant Tom O'Day and his wife, Stephanie, and his daughter, Callie. The files on Freddie Cooper and Isaiah Rincon and Jorge Velez and Jonathan Bell, who has a wife and daughter living in Burlington, Vermont.

If he moves quickly, he can be there in four hours.

He moves quickly.

Chapter Twenty-Eight

THERE ARE A lot of things Athena has come to like about living in Vermont — Burlington in particular. It's a total college town, so there's always something to do, somewhere to go, something to see. It's easy to get around without Mom needing to drive her everywhere, at least when they're not all up to their ears in snow. The winters are spectacular, even if they're cold as hell, and last autumn was blazing in its beauty. Then there's the school, Hollyoakes, which is why Mom moved them there in the first place, and as a veteran of more than a few schools in her sixteen years, she can say that it is hands-down the best.

But she can't go to the movies.

Or, more to the point, she could totally go to the movies if she wanted to sit there and try to figure out what it is she isn't hearing. Because not one fucking theater in Burlington, in a goddamn college town, has a theater with audio assistive technology. Not one of them. They've got a fucking school for the deaf not more than two miles south of the University of Vermont, but not one place where she and her friends and anybody else who attends Hollyoakes can go to catch the latest thriller or blockbuster or romance or comedy or any of it.

Which pisses her the hell off, to say the least.

*　　*　　*

Friday night, she and Lynne are at Gail's, and because there is no point in going to Merrill's Roxy or the Palace 9, they're watching movies on the big flat-screen television Gail's parents bought for the Super Bowl last year. Gail's parents have money, but they're cool about it. Both her parents are doctors; her mom's an ob-gyn and her dad's a pediatrician, which means that Gail is always full of information she's dying to share about the human body.

When Athena arrives at five, Lynne's already there, and Gail's parents have ordered pizza for dinner. They sit around in the TV room eating and watching a Pixar movie on Netflix, and the captioning is good, and they half pay attention. Mostly they talk. Gail's parents come down just past seven to say they're going out to — yep — see a movie, and they'll be back before midnight.

Be good, Dr. Gail's Mom signs.

We will.

So they finish the pizza and they finish the movie, and they're trying to decide what to watch next when Lynne says it should be a romance, and Gail sticks out her tongue like she's going to puke.

No romance.

Athena wants a romance. Lynne grins like she's got a secret.

Athena has a romance.

Athena shows them both the middle fingers on each of her hands, and they laugh.

So have you and Joel done it yet? Lynne asks.

Now it's Athena's turn to grin like she's got a secret. Gail's eyes go wide, and she scoots closer, and Lynne gapes.

No way. Gail signs. *You have not had sex he just had surgery.*

Athena bursts out laughing, and Lynne socks her in the shoulder.

Not funny.

Very funny, Athena signs.

Gail goes serious. *You thinking about it? How far have you gone?*

Just fooling around. Not all the way.

Thinking about it?

Athena nods, feeling suddenly shy about the whole thing. She went down to Planned Parenthood yesterday, but chickened out at the last minute, convinced that no one inside would be able to understand her. The idea of trying to lip-read someone, to try to get that person to understand that she was after birth control, was mortifying.

You should wait, Gail signs.

Maybe we made out a lot on Wednesday and it was hard not to do more I really wanted to do more.

It was hard? Lynne waggles her eyebrows. *How hard was it?*

Athena gives her the finger again.

That is hard but small.

Asshole.

Joke.

I know.

What do we want to watch? Gail asks.

Lynne and Athena both find themselves signing pretty much the same thing.

No guns.

It's after ten when Athena texts her mother to say she's on her way home.

> Should I come and get you?

> Bike remember?

> I can put the bike in the car.

> Ill ride.

Be very careful. Also "I'll" ride.

:P

The night is brilliant, clear and so full of stars, and Athena takes a moment before mounting her bike to just stand in the driveway of Gail's house and look up. There's no moon, and the Milky Way is distinct, and she thinks about the fact that right this moment there are people living up there on a space station, that there are spacecraft that have left the solar system, that there is so much out there. She read a physics article once that talked about infinite universes and how if the universes were really infinite there would be another one of her, just like her, out there somewhere. Another deaf Athena, and a hearing one, and one who never met Joel, and one who had already lost her virginity to him, and one whose parents weren't divorced.

She climbs on her bike and starts pedaling, taking it slow because of the darkness. She's got flashers on her bike, front and back, and she's wearing her helmet. It's still warm, but the humidity has dropped, and as she rides she feels the slight, pleasant breeze on her arms and through her T-shirt.

Athena turns onto Edinborough, and the first thing she notices is that the Mazda isn't parked down the block anymore, and neither is the Toyota. It's dark, so maybe she's wrong, or maybe they've left. She knows that Mom had a fight with Dad the other day about the people watching them. She's still not entirely sure what she thinks about that whole thing, the idea of them being under surveillance, as Mom put it. On the one hand, it's definitely creepy, knowing someone is following you and watching you; Athena's been very careful about not changing clothes anywhere near her windows. On the other hand, there's something reassuring about it, in feeling that you're being protected.

She's just about reached her house when she sees the slant of light from the front door, realizes it's ajar. Her first thought is that maybe Leaf has snuck out, but she doesn't believe it even as it comes to mind. She stops on her bike, feet on the ground, searching the street once more for either of the cars she now knows belong to people who are meant to protect her and her mother. She is more sure than ever that the cars are simply not there.

Dismounting, she guides her bicycle across the lawn, rests it against the elm tree. She makes her way across the grass, climbs the stairs to the porch, careful where she sets her feet. She wishes, just for once, that she could hear the world, that she could know if there were voices or silence coming from inside, if the wood beneath her feet was creaking. She thinks of all the stories she's read in which a footstep is betrayed by its sound, and she is certain that it's happening to her now. She thinks she's being silly, that she's worrying about nothing. The door is simply ajar, nothing more.

All the same, Athena holds on the porch, slides her feet sideways until she can see through the gap between the door and the frame. It's a straight view down the hallway to the kitchen, the source of the light, and she can just make out her mother seated in a chair that should be out of sight, at the kitchen table, but isn't. Her mouth is moving, and Athena sees that her mother is sitting with her hands in her lap, and her back is straight, as though her spine is tied to a plank, and her chin is tilted just that much up, and it's a posture, or, more precisely, a manner, that she has seen before. It's a manner she will never forget.

It's the same way her mother looked at the men who made them their prisoners at WilsonVille.

The apprehension Athena Bell feels spasms, turns into fear. Whoever her mother is talking to, that person is not a friend. Whoever her mother is talking to, that person is dangerous.

She takes a step back, then another, runs into the porch railing, startles herself. Certain she's made noise, she vaults back onto the lawn, rolls on the grass and to her feet, runs around the near corner of the house, into deeper darkness. Her heart is pounding, and she stops, dares to peek back around to look at the front door. Nothing has changed. She feels for her phone in her pocket, frees it, snaps the screen open. Her thumb hits 9 and then 1 and is about to hit 1 again before she stops herself. Her cell provider has no text-to-911 system; there's no way for her to communicate without third-party assistance or TTY. She could call, try speaking, try to pronounce the words in a way that will be understood, but she's afraid of the noise she will make. Just calling without speaking — maybe they would try to trace it, send the police, and that would be good, but then she thinks that maybe it wouldn't be, either. Calling the police but not being able to tell them that her mom's inside their house and she's in danger.

She wants to believe that she's overreacting. That would be the best thing, and it would make sense. Everything in WilsonVille, everything with Dad — maybe it's her imagination. Except those cars that are supposed to protect them, they're not there anymore. But maybe there are new cars. Maybe they're on break or asleep.

Athena thinks about texting her dad, but what if she's wrong? If she really is overreacting? Mom had texted her just half an hour ago, not that long ago. Could so much have changed in just thirty minutes?

She peeks around the side of the house again, and still the front door is just that little bit ajar, she can see from the light. Everything on the street looks so quiet.

It's the thought that her mother is in danger that ultimately moves her, that decides her course of action. The thought that her mom is in trouble and that her dad would know what to do. Shoving her phone back into her pocket, Athena continues along the side of the house, toward the backyard, peers around the corner. She can see the kitchen window, and now she can see another shape in there, and it's definitely not Mom but a man. He's wearing a white shirt and a blue tie, sitting at the table, his jacket hanging from the back of his chair. Athena edges closer, trying to adjust the angle to get a better view, and the man moves his left hand, speaking, a very calm and reasonable gesture, and she would let that persuade her that she is, in fact, overreacting, except that resting on the table beneath his right hand he has a gun.

Athena steps back, catches her breath. Her stomach hurts. She wants to be sick.

The stairs down to the basement door are just ahead of her, six feet that she covers with her back flush against the side of the house to keep from being seen from inside. She turns, drops down into the darkness, lands on the bottom step, falls forward, hands out. Catches herself on the door, and she can feel a vibration from behind the wood, an irregular pulse, and she thinks she knows what it is. She tries the knob, but it's locked, and she has to dig for her keys, feel her way to the keyhole in the handle, for the moment both blind and deaf. She feels the bolt turn, and as quickly and as quietly as she can, she shoves it open, steps through, and shuts it behind her. Leaf is immediately at her hip, nosing her, and she can tell he's barking, she can feel it in the air. Someone put him in the basement, the man or Mom, and Athena thinks it must've been Mom, because the light over the dryer is on, and if the man with the gun did it, he wouldn't care if there was light for the dog.

Athena hopes to God that Leaf's been barking the whole time, not because of her arrival.

Do what Dad would do, she thinks.

She goes to the stairs, climbs them quickly, Leaf following. He's still barking, and she wonders if that's enough to cover the noise. She pushes him back, gives him the hand sign to stay, and he backs off, then comes forward again. She repeats the sign, and he lowers his head but doesn't move, and he stops barking. Athena sets her hand on the doorknob, turns it slowly, feels it rotate without resistance. She doesn't open the door, not yet.

Do it like Dad would do it.

She takes a deep breath, lets it go, takes another, and opens the door as smoothly as she can. Slips through, shuts it again, turns right, three steps, and she's at the linen closet opposite the bathroom.

From the linen closet, it's another right around the corner, past the guest room into the kitchen. She rounds with the shotgun coming up, tucking the butt high on her shoulder, the way Dad and Uncle Jorge showed her that one summer. Mom is facing her, in her chair, and she sees her at once, but it's the man at the table that Athena is aiming at, and she has her finger on the trigger, and she's saying some of the words that Uncle Jorge taught her to say when Mom and Dad weren't paying attention.

"Hello, motherfucker," Athena says.

Mom is signing, speaking at the same time, but Athena isn't paying attention to her. The man at the table looks at her, and she's kind of surprised, because he doesn't even look afraid. She can see that his clothes are a little rumpled, like he's worn them for a day too long, that the tie is loose, the top button at his collar unfastened. His right hand rests on his gun, the gun on the table. He spreads his fingers, raises his hand, leaving the weapon behind, and Athena takes another step toward him, the barrel never wavering.

"Limp-dick motherfucker," Athena says, trying to get the sounds right, biting each word, like Uncle Jorge taught her. He spent a long time teaching her that one. "Fuckbag."

The man glances at Mom, then back to her, his mouth moving. He speaks slowly, like he knows she's deaf. He speaks slowly, she realizes, so she can read his words.

You must be Athena, he says.

Athena risks a glance at her mother, sees that Mom is on her feet, holding out a hand, and for a moment Athena thinks she wants the shotgun. When she looks back to the man, he is shrugging, then slides the gun on the table toward Mom. She picks it up like it's a diseased rat, points it at the floor. When her hands are done with it, the gun is empty, the slide locked back, and both the weapon and its magazine and a shining brass bullet are on the counter. She turns to Athena, signing again.

Give shotgun.

Athena does not give her the shotgun, still pointing it at the man. With it in her hands, she cannot sign, so she puts it all in her expression, hoping Mom can read it the way she knows that Gail and Lynne and Joel would.

Fuck that.

Mom signs again, angry.

Give weapon now young lady so help me.

Athena looks from the man to her mother. The man is far too calm for her liking. Mom looks like she's going to start spitting flames at any moment. Her hands fly, speaking quickly.

Man wants talk Dad. Give shotgun N-O-W.

Confused, Athena hands the weapon to her mother. She's even more confused when Mom brings it up to her shoulder and points it at the man at the table, exactly as Athena has done.

Very slowly, so Athena can read each word, her mom says, *Call your father.*

She gets out her phone and begins typing.

Hey Dad? she writes. *Mom's pointing the shotgun at someone here who needs to talk to you right away.*

Chapter Twenty-Nine

JORDAN WEBBER-HAYDEN doesn't stop crying.

From the moment the cuffs are on her, to the transport, to the unloading and the second search and trying to bandage the flesh wound along her side, through processing and right into interrogation, her body shakes, and she sobs, and the tears flow, and mucus spills from her nose. For Bell, who has seen trauma and grief in more places and more phases than he can count, it verges on awe-inspiring. Jordan Webber-Hayden, he decides, is either out of her skull with grief or simply out of her skull.

He's sincerely hoping it's the first, because if it's the second, they're shit out of luck.

"We've got a team going through her residence," Ruiz tells Bell. "Heath's leading on it. Wallford is on his way over."

Bell looks through the one-way glass at the woman in the interrogation room at Fort Belvoir. Her hands have been cuffed and joined together by a chain that runs through a D ring on the table. Her head is down, a spill of brown hair, and her shoulders are visibly shaking.

"She's been like that the whole time," Bell says.

"She say anything?"

"Just the one word in Russian."

"You think she's talking about Brock?"

"Maybe."

"We need to find out," Ruiz says. "My watch says it's fifteen fifteen, it's Friday, and we're looking at our only lead on this thing."

"Nothing else on the names?"

"Nothing after Ledor." Ruiz pauses. "We found a note on the general, in his coat. Handwritten."

"Saying?"

"Saying he had betrayed his country and could no longer live with what he'd done. Some other things."

Bell waits.

"Had her home address in the West End and a list of five names. One of them was Lee Jamieson."

"Who were the others?"

"The kind of names you don't want to ask me about, Master Sergeant."

Bell thinks about that, thinks about names like Lee Jamieson's on a list left by a man who had planned a murder-suicide.

"You want me to run at her?" Bell asks.

"Soon as the chief gets back." Ruiz indicates Jordan Webber-Hayden with his chin. "Maybe she'll calm down."

"Don't count on it," Bell says.

"You could always talk dirty to her."

"You're a funny guy, Colonel."

"I've got a brigadier general who was leaking top-secret information shot dead in a Hilton near BWI, a hysterical suspect as my only lead to a terror attack on home soil in the next eighteen or so hours, maybe, and my Indigo First Team leader is whispering naughty sweet nothings over the net to our very own Mata-fucking-Hari. I'm about to piss myself, I'm so funny."

"Situation normal," says Bell.

"All fucked up," Ruiz says in agreement.

*   *   *

Nessuno enters with Wallford a couple minutes later. She's cleaned her-self up and bandaged the claw marks on her wrists, and she gives Bell a weak smile as she enters. He wonders if he looks as fatigued as she does and suspects that he looks far worse.

Wallford, for his part, comes with the same energy as ever. As Nes-suno moves to Bell's side, Wallford goes to the glass, puts his hands and face against it as though he were a five-year-old visiting an aquarium. He taps the surface with his fingertips, drums them, and in the inter-rogation room, Jordan Webber-Hayden doesn't look up, just brings her hands together as if in prayer, shifts her head. Her shoulders continue to shake.

"Jordan Webber-Hayden," Wallford says.

"So it appears."

"Scrubbing the residence?"

"As we speak."

He turns, puts his back to the glass, grins at them. "No known aliases, no record, no nothing."

"Helpful," Ruiz says.

"This is. She bought a Walther PPQ yesterday morning from a dealer in Alexandria."

"No gun on her," Nessuno says.

"Single use, maybe."

"Jesus Christ," Bell says. The thought that he's looking at the same person who put a bullet in Tom O'Day, who murdered O'Day's wife and daughter, is sickening. He feels the anger again, feels any dribs and drabs of sympathy her tears might've engendered evaporating with its heat. "What the hell is she?"

"She's a pro," Nessuno says. She looks at Wallford, then at Ruiz. "I want to talk to her. Can I talk to her?"

"You want to go in alone?"

"Better with a partner." Nessuno now looks at Bell, and Bell hesitates. What he wants and what he needs are two different things, and for a bitter instant, he resents his duty above all else.

"Got your back, Chief," he says.

Nessuno fills two paper cups with water, and Bell carries a box of tissues. Jordan Webber-Hayden doesn't look up when they enter, and as soon as they're through the door they can hear her wheezing, her sobbing hoarse and weak. Bell sets the tissues on the table, and Nessuno sets one cup down, then the other.

"Jordan," Nessuno says. "My name is Petra. Have something to drink."

The woman doesn't move, doesn't acknowledge them at first. Nessuno takes one chair, and Bell takes the other. Nessuno reaches out to him, touches the back of his hand, and Bell looks at her, confused. Nessuno uses her eyes to indicate the woman.

"I'm Jad," Bell says. "It's all right."

She lifts her head, looks at him, her eyelashes matted and her eyes rimmed red. A pool of snot has formed on the table; a string runs from it to her nose. She snuffles, but the sobbing subsides. Bell pulls a tissue from the box, reaches out, and wipes her nose. The woman coughs.

"Thank you."

Bell crumples the tissue, tosses it into a corner, pulls another one free. He reaches out again, this time cleaning up the table.

"Don't worry about it," he says. "We all have bad days."

She snuffles again, makes a sound as if trying to laugh. He discards the tissue, offers her the box. She takes one, wipes at her eyes, then her nose.

"You're not police," she says.

"No."

"FBI?"

"Jordan," Nessuno says. "Who is *dorogoy?*"

Jordan Webber-Hayden drops the tissue, takes another. She blows her nose. "My lover."

"You mean General Brock?" Bell asks.

"He was going to shoot me. He was going to kill me and himself, I think."

"Why would he do that?"

"Because he loved me."

"Strange way to treat someone you love."

She shakes her head. "You do not know."

Nessuno tilts her head, studies the woman for several silent seconds. Bell, sitting beside her, understands that she's heard something that he's missed.

"How long?" Nessuno asks.

"What?"

"How long have you been under, Jordan? Do you even know?"

The woman won't look up from the table.

"Do you remember your name?"

"Jordan Webber-Hayden."

"Your real name, I mean."

She doesn't respond.

"I'm only starting to remember mine," Nessuno says. "Sometimes I wake up and I have to actually think about it. It's getting easier, but I still have to think about it."

"You don't know."

"It'll come back to you. It just takes time."

"You don't know."

"I'll tell you the worst part, though," Nessuno says. "The worst part is that sometimes I don't want to be me, I want to be her again. Not the fear, not that. Not waiting to be discovered, not like that. But she was so much…more exciting than me. She was wealthy, she ate in fine restaurants. She wore expensive clothes, not like this, not jeans and a T-shirt and sneakers. She was special. She was loved. Maybe not the way she wanted to be, maybe not really at all, maybe only truly desired. But she could believe that was love. And now I've lost her, she's gone, and I'm trying to be just me again."

Jordan Webber-Hayden takes a new tissue, begins tearing at it with her fingernail.

"Have some water," Nessuno says.

The woman hesitates. Then, still holding the tissue, she takes one of the cups in both hands. She empties it, sets it down, takes the second one.

"I can't help you," she says.

"Sure you can, Jordan," Bell says. "I know you can."

She shakes her head. "I won't help you."

"Is he worth it?" Nessuno asks. "Your lover?"

Jordan Webber-Hayden looks into the water in her cup.

"He is everything," she says.

They leave her alone for an hour, fall back to the observation room. Ruiz has left, but Heath has arrived, and Wallford has remained.

"What was that?" Wallford asks Nessuno.

"That's called empathy," Nessuno says. "You should try it sometime."

"Her lover is Brock. Was Brock."

Nessuno shakes her head. "No way in hell would she do what she's done for Brock. Kill Steelriver's family? She's talking about Echo. She knows him. Tohir didn't even know him, but that woman in there, she's been in his bed. She's in love with him."

She points to the glass, where Jordan Webber-Hayden is now sitting upright in her chair, her hands together in front of her. She's tearing another tissue into tiny fragments, a snowfall of them beginning to pile on the table.

Heath leans against the far wall, arms folded. "She didn't limit herself to working General Brock, from what we've gathered at her residence. There's a half dozen lovers at least, and her bedroom is wired for sight and sound, too, feeds into a hard-drive system in the walls. We got a laptop out of her car, and tech has been bashing its head against it for the last few hours, too. We can break the encryption, maybe, but it's going to take more time than we've got. We're going through everything, but there's no telling what, if anything, will lead us to Echo."

"Echo is secondary," Bell says. "We need something actionable."

Nessuno shakes her head. "She's not going to know."

"We have to ask."

"Feel free, but I'm telling you she's not going to know. That woman in there, she's me. She's purpose-built, she was trained for this. She ignored me initially and responded to you. That's not because you're nicer. It's because she's trying to bond with you, she's trying to work you."

"She killed three people."

"That we know of, yes, and maybe more. But that's not her primary mission. Her place was wired, Jad, and she had a list of lovers. She's asset acquisition for Echo — that's her primary, to gather intel and feed it back to him. If it weren't, if she were an assassin, she'd have killed me with her bare hands. She had the drop on me, she had me cold when I came around that corner. Someone taught her how to shoot and how to fight, but that's not her MOS, it's not her job. I know what I'm talking about here. I'm fucking looking in a mirror."

"It's a distorted reflection," Bell says.

Wallford clears his throat. "How long you want to let her cook? Because there is a time constraint, you may be aware."

"She needs to stew," Heath says. "The chief's right about this. We give her a bathroom break, we ask her if she needs anything, we give her something to eat. We need to make friends with her."

"Not us," Nessuno says. She points to Bell. "Him."

"Because she's trying to work me?"

Heath puts a fingertip to her nose.

*　　*　　*

Bell waits and finds it difficult. Nessuno and Heath go in and unchain her and take her to the shitter, bring her back, lock her up again. They bring her a cup of tea, and a sandwich, then leave, and the door to the observation room opens and Nessuno comes in. Wallford has left for the moment, and they're alone.

"That's not you," Bell says.

"I don't need a pep talk."

"There's a difference between her and you."

"You think so? Why? Because I did what I did for God and country and she's doing it for Echo?"

"That's not it."

"Look, you can dress it up however you want to, Master Sergeant. You can make me your battered damsel or you can make me a victim, but the fact is she and I are the same, just with a different coat of paint."

"That's the difference," Bell says. "You're not a victim."

"No?"

"No, and you know it. You're battered and you're maybe even broken, but so am I, because nobody gets out of combat unharmed. But in spite of everything you've been fighting since coming up for air, you still own yourself, and she's owned by him. I believe everything you're saying about her, Chief, right down to the rivets. But you do yourself dishonor if you think what she is and what you are match."

Nessuno fingers the small medallion on its chain, stares through the glass at Jordan Webber-Hayden. "I think I'm falling for you," she says.

"Thank God."

"Did you mean what you said? Outside the Hilton?"

"Every word. I was never any good at talking dirty."

"Maybe I can help you with that."

"Maybe you don't need to."

"You should get back in there."

"She gets her claws into me," Bell says.

"I'll rip 'em right out," Nessuno says.

"A lot of people are going to die," Bell says.

"I'm sorry," Jordan Webber-Hayden says. "I don't know anything about it."

"But your lover does?"

She nods slightly, leans forward so she can bring her hands up and brush hair away from her face. The dress draws tight against her chest when she moves, and Bell makes a point of not looking.

"So tell me about him."

"You're nothing like him."

"Does he have a name?"

She smiles. "I don't know it. Do you believe that?"

"No."

"But it's true. He never told me his name, and I understood that I was never to ask. So I gave him one."

"*Dorogoy.*"

Her smile brightens. "Yes, exactly."

"What's your name?"

"Jordan." Her eyes shift past him, to look at the window, the one-way glass that only shows their reflections. "Zoya."

"Russian?"

"Yes."

"Is he Russian?"

"I don't know." She shrugs, smiles again. "It doesn't matter."

Bell shifts, leaning forward. She copies him, coming closer.

"Jordan, you need to listen to me, because I'm trying to help you now. But you're not helping yourself. I don't care about your lover, you understand? This isn't about him. But people are going to die, and if you can help me keep that from happening, anything you can say, anything you can do or offer, that'll go a long way."

"You want to be my friend?"

"I'm the only friend you have."

"You'd probably be a good friend to have," she says. "I could make something up, I suppose. Try to tell you what you want to hear. But I don't know anything about that; I told you the truth. That wasn't what I did. That's never been what I do."

"You understand what's going to happen to you?"

"I imagine I'll go to prison," she says. "Prison doesn't frighten me."

"It could be worse than prison."

"You don't understand," she says. "You've already done the worst you can to me. You've taken me from him. I'm already dead."

Bell doesn't know what to say, is spared the silence by a tapping on the glass over his shoulder. He slides his chair back.

"Anything you can give us," Bell says. "Maybe you can see him again."

"Don't you think if I could make that arrangement with you I already would have tried?" she asks.

Bell leaves, enters the observation room. Nessuno and Heath are there, and he can feel that something's wrong the moment he steps inside. Nessuno holds out his phone.

"Just came," she says.

Bell reads the text message from his daughter.

"Who is this?"

"Master Sergeant Bell?"

"Yes. Who is this?"

"You sound alarmed. Don't be. Your ex-wife has a shotgun pointed at my head, and it's very clear she knows how to use it. Very clear your daughter does as well."

Bell looks at Ruiz, who has a phone of his own pressed to his ear.

"You're wondering about the security team on your house," the man says. "They won't be coming."

"They're dead?"

"That's not relevant, and I am not going to waste time while you try to get a response to your house. Listen carefully. I am going to tell you something, and then I am going to ask a question, and then you will tell me if we can deal. If we can deal, I am going to walk out of your house and leave my phone behind for you. If we cannot deal, your wife will have to kill me."

"Let's hear it."

"In just under eighteen hours, a group of armed men are going to enter a very public location and open fire. These are trained, motivated men. It's going to make what happened in Mumbai look like a parlor game. I can give you everything you need to stop them before they begin. Now the question. Is Jordan Webber-Hayden alive?"

Bell looks to Ruiz. Ruiz nods.

"She is."

"Then I have something you want, and you have something I want. I'm leaving your house now, Master Sergeant. I'll contact you in four hours."

Bell hears Amy's voice, the clatter of the phone as it's picked up. "Jad? Jad? What the hell—"

"Let him go, don't let anyone in until I get there." He hangs up, already rising, says to Ruiz, "We willing to do this?"

"I'll know by the time you get there," Ruiz says. "For this to work he's going to have to offer himself up."

"We give her up to get him and shut this down, I can live with that," Bell says.

"Wait a fucking second," Heath says. "You really think Echo's willing to lay it down for his piece of tail in the interrogation room? Why in fuck's name would he do that?"

"Here's a crazy thought," Nessuno says. "Maybe he loves her back."

Chapter Thirty

THE ARCHITECT HAS a horrible moment, walking out of the house, when he fears that he has miscalculated and that Amy Kirsten Carver-Bell is going to shoot him in the back. Then he steps out into the Vermont night, and the door closes behind him, and he hears the locks being thrown. He stops on the lawn and sees the ten-speed bicycle that he presumes Bell's daughter had been riding before coming home. He walks it to the garage, props it against the front, then heads back down the sidewalk and around the bend, through the trees to where he left the car from which the CI men had been watching the house. The car smells of their blood and other fluids.

He had taken their weapons and their phones and wallets before disposing of their bodies. He collects them all now, including his own laptop bag. On each phone, he can see multiple missed calls, no doubt attempts to raise them while he was speaking to Bell.

He leaves the car and starts walking, checks his watch, and sees it's nearly midnight. With military transport and all the stops pulled, he expects Bell to be at his wife's home by two thirty in the morning at the latest, but he tells himself he'll wait until three to make the next call. That's as late as he's willing to push it; time is enemy and ally at once in this, for both Zoya and himself, and for Bell.

He walks in the darkness and sees nobody. He takes his time, mindful, ducks out of sight when the glow of headlights rises in the night. Once, a police car passes him by, but he had warning as it came around the bend, and he is certain no one saw him.

He makes it to the Church Street Marketplace by one in the morning and is pleased to find lights shining and people about, and then he remembers that it's a Friday night. He stops at a food stand and buys himself a kebab and a soda, finds a place to sit and people-watch while he eats. By the time he's finished, the night is catching up with his surroundings. He resumes walking, heading back toward Lake Champlain, and he's at the shore and listening to the water when his watch tells him it is three.

He uses one of the two dead men's phones and dials his own number.

"Bell."

"Neither of us has much time if this is going to work," the Architect says. "Obviously you do not trust me, and I would be foolish to trust you. What I propose is that you come and meet me. I passed a preschool on my walk on Lake Street, called Heartworks. Meet me in the parking lot there and we can get this process under way."

The Architect throws the phone into the water without bothering to disconnect. Then, one after the other, he sends the collection of wallets and weapons in after them.

He waits until almost three thirty before heading toward the preschool. In the silence, listening, he can hear the sound of the car arriving, stopping, the door opening and shutting. It makes the Architect wonder what he isn't hearing, if there aren't a dozen other men closing on his position right now, if a black helicopter isn't silently watching from above. This isn't paranoia; this is, to him, only logical.

Security lights illuminate the preschool parking lot, creating an orange sodium-vapor glow that catches the moisture in the air and refracts it, making it all seem brighter. He can see the man waiting, light in a pool around him. He's a big man, wearing jeans and a jacket, hands in his pockets. The moment the Architect moves, the man's head turns, finds him almost immediately. But his hands remain in his pockets, and he says nothing as the Architect approaches.

"Jonathan Bell?"

"Yes."

"I want it noted," the Architect says. "I did nothing to your family. I went to them because it was the quickest way to reach you."

"You think that buys you something?"

"I think it's something for you to consider. Let's walk."

Without waiting for a response, the Architect turns, heading south. Bell matches his pace.

"Let's hear it."

"You're going to let Jordan Webber-Hayden go free," the Architect says. "Before you do, you're going to give her your phone number. She is going to send two text messages to your phone from numbers that I will recognize. The first message will be proof that she is free and under way. After that message, I will give you a piece of intelligence to demonstrate good faith. The second message, from a different number, will provide proof that she is safely out of your reach. At that point, I will give you everything you need to stop the attack before it begins."

"You're talking time," Bell says. "We release her right now, how long does it take for her to reach wherever she's going and send that second message?"

"You're worried the attack will occur before she verifies her freedom."

"Correct."

"The attack will commence at eighteen hundred hours in zone."

"Which zone?"

"Not yet," the Architect says. "It's almost four now. Do the math yourself."

Bell answers without pause. "Fourteen to seventeen hours."

"Yes, but I'd advise viewing it as somewhat less than that. You'll need to get your people in position, after all."

"Or we could just grab you."

"You could do that," the Architect says, agreeing. "You could black-hood me and pack me off to Gitmo or anywhere else. You could take my laptop and attempt to breach its security. You could pull out my finger-nails and waterboard me. And you might well get what you want, and you might even get it with time to spare. But if you don't, I guarantee you, hundreds of American lives will be lost today. Conservatively. This isn't hyperbole."

Bell is silent for a moment, and the Architect suspects he's listening to traffic in his ear. "I believe you."

"Then let her go. Do it now."

There's another silence, and then Bell says, "She's being released and your instructions are being relayed. Can we give her a lift somewhere?"

The Architect laughs. "That's very generous of you, Master Sergeant. But she's a big girl, and she knows what to do."

"She's a messed-up girl."

"Well, I'm a messed-up boy, so what can you do?" The Architect stops, looks out at the lake again, and Bell, likewise, halts. "It's a big, messed-up world."

"You're not helping unmess it."

"I am, actually. But you wouldn't understand. You're part of the problem."

He turns away from the water.

"We've got a lot of time to kill," the Architect says. "Let's see if we can't find someplace where we can kill it."

They find a café on the corner of South Winooski Avenue and Cherry Street, loiter outside for twenty minutes before it opens at a quarter of seven. The sun has been up long enough for the Architect to take a good look at Bell, and his first impression is of incredible fatigue. The man's eyes are faintly bloodshot, the bags beneath them a haze of bruised purple. There is stubble, at least two days' worth, and a faint if unmistakable scent of sour sweat and overworn clothes. There is a tattered bandage around his right palm; the cloth tape that holds the gauze in place is dirty and peeling, and when they walk, the Architect sees hints of a further injury to his left leg or perhaps his ankle. The Architect himself is feeling tired, but Jad Bell looks like he's running, literally, on fumes.

"You should get some sleep."

"Tell me what I need to know and I'll be able to."

They get a table, each of them ordering coffee.

"You're paying," Bell says.

"More than you can imagine. You should get your phone out."

Bell takes his phone off his hip, and the Architect can see the pistol riding there. He expected nothing less. The coffee comes, and Bell lays the phone beside his mug. The Architect looks at the menu, orders the gingerbread pancakes. Bell orders eggs over easy and wheat toast.

His phone chimes, and Bell looks down at it, then shows it to the Architect. "That the number?"

The Architect lowers his mug and looks at the screen. The number matches.

In transit, dorogoy.

"So far so good," the Architect says.

"Your turn."

"You have more time than you think. The target is in the western United States."

"You have something against Californians?"

"I did not say it was California."

Bell pushes back from the table, taking his phone with him. "I'm going to make a call."

"Of course you are." He watches as Bell steps outside. The café is filling up rapidly, even given the early hour. The Architect finishes his coffee, finds that he's feeling remarkably calm. Of course, he realizes, this is the easy part. Bell and those he works for will play him along until they have what they need.

He thinks about Zoya, wonders which of the caches she's cleared, what route she is taking. It doesn't matter much, only that she gets clear of the country. The first number, the message that just arrived, he recognized. The second that comes he won't, but Bell has no way of knowing that, just as Bell has no way of knowing that Zoya's run, now, is simply that. When she feels she is safe, she'll let him know.

That she will be safe isn't a question. The calculus of the scenario is absolute. In the grand scheme of things, Zoya means nothing to Bell and his owners, only to the Architect. In the grand scheme of things, they are trading her for him, and he is the prize of greater value.

The Architect watches as Bell speaks on the phone, then he directs his gaze around the café as his mug is refilled. From Brock's files, he makes at least one of the men present as another of Bell's team, the one called Chaindragger. He ignores him, and his pancakes come, and the Architect attacks them with vigor.

Bell returns to find his plate waiting for him. They eat in silence.

Finished, the Architect lays a twenty on the table.

"My treat," he says.

Chapter Thirty-One

BELL DOESN'T KNOW what to think.

At first he thought the walking around was Echo's way of flushing coverage, of identifying and counting the surveillance, but the man genuinely doesn't seem to care how much of how many are watching them. They've had breakfast, walked much of downtown Burlington, and ended up on a pedestrian mall that has too many people and no vehicle access, and Bell thinks that if Echo wanted to run, this would be a pretty good place to start the race.

But Echo gives no sign of fleeing. He gives no sign of anything, just maintains the complacent calm of a man who knows how to wait. What little he's said seems to both mock and defer, as if he holds Bell in contempt but somehow feels sorry for doing so.

Now it's eight minutes to ten in the morning, and Echo wants another cup of coffee. Bell is happy to oblige, mostly because he can't feel the caffeine anymore. They get their drinks at a shop on Church Street, and Echo himself suggests they take a table outside.

"Easier on the surveillance teams, I should think," he tells Bell.

"Jesus fuck," Heath says in his ear. "This guy is ice."

"Brickyard," says Ruiz. "Status."

"I've got eyes on." Cardboard now. "Still at Church Street, sharing a table."

"Blackfriars," Nessuno says. "Coming up from the south."

Bell looks past the Architect, sitting opposite him, sees Nessuno, wearing a baseball cap and carrying her jacket over her arm, coming up the pedestrian mall toward them. She stops, window-shopping, and Bell focuses on the Architect, finds the man staring at him again. Every time he looks at him, Bell feels like he's being weighed, measured, and itemized.

"Radio chatter?" the Architect asks.

"You know it."

"It's interesting. I had thought about approaching you before."

"For?"

"I lost a good man in Tohir. I need to replace him."

"You wanted to recruit me?"

"I considered it. You have exceptional skills. You're smart, or at least smart enough. You're dogged. You don't posture. You're loyal, as evidenced by the trouble you went to in an attempt to preserve your marriage. Amy seems a remarkable woman, by the way."

"You're well informed."

"I had help."

"Brock."

"Obviously. I considered it, as I said. And rejected it. It's clear you would have refused."

"How would you know if you never asked?"

"Because you're a good soldier, Jonathan. Even if the people you soldier for aren't."

"You're telling me you're the good guy?"

The Architect waves a hand as if shooing a lazy fly. "I'm long past measuring things in terms of good and bad or, worse, good and evil. Frankly, I'd have thought you were, too. But I've never understood patriotism. It requires a willful blindness I find difficult to stomach."

"Zoya said she's Russian," Bell says. "She says she doesn't know where you're from."

"Where do you think I'm from?"

"I don't know." Bell considers everything he's seen of the man, everything he's heard him say, tries to collate the information into something that resembles an informed opinion. "Your English is excellent, accent sounds native. It's a little stiff, fluctuates between almost colloquial and formal. You've got some European manners. You've clearly traveled extensively, you're clearly educated. First World child."

"Would it surprise you to learn I'm American?"

"Are you?"

The Architect smiles at his coffee. "I'm going to need a bathroom. Can I go alone? Or do you want one of your men to follow me?"

Bell holds up his cell phone. "I think you'll come back."

"Yes, I certainly will."

The man rises, disappears into the building. Bell stretches, arching his back. The sunlight is too bright, hurts his fatigued eyes. He thinks he's slept all of four hours in the last forty-eight.

"Status?" he asks.

"You are prepped and fueled," Ruiz says. "Soon as we have the intel, you are go."

"Capture team?"

"Waiting on the word."

Cardboard, in his ear, cuts in. "What?"

"This is open for discussion?" asks Nessuno. "This is a debate?"

"Priority is his intel," Ruiz says. "We are waiting on the word to bag him."

There's something in the way he says it that makes Bell think there are others on the net, other people listening in aside from Heath and Ruiz and Nessuno and the rest of his team. Brock had a list, he remembers, and it wasn't one the colonel had been willing to share. Bell thinks again about the authorization required to go after Brock, about how high up the chain of command this must now reach. If everything they're doing now isn't feeding straight back to the White House Situation Room, he'd be surprised.

The Architect returns.

"Message?"

Bell shakes his head.

"You didn't do something stupid, did you?" the Architect asks.

"Stupid like what?"

"Put a tail on her. Try to track her. Bug her."

"We did not."

As if in answer, his phone chimes. He doesn't recognize the number.

Safe.

The Architect is leaning forward, he's responded to the noise, and Bell hands him the phone, watches the man's reaction. When Echo smiles, his face moves just a little wrong, and Bell can see the effects of cosmetic surgery, but only just. Whoever did it was very good and therefore very expensive. Bell would put the man in his forties, close to his own age, if he felt he could trust what was before his eyes.

"Happy?" Bell asks.

"Pleased, rather." The Architect hands him back the phone.

"Let's hear it."

"Before I do —"

"No," Bell says. "Now. That's our deal."

The Architect nods once, reaches into his coat, and comes out with a fountain pen that he uncaps. There's a paper napkin on the table, and he writes on it, the ink leaching through the fibers, spindly fingers crawling out from letters and numbers. He hands the napkin to Bell, screws the cap back on his pen.

"That is the address of a house in Las Vegas, Nevada. That is the staging house. Inside are six men. Those men are armed with fully automatic weapons, small arms, and twenty-four hand grenades. At eighteen hundred local, they will depart from the house in three vehicles, three teams of two, and proceed to the Strip. At eighteen forty, they will launch an attack from entry points to the north, east, and south of the major casinos on the Strip's west side, one team entering at the Bellagio, another at Caesars Palace, and the third at the Mirage. They will first attack the casino floors, where the sight lines are almost entirely unobstructed, for maximum chaos, then they will move into the casino's shopping areas to group up and take defensive positions. Their targets are anyone who moves."

Bell puts a hand to his ear. "Got all that?"

"Confirmed," Ruiz says. "Second Team is rolling."

The Architect starts to rise, and Bell reaches out, takes his wrist, pins it to the table. "Hold on."

"I'm leaving," the Architect says.

"No, you're not."

The Architect sits heavily, sighs. "You've not thought this through. Hopefully others have."

"You're not walking away."

"I have given you exactly what I promised. As I said, you *can* stuff me in a van and cart me off and put me in irons and sweat me for months. You have that power, I recognize that. You will certainly shatter my network, you will certainly get more out of me than you have done already."

Past him, Bell can see Nessuno is moving up. He sees her mouth move, hears her saying, "Take him."

"But you will not get much more," the Architect is saying. "And you will lose what I can provide you. You will lose the intelligence I can gather and would be willing to share. You will lose an asset."

"You're an enemy of my country," Bell says.

"No. Your country was just the arena in which I was paid to operate."

"Hold," Ruiz says. "Hold."

"I'm going to walk away, now, Jon."

"You're not going anywhere."

Chaindragger's voice, soft, "I have transport, exfil north side."

"Hold," Ruiz repeats.

"Take him down." Nessuno's voice, hissing. "Jesus Christ, take him down!"

The Architect doesn't move, doesn't pull, just looks at Bell with surprising resignation.

"They're going to order you to let me go, Jon," he says.

"Cut him loose," Ruiz says.

Nessuno's voice comes from behind the Architect as much as in Bell's ear. "Are you fucking kidding me?"

"This is from the shiny on-high," Ruiz says. "You are ordered to release target Echo and clear your AO; repeat, you will release target Echo and clear your area of operations. Proceed to ANG local for immediate loadout and transport. I require confirmation."

Nobody moves.

"Warlock, I require confirmation."

Echo smiles sympathetically.

"Warlock, confirm."

"Warlock," Bell says. "Confirmed."

He lets go.

Chapter Thirty-Two

THE GULFSTREAM G650 eats the sky at a top speed of 704 miles per hour, covers the distance from Burlington to Las Vegas in just under four hours, sets down at McCarran just after 1500 local. Bell, despite thinking he wouldn't, manages almost three hours of sleep on the plane, then leads the team off and into the back of the waiting van. His team is light. There will be running, there will be gunning, and this will be a speed strike, and that means Jorge — Bonebreaker — is once more out of the action on this deployment because of his injured ribs. The Second Team, once commanded by Tom O'Day and now being led by Sergeant Josiah Henry, is waiting for them at a staging area four blocks from the house, at the edge of the perimeter established by local law enforcement.

Bell, Chaindragger, and Cardboard are all geared and ready to roll by the time the van comes to a stop. In the absence of Steelriver, and with Henry's consent, Bell has command. He steps up to the command post — more precisely, another unmarked van — and Henry gives him the briefing book.

"By-the-numbers parakeet op," Henry says. "If it's not a friendly and it moves, it dies."

Bell looks over the blueprints. He reviews the plan of attack. He reads over the list of operator call signs, the number of Indigos in each element. Eight men could do this job well. Doctrine says that twelve would be ideal. They have seven, and Bell took the house in Tashkent almost a week ago with only four.

Seven will be more than enough.

"We're buttoned up on this?" Bell asks.

"We've had command as of fourteen fifty local." Henry understands what he's asking without needing explanation. This is an Indigo op, he's saying; we are secure.

Bell takes the secure phone handset from its rig, keys the mike. "Indigo oh-one actual, we are in position and standing by."

"Brickyard, actual." It's Ruiz, not the duty officer, not some CWO or staff sergeant, in the TOC. "You are go."

The Second Team makes their breach at the front, hydrocharge on the door and following with their 9-bangs. Bell, Chaindragger, and Cardboard take the back; this was Bell's call, made because he's still missing Bonebreaker and because he expects lighter resistance at the rear of the house. He effects entry with a ram, knocks the back door clean off its fittings. He drops the ram and pivots, Board, then Chain, taking the entry as he swings up his own submachine gun to follow. There's steady chatter on the radios, the dulled concussion of the grenades. Their weapons are suppressed, and Bell can hear no gunshots, but Henry comes through almost at once with a "Tango down," and another on his team gives a "Clear."

He steps in, weapon ready, hears Cardboard calling a splash, sees the man Freddie has killed laid out on the floor. The tango is in a vest, threat level II, possibly identical to the one found in Michael Ledor's apartment back in Provo, and a combat harness, and his dead hand rests on his chest, half an inch at the most from one of four fragmentation grenades worn there. Cardboard took him down with a shot to the face.

Chain hooks left, and Board has his slice covered, and Bell takes the door. The banger goes in but fails to detonate, and Bell snaps one of his own free, sends it through after. The blast comes, chasing another man, same vest and harness setup as before, a pistol in his hands. He never makes it through the door; Chaindragger drops him with a double-tap.

Bell makes his sweep, Chain on him, then Board. They're hearing the calls from the Second Team, no more vibration from gunfire or grenades. Clear, clear, clear, clear.

"Clear," Bell says.

The house is secure.

He checks his watch.

Sixteen seconds.

Bell emerges through the front, steps out into a Las Vegas twilight. He pulls his mask from his face, inhales the fresh air. He feels like he's been here before, the twilight not so far removed from predawn in Tashkent.

He can't remember how many days ago that was. Five? Six? A week, maybe? He doesn't know.

It feels like years.

The Architect leaves the Church Street Marketplace and makes his way to Burlington International Airport via taxi, catching the first flight he can out of town, not much caring where it will take him. He knows he's being followed; if he's not under close surveillance then at least he's somehow being tracked. There's an 11:20 departure that takes him to Chicago, and, like Bell, he manages to grab a few hours of sleep on the flight. He leaves the airport and heads into the city, where he takes a room at the downtown Marriott, still traveling under the name Willem Smart. It unsettles him to continue using the Smart identity, but he has only one set of papers remaining on him, and he wants them clean when he leaves the country.

His rolling bag with his wardrobe has been lost to him, left behind at the Watergate, and after checking into the hotel he heads out immediately for some utility shopping, clean clothes and necessary toiletries.

He returns to his room, showers, then sits on the edge of his bed, feet flat on the floor, debating what to order from the room-service menu. He doesn't like any of the choices, finally settles for a grossly overpriced chicken Caesar salad. He turns on the television, flips through the cable news offerings, and sees absolutely nothing at all about happenings in Las Vegas, Nevada, or, for that matter, about the death of a brigadier general outside of Baltimore, Maryland.

He eats his salad with the room-service cart fully opened as his table, resists the call of his laptop until he is finished. Once his meal is completed, he succumbs, sending his programs out into the world to do their work, responding to the correspondence that demands his immediate attention. There is an e-mail from Zoya, and it's with difficulty that he saves it for last.

Her message is short. She is in Montreal, she is free, she loves him.

He sends her a response with the address to their house in Narbonne, in the Languedoc-Roussillon region of southern France, only fifty miles or so from the border with Spain. He tells her he loves her and that he will never, ever, risk her like this again.

The room phone rings. The bell surprises him, but the call itself does not. The Architect looks at the unit, at the message light flickering red in time with the annoying bleat. He watches it do this twice more before answering.

"Mr. Smart," a man says. "I'd like to buy you a drink and discuss a business proposition."

"I've had a long day, and I'm very tired," the Architect says. "If you would like to leave me a number at which you can be contacted and a name to ask for, I would very much appreciate it."

The man on the other end of the phone agrees, apologizes. He leaves a number and a name. The name is Wallford.

The Architect hangs up, then makes notes about the call before proceeding to the rest of his work. He shuts down his laptop, turns off the lights, and climbs into bed. There are enough pillows for him to arrange them to his liking, the way he has done every night without her, the way he will, very soon, never have to do again.

"Goodnight, my love," he whispers, and settles into sleep.

It's into the small hours of Sunday morning by the time Bell gets to the house in Hailey, the house that's too big for just him alone. He's called Amy three times before leaving Las Vegas and texted Athena twice that many times, and the only answer he's gotten has been from his daughter, a terser-than-usual text message telling him that she's going to sleep. He sends one back, *sweet dreams,* and gets no response.

He unlocks the door to the house and drops his bag, fumbles his way to his bedroom, halfheartedly undressing as he goes. He can no longer tell which is greater, his hunger or his exhaustion, and he feels like his body is turning to parchment, thin and brittle. He finishes stripping in the bathroom, showers in less than two minutes, towels off, and heads for his bed. He's closing his eyes when he sees Nessuno standing in the doorway. He shifts, pulls the covers back, and she climbs in beside him.

She puts her head against his breast, and he puts his arm around her shoulders, finds them strong and warm, feels her relax, and then he's asleep.

He dreams of shadows.

Acknowledgments

This novel would not have been possible without the assistance of several people.

Gerard Hennelly, Eric Trautmann, Evan Franke, Nunzio DeFilippis, and Christina Weir remain stalwart and endless fonts of knowledge, support, critique, inspiration, and friendship. It is on your collective shoulders I have stood to reach the high shelves. I am grateful to be able to call each of you friend.

Once more, heartfelt thanks to Heather and Daniel Perkins, not solely for their assistance, but for their efforts to teach me about the life of the deaf. I still fear I do not have it right, but I sincerely hope I'm getting closer.

My thanks to Patrick Weekes, who served as an early reader when one was desperately required. He helped far more than he thinks he did. Sometimes, you just need someone to talk to.

A quick thank you to all on Twitter who responded to obscure questions at odd hours, foremost amongst them Natalie Stachowski, who knows many, many things, and not all of them are about nugs, the Sith, and N7 training.

As always, to David Hale Smith, and to Angela Cheng-Caplan. There is no such thing as "only business," and I am humbled by your dedication and devotion to your work, and your unflagging faith in my own.

ACKNOWLEDGMENTS

To Ben, who will read this and think it silly because he has lived and witnessed the Real Deal™, but who put the idea in my head. Through all the years and all the miles, your friendship still holds its notes, still rings clear and true. Someday, I sincerely hope we will be in the same place, at the same time, and that you'll be buying.

To Jennifer, my bandit. Always and forever.

Last, to those who offered insight and information, but who asked not to be named. Your service is remembered.

About the Author

Greg Rucka is the *New York Times* bestselling author of almost two dozen novels, including the Atticus Kodiak and Queen & Country series, and has won multiple Eisner Awards for his graphic novels. He lives in Portland, Oregon, with his wife and children.

MULHOLLAND BOOKS

You won't be able to put down these Mulholland Books.

YOU *by Austin Grossman*

OVERWATCH *by Marc Guggenheim*

THE SUSPECT *by Michael Robotham*

SKINNER *by Charlie Huston*

LOST *by Michael Robotham*

SEAL TEAM SIX: HUNT THE JACKAL
by Don Mann with Ralph Pezzullo

ANGEL BABY *by Richard Lange*

MURDER AS A FINE ART *by David Morrell*

WEAPONIZED *by Nicholas Mennuti with David Guggenheim*

THE STRING DIARIES *by Stephen Lloyd Jones*

THE COMPETITION *by Marcia Clark*

BRAVO *by Greg Rucka*

DEATH WILL HAVE YOUR EYES *by James Sallis*

WHISKEY TANGO FOXTROT *by David Shafer*

CONFESSIONS *by Kanae Minato*

Visit mulhollandbooks.com for
your daily suspense fiction fix.

Download the FREE Mulholland Books app.